SHIFT OF MORALS

2

SHIFTER LORDS

S.E. BABIN

CHAPTER
One

Moira and I stared down at the shriveled plant lying on top of my new worktable. I'd experimented for weeks to nurse the vine back to health, but nothing I tried had worked. I'd gone from a gentle nudge to something more substantial before attempting a full-blown magic blitz.

Nada. If plants had tongues, this one would be nana booing me.

"Why won't it get any better?" the vampire asked. Moira was my best friend and shop employee. A lock of dark hair fell over her eye as she bent forward to peer at the poor thing.

"There isn't much I can do for a plant that refuses to live."

Moira blinked and looked up at me. "You're just going to let it die?"

I held my hands out. "Contrary to popular belief, I am not a plant god."

She frowned and reached out a pale finger, gently touching one of its leaves. "But you kind of are."

"It's not that simple. Sometimes things don't want to live. I can nudge and encourage, but I never force. Even if I did, any boost would be temporary. If a plant decides to die, there's nothing I can do for it."

She gave me a sideways glance. "And this one has decided?"

"Looks that way." I sent a soft pulse of magic into the heart of the plant and felt its flickering life force against my mind.

Moira's expression as she stared at the lifeless plant twisted my heart, so I pulled my magic away and turned to grab a small pot from the shelf behind me. I set it before her and pushed the special pot of soil next to her. "All I can tell you is to give it the best possible environment to grow, put it in a window with lots of natural light, and keep the top layer of soil moist. If you want to go the extra mile, play it some Beethoven a few times a week. We'll revisit in a month, okay?"

Moira tugged the pot closer. "Think it will work?"

I didn't want to give her false hope. "Love and care can turn the worst situation around. All you can do is try."

Moira nodded and straightened, grabbing the soil scooper. I left her to tend to her new project and headed back over to the register. Tess was there, wearing new sparkly barrettes in her hair and new lip gloss. I'd been dying to say something all morning, but I didn't want to embarrass her.

Things between her and Ash were progressing at a glacial pace, but then things like this happened, and I knew she and the dryad were well on the way to a warm and cozy romance. "How's it going?" I asked as I came up beside her.

"Fine," she said in her monotone voice. "It's not very busy today."

Tess wasn't wrong. Ever since Caelan had stopped coming around so much, it was like the townspeople were too scared to pop by, thinking I'd fallen out of favor with the Shifter Lord. This couldn't be further from the truth as he (or someone at his Keep) had requested I do the flowers for his upcoming wedding.

The wedding I tried not to think about. After the disastrous dinner party where Finn, the attacker who'd turned me into a Chimera, had shown up and tried to get me to make amends and become his …I had no idea, actually, things had gotten real weird.

Everyone in Joy Springs was abuzz about the identity of

Caelan's mysterious fiancée, but no one had seen her yet. Not even me, and I was part of the wedding planning team. I'd spent way too much time thinking about what she must be like if she'd caught the Shifter Lord's eye.

Beauty was the obvious choice. But she was probably smart and politically savvy, too. She had to be to keep up with Caelan. The question I'd had in my mind since the second Simone walked into my shop and broke the news was why. Why would Caelan pursue me and make me feel like he wanted me, then abruptly go and get hitched?

It made no sense.

My life over the last several years made no sense.

Par for the course, I guess.

"You alright?" Tess's querulous voice nudged me from my maudlin thoughts.

I blinked and straightened. "Yes. Sorry. I have a lot on my mind."

The banshee fidgeted with the ink pen by the register. "Caelan getting married is a good thing," Tess said. Her words were slow and even, as if gauging how I might react once she said them.

My stomach clenched. His upcoming marriage *was* a good thing. Every strong leader needs a partner, and Caelan had been running this region by himself for a long time. He deserved one.

So why was I so bothered by the thought of his wedding?

I forced a smile. "Of course it's a good thing. I hope Caelan and his new bride are very happy."

A dry laugh sounded from behind. "You hope a meteorite strikes the wedding."

I stifled my grin. "Ash! How terrible. I would never."

"You would always," he corrected. "God might not be petty, but you sure are."

I laughed as Ash sauntered over and placed two coffees on the desk. "A cortado for Evie and a saltwater taffy latte for you."

Tess gave a shy smile and slid hers closer.

"Thanks!" I popped the tab off my cup and took a sip.

The banshee grimaced. "I don't know how you drink that."

A cortado was my new favorite discovery. As coffee drinks go, it's a simple one. Equal parts espresso and milk, and I took mine with zero sugar. The only downside was its size, and that's because I was more American than anything these days. Four ounces of deliciousness was a small amount, but two ounces of espresso was enough to get me going.

Tess's latte, on the other hand, was a monstrosity of artificial flavor and whipped topping goodness. I tasted it once and felt my mouth pucker, but the banshee drank one a day. I suppose it's a good thing sugar doesn't affect people like us as it does humans; otherwise, Tess would have fallen into a sugar coma months ago.

Ash sipped his coffee, a simple black breakfast roast. He might be a dryad, but his taste in coffee was simple. Moira, though, was all about the tea and turned her nose up every time she spotted one of us with the blue paper cups with the adorable Brewtide Beans logo.

The merfolk-owned coffee shop stood a few blocks from the flower shop and served up the regular offerings for the tourists, along with a few quirky offerings they could talk about once they got back home. There was a secret menu for the residents, serving up delicacies for the vamps and wolves, and Tess's special order saltwater taffy latte.

Mine was one of the touristy drinks, but Lir, the main barista and owner, told me he was coming up with something extra special for me, and he'd have a sample to try soon. I was weirdly nervous about it because I had a human palate. What could he possibly make for me that would suit my unique biology more than a cortado?

Espresso and milk. Goddess bless the combo.

"What do we have on the docket today?" Moira asked, nose wrinkling when she spotted our cups. She held a delicate teacup, dotted with blue and pink flowers and a thin layer of gold coating around the rim. A light floral fragrance steamed upwards and tickled my nose.

Bergamot. One of Moira's Earl Grey blends.

It smelled delicious, and I liked tea, but I loved coffee even more.

"That bouquet is still in the walk-in," Ash said. "We're already two weeks behind. Maybe we should move that up the priority list."

"Ugh." That bouquet was cursed. We'd stuck it in a magic dampening pouch several weeks ago and pushed it to the back of the storage fridge. I meant to take it out much earlier to take another look, but every time I got near it, I got a bad case of the heebie-jeebies.

Men normally didn't touch their bride's bouquets, but this one possessed a distinctly male, oily, malevolent feeling. A magical feeling, one not belonging to the natural world.

I went to the fridge and fetched the bouquet, keeping it at arm's length as I carried it back to the desk. We gathered around and stared at the pouch.

"We should open it," Tess said. "It's hard to feel how bad the magic is with the dampening sack."

"I don't want to," Ash muttered.

"She's right." Moira sipped her tea. "It's too late to turn down the job since Evie has already put the client off twice."

I winced. "I've been busy."

Ash snickered. "Pining over an emotionally unavailable Shifter Lord."

"Don't forget engaged," Tess said.

"He was not engaged when all this nonsense started," I muttered. "But you're right." I threw up my hands. "Fine. Let's get to the bottom of this creepy bouquet so we can restore it and get it out of our fridge."

I reached for the pouch, but Moira slapped my hand away. "I'm the least vulnerable to rogue magic, so I'll do it." She undid the zipper and shook the bouquet out. All of us stepped back, expecting something to go boom, but nothing happened other than a rose head snapping off and plunking onto the table.

Ash cringed. "Can you fix it?"

"Not sure. I'll have to figure out what's causing it first. The preservation spell should have held." I grimaced as I turned the bouquet over, and two more flowers fell off. It was decomposing before my eyes.

As wedding bouquets go, it was simple but tasteful—a mix of blush roses, cream peonies, baby's breath, and several other filler flowers wrapped with floral tape and blush-colored ribbon. Probably middle of the range in terms of cost, but cookie-cutter.

I'd guess the bride used a popular wedding planner who earned kickbacks from all the local businesses in the town. We had a planner in Joy Springs, but there was no way to tell where this bride had gotten married. Our shop was well known throughout the state, and our customers came from all over.

Our town's planner had a touch of magic, so she should have sensed something if she'd met the groom. While it wasn't her responsibility to warn the bride, I'm not sure I could have stopped myself. Inserting myself in other people's affairs seemed to be my current M.O. One I hoped to correct very soon.

"Are we just going to stare at it and hope it does something?" Tess said in the silence.

Ash laughed. "Evie was in deep thought."

"Probably wondering how to break a shifter engagement," Moira said, laughing when I swatted at her.

"I'll take this over to the worktable in the back, just in case it gets rowdy. In the meantime, what else do we have going on today?"

Moira checked the schedule. "Normal business, but Hattie called yesterday and asked for her order a day earlier than normal."

"Any special requests?" I tucked the bouquet back into the dampening bag, careful not to disturb the weakest parts.

"She asked for oranges and yellows." Moira shrugged. "Normal seasonal flowers."

"It's a little early for fall colors, but we're edging closer to autumn, so I'll see what I can do." Hattie had been a customer for a while now and ordered a weekly, seasonally appropriate bouquet. I'd helped her out with some landscaping not too long ago and didn't charge her, so she'd called and requested I bump the size of her bouquets up by 25%.

After that, we'd gotten a few more similar orders like Hattie's, though most people chose biweekly instead of weekly.

"Tess, can you check the main fridge first for orange and yellow flowers? If we don't have enough, can you run over to the greenhouse and see what's ready?"

To keep my mind off Caelan, I'd thrown myself into restoring my greenhouse, a project I'd neglected for far too long. With a little elbow grease from me and Caelan's handsome healer, Ben, the place was back in fighting shape, with brand new hydroponics to prove it.

A small smile tugged at my lips when I thought of Ben. He was wildly different from Caelan—gentle, caring, communicative, and careful with my feelings. He never pushed or tried to coerce me into giving more than I could, and he respected my boundaries.

Maybe a little too much. We'd done nothing more than kiss, and that was fine, but something was holding him back. Something always held me back, but I was used to being the problem.

Ben and I were both the problem in this relationship. Or whatever it was.

Tess cleared her throat. "Lost in your thoughts again, Evie?"

Shit. "No. Yes." I waved a hand. "There's a lot to think about. Fridge first. Greenhouse second. Got it?"

Tess nodded and glanced at Ash. "Want to come with me?"

"To the walk-in?" Moira asked, rolling her eyes at young love.

Tess let out a soulful moan. "To the greenhouse, vampire."

Ash's lips twitched. "Of course. You may need some help carrying the flowers back."

It wasn't that big of a bouquet, but I let it go.

"Moira, you man the front. Ash, can you check on the deliveries and make sure we have enough stock to last a few weeks?"

The dryad nodded. "Of course. Don't forget I'm leaving in a few weeks to return to ground."

I snapped my fingers. "Right. Almost forgot. We need to make a family calendar." Turning to Moira, I opened my mouth, but she cut me off.

"Got it. Make a calendar. Electronic or hard copy?"

"Hard copy," all of us said at the same time.

Technology might be awesome, but we were all pretty old school. I liked to look at my schedule on a wall, not down at my phone. "Make it big and monthly, with large enough space to write in the blocks. Also, make sure there's a side area to write upcoming shop events."

Moira nodded. "Will do. There's a good spot in your office to hang it. But everyone has to remember to update their schedule."

"I won't forget," Tess said. "We're still keeping the digital work schedule though, right?"

"Yep. That won't change." Something niggled at the back of my mind. "Ward it from prying eyes, would you, Ash?"

His eyes widened. "Good idea. Once it's up, I'll take care of it."

No one needed to know any of our personal business. Not with Finn still roaming around. A shiver went down my spine when I thought about our last encounter.

Posing as Halvar, one of the Shifter Lords, Finn had infiltrated Caelan's stronghold and accosted me at one of the events Caelan had hired me for. No one saw what happened because I'd encaged us to keep my secrets, but I'd wounded Finn and he'd escaped before I could finish the job. But not before he almost took me down with him.

He and I weren't done with each other. I felt the knowledge in my bones as strongly as I did that extra power he'd fed into me that night. Even now, I felt Finn's presence inside and outside, all around me. His and the Chimera's magic seeping into my bones, preparing me for...I had no idea. But I'd noticed odd things happening with my Floromancy and more urges than normal.

More hunger, physical and emotional. And the urges...

Well, let's just say it's a good thing Ben doesn't come around all the time, because I might have him laid out like my own personal buffet.

And he seemed way too proper for that.

Once the bouquet was on the worktable and everyone had dispersed to go about their assignments, I cleared my thoughts and turned on streaming music. I preferred the worktable in the front, given to me by Ash's uncle, a powerful dryad named Septimus, but this one was safer.

If something went awry during the preservation process, no customers would be in the blast radius. All the magic would stay contained to this area thanks to the wards I'd just activated around me and the table, pushed out in a four-foot radius.

Of course, I might get blown to smithereens, but everyone else would be safe.

Chris Stapleton's bluesy, soulful voice came through the speakers, and peace settled over my shoulders. I took a few deep inhales, steadied my magic, and opened the pouch.

The preservation spell wasn't exactly successful, not without tapping into some hefty Floromancy. I wasn't charging the woman nearly enough to do that, so once I had the bouquet stable and the flower heads reattached, I stepped outside the wards to find the others.

Moira was just finishing up with a customer, and Tess was busy putting together the beginnings of Hattie's flower arrangement. Ash was next to her, scribbling something in the ledger.

"It looks a little better," Moira hedged, keeping her distance.

"But it still feels the same," Ash said.

"He's a bad man," Tess remarked, the words an earlier echo of when the flowers had first come through our doors.

Tess was right. Whoever this groom was, he hurt his bride. Repeatedly. I couldn't get a strong enough read on the flowers to tell exactly what he was doing to her, but I felt the need to find out who he was and inform his Alpha. All I could hope was that his Alpha wasn't Caelan. "I think he's a shifter."

Moira's attention snapped to me. "One of Caelan's?"

"Impossible to tell. Can we get the mom in here?"

Moira held up a finger. "Let me get the book."

She was back in less than a minute, flipping through the

orders. "Here. The mother's name is Amy. Would you rather I email or call?"

"Put this one in writing. Do we have the lines set up to record?" It was one more security touch I added after the run-in with Finn.

"All we have to do is push the button," Tess assured me.

"Good. If Amy or the bride calls, make sure you push record."

"Will do, boss!"

I glanced at Tess. The banshee never sounded cheery, and this response was way too chipper. She gave me an awkward smile, which made my brow furrow.

"Okay," I said slowly. "Moira, let me know what she says. I'd like to know if she used a wedding planner and the person's name. Asking the groom's name might make her suspicious, so maybe just ask the wedding date and the location. If she asks why, tell her we're making a plaque."

"Alright. I'll forward what she says." She frowned at the bouquet and shivered. "That thing gives me the creeps."

"Me too. The spell should hold for now, but the residual magic keeps breaking down the preservation. It needs to be cleared."

"Can't you take care of it?" Ash asked.

"I can, but I'd like to wait for Hazel. She has more experience with magic like this." A frown curved my lips down. "Although I'm not sure if it's magic at all or maybe just the groom's essence. Evil is ingrained into the very heart of these flowers. Having all the information we can about the groom will only help." I shrugged. "And if it's one of Caelan's people, I might hand this over to him and let him handle it before Hazel arrives."

Washing my hands of the thing was my preference. Getting involved in the Shifter Lord's world wasn't something I'd be foolish enough to attempt again, even though I'd been roped into doing his wedding. Our negotiated contract would keep me out of the limelight and relegated to the shadows, which is exactly where I wanted to stay. He and his bride would have stunning flowers. I'd receive kickback business from cleverly placed logos on the table centerpieces, and he and his new Lordette could ride off into the sunset and have tons of shifter puppies to dote on.

"Once we leave here, I'll put the wards back up, tightly contained to the table. Try not to disturb them. Once we hear back, I'll figure out the best way to go about getting this out of our shop." I gave them a hopeful smile. "Sound good?"

"The sooner the better," Tess said as she floated away.

"Agreed." Ash followed her out, leaving me and Moira alone.

"And you?" I said.

She grinned. "We both know I agree with them. That thing is super creepy, and I love flowers. And weddings."

For a vampire, Moira was a softie. "Hazel should be here in a few days. She'll know what to do."

She gave me a curious glance. "I think you already know what to do. You're hesitating. Why? That's not very Evie-like behavior. Especially over the last couple of months."

I snorted. "I think you answered your own question. Look what's happened over these months."

Moira's eyebrows flicked up. "Uh. A hot Shifter Lord cast his eyes upon you, and our fearless protagonist, one Evangeline Quinn, found her shiny spine."

"And her ex-boyfriend came back and tried to kill her. Again."

"Semantics," Moira said with a flick of her fingers. "He didn't succeed."

"It was close. Too close."

She grinned. "You still kicked his ass. I bet his rear was hot for days."

With his healing abilities, any burns would have sealed within a few minutes. But ...it was satisfying to chuck him right into an open flame. "Your faith in me is a little unsettling," I said after a moment.

"Not misplaced, though. You underestimate yourself. Few people could have kicked a Chimera's ass, but you did it and sent him packing."

"It was mostly due to terror," I said dryly.

"Yes, well, imagine what you can do when you know what you're fully capable of." Moira waved at the bouquet shimmering with malevolent magic. "Lock that thing down and come out and have lunch with us. We'll check on Hazel's progress."

I nodded as Moira headed toward the front. Hazel would get here when she got here. She'd never been great with time or a schedule and seemed to show up at the exact time she was needed, regardless of whether you agreed you needed her.

Shaking my head, I resealed the wards and headed to the front.

AFTER A HEARTY LUNCH of chicken salad croissants and chips, Tess and Ash went to the greenhouse to gather more flowers for Hattie's bouquet, leaving me and Moira at the register. A slow but steady trickle of customers kept us busy, but things died down around three o'clock. I made a pot of dark roast coffee and popped a few frozen chocolate chip scones in the air fryer to bake.

But when the bell over the doorbell jingled, and Moira turned to give me a sympathetic wince, I knew the day was about to change for the worse.

Simone Ashmoore, Caelan's Omega, and high up in the Shifter Lord's pack, walked in, her normally smiling green eyes sweeping the entrance for potential threats. When our eyes locked, her lips tightened before relief filled her face.

"Evie. Hi. You're just the person I came to see."

"I'd hope so," Moira drawled. "You are in her shop."

Simone's nostrils flared.

"Moira," I said in quiet rebuke. The vampire rolled her eyes and returned her attention to the inventory list Ash had left her.

"Simone, please, come on in. Do you want some coffee? Scones will be ready in a couple of minutes if you want one of those too."

She gave me a grateful smile but shook her head. "No, thank you. I'm only here for a moment."

Not too long ago, I thought I might have a friend in this

woman, but things had changed once she'd popped into the shop to announce Caelan's engagement. It wasn't her fault, but a wedge was driven between us at that moment, and we were at an odd impasse.

Simone was and would always be loyal to Caelan, and I was simply Evie, a florist with mixed-up heritage doing her very best to stay under the radar in a world that kept trying to drag her into the spotlight.

"If you're here about the wedding, I have some ideas sketched out if you want to take them back. I didn't have too much to go on, but I figured a Shifter Lord's wedding was big business, so I drew up some extravagant arrangements and some middle of the road ones. He and his future bride will have to choose the flowers and whatnot, but I think either should work."

Simone's smile didn't reach her eyes. "I'm sure they're beautiful, but I'm here to invite you to the Keep in two days' time for a meeting to finalize the happy couple's vision."

My jaw tightened at her words. Considering I had Caelan in here backing me against a wall with sexual tension crackling over my skin just a few weeks ago, was the couple really happy, or was this yet another political game I couldn't get caught up in?

"I'm not sure why I need to attend a meeting, Simone. I've drawn up sketches, prepared mood boards, and have a few samples awaiting their perusal in my walk-in fridge. I'm happy to send those back with you. The happy couple is more than welcome to make additions or subtractions, change colors, or anything they like."

"I'm truly sorry," Simone said, and to her credit, she did sound remorseful. "I'm sure the samples are wonderful, but the Shifter Lord insists you attend in person."

"Of course he does," I muttered.

Moira snorted. "Since when does the Lord give a shit about hydrangeas or peonies? He was perfectly happy to leave that all up to Evie the last time she worked for him. Seems strange he'd suddenly develop an opinion overnight about floral choices."

One of my eyebrows rose as I waited for Simone to address Moira's words.

Her polite smile faltered. "Evie, you know I am just the messenger." She blew out a breath. "Listen," she said urgently. "I cannot divulge any information, but please don't be difficult about this. There are things in play you cannot possibly imagine. If you don't want to attend because of Caelan, please consider it a personal favor to me." Simone cleared her throat. "Plus, Lord Rowan will be there, and he has personally requested to see you again."

I had a soft spot for Rowan. Our magic was not dissimilar, and he seemed like he was a good dude. For a Shifter Lord, anyway. But Simone was acting strangely. "Is everything okay?"

Simone nodded. "For now." She pulled an iPad from her purse and opened the case. "Can I count on your attendance?"

I sighed. "Fine. What should I bring besides the sketches and samples?"

Simone's shoulders sank with relief. "Just any ideas you have and any examples. Thank you so much, Evie. I won't forget this."

"You better not," I grumbled.

This time, the smile reached her eyes. "For what it's worth, this took us all by surprise," she said softly. "Even Caelan."

Before I could respond to that bombshell, Simone had turned and breezed through the door, a scent of jasmine perfume in her wake.

I turned to Moira, feeling completely befuddled.

Moira had the same look on her face I assumed I was wearing.

"Huh," she said. "Is this a shotgun wedding or something?"

I laughed, the sound breaking the awkward silence. "No idea. It's pretty difficult for shifters to get pregnant, isn't it?"

Moira shrugged. "They can't get diseases, so you know none of those horndogs are wrapping up their wieners."

"No one says wieners anymore, you ancient idiot." I snickered as I went over to the register to grab my cell so I could add the appointment onto my calendar.

"It feels way too much like a romance novel to say cock."

I held up a hand. "Please. No."

She tapped her pen on the wood. "Have you seen the bride before?"

"Never. There aren't many women in the Keep to begin with. But when he came to the shop and even when he was at home, I never saw any females other than Simone and one of his mated shifters around."

"Maybe she's not from the Keep."

"It doesn't matter. She's Caelan's fiancée, and we'll meet her soon enough."

Moira grinned. "I can't wait to see how this meeting goes."

I crumpled a duplicate receipt and tossed it at her. "You'll behave. Caelan is throwing enough money at us to sustain the shop for years. We will both be on our best behavior. Promise?"

Moira sighed but made an x motion over her chest. "Cross my heart."

I narrowed my eyes, but Moira wore an innocent expression. "Two days from now," I reminded her. "Wear business professional."

"I'll look like a million bucks."

I slung my purse over my shoulder. "Just look normal, please. And like we know what we're doing."

"That too." She nodded eagerly, and a knot of worry uncurled in my stomach.

"I'm heading home. Mind closing up shop?"

"Not at all. Tess and Ash should be back shortly. We'll work on Hattie's bouquet, so you won't have to do as much tomorrow."

I shot her a grateful smile. "Thanks."

"You got it, boss." She waved me away. "Get out of here. We've got it under control."

I'm glad one of us did.

CHAPTER
Three

S eeing Simone rattled me more than I thought it would. She was a harsh reminder of Caelan. His power, his presence, his ability to influence my life in ways I hated…his Omega was only one piece of his power. I liked her, but I wouldn't be upset if she stopped coming around.

Not that she would. Simone was Caelan's official messenger for wedding info.

I sighed and tapped my fingers against the steering wheel. My greenhouse awaited me. I couldn't wait to dig my fingers deep into the soil and rid myself of thoughts of Caelan and all the conflicting feelings he inspired in me.

But when I pulled into my driveway, a sleek black car sat in my spot. I tensed, carefully navigating around the vehicle so I wouldn't block it in. The thing could only belong to one person, and I wasn't in the mood to deal with him.

I sat in my vehicle for a long moment contemplating leaving again, before sliding out of the seat and heading straight for my greenhouse. Caelan's presence tickled against my awareness. He wasn't inside my house, but he wasn't on the front porch either.

I made my way through the yard, unsurprised when Caelan

stepped into my path from the side of the house. Veering around him, I kept walking.

But his presence struck me like lightning. I hadn't seen him since the night Finn had found me—the night Caelan had given me the tools to save my life in the form of a dress attuned to my unique magic.

He was tall, broad-shouldered, and lean. Tousled dark hair framed a stunning face with high cheekbones and generous lips, but the thing that had always made me mute was Caelan's eyes. Storm gray and gold-flecked, those eyes had always stopped me in my tracks.

The Shifter Lord's form was barely restrained violence, his staggering magic tightly leashed. To my surprise, he looked tired.

My lip curled. His future bride must be keeping him up at night.

"Evie," his voice rumbled, caressing my skin.

I schooled my face, controlled my heartbeat into a steady, calm rhythm, and lifted a brow. "Stalking your wedding florist, Caelan? You can leave me a bad review if the flowers disappoint you. No need to show up at my house unannounced."

He fell into step beside me, his hands shoved into the pockets of his jeans. "Just wanted to make sure you didn't plan to poison the bouquets."

My lips twitched. "Only the boutonnieres."

"But not Rowan's?" he drawled.

The Shifter Lord knew I had a soft spot for the Pacific Northwest Lord. "He'd sense it beforehand, but no. Never Rowan. Not many people possess similar magic to mine. The Lord is deeply tied to the flora and fauna of his land, and the earth needs as much care as we can give it."

Caelan grunted in agreement. "And never Ben," he added softly.

His gaze rested on my face like a brand.

I stopped at the door to my greenhouse, hand resting on the

knob. The best path was ignoring that loaded question. "Why are you here, Lord?"

His low growl sent the hair on the back of my neck standing up. "Caelan," he snarled.

"You are the Shifter Lord of Texas and the Borderlands and newly engaged. I am an unmated woman." I turned my head to stare at him. "As such, it is inappropriate to use your given name." A tight smile, and I returned my attention to unlocking the door. "You should know this," I said as I breezed in.

Caelan followed, allowing the door to click shut behind him. Motion-activated lights buzzed and flicked on, casting the greenhouse in a warm, inviting glow.

Caelan blinked and sucked in a breath. "Evie," he whispered in awe.

Yep. I knew how he felt. My greenhouse was insanely decked out, both with technology and with flora. Dozens of structures hung from the ceiling, filled with baskets holding twining vines blooming with brightly colored flowers on one side of the greenhouse. On the other was an entire wall of baskets filled with newly budded strawberries. The back side of the wall held baskets of Dutchman's pipe, most teeming with Pipevine swallowtail butterflies. That setup took a while to perfect and ended up requiring a specific spell I had to refresh each season. I didn't want many insects in my greenhouse, but I was growing a ton of butterfly host plants and didn't want them to go to waste when I could invite the butterflies in to help their population.

I had them growing outside too, but Texas was hot as hell during the summer, and our part of the state was in drought more often than not. I might be a Floromancer, but I tried not to compete with Mother Nature. Here in the greenhouse, though, I was the mistress.

Six long planting benches stretched the greenhouse's entirety and went along all the walls, including the back. I used the middle two for planting, and the rest were storage for currently growing plants, seed starting, and miscellaneous other projects. I grew many things for my shop, but I also had things for my own use. Fruits and vegetables, cut flower varieties, plus blueberries and raspberries.

"This is something," Caelan murmured.

"Thank you. It took a while to complete, but the project was worth it." What I didn't add was Rowan had given me some great notes to help me keep the temperature controlled without skyrocketing my light bill, and he'd given me some apple tree starters. I was still on the fence about whether they'd grow or not, but Rowan had assured me he'd given them a boost.

Apple trees normally needed a sustained period of cold before fruiting, but Rowan said they could skip it this year, and he'd return next year and give them what they needed to produce.

So I planted them, keeping them close to the coolest part of the greenhouse, and they were still alive and had even sprouted a few new leaves.

"Seymour is still ornery as usual," Caelan murmured. "Two weeks ago, he gave me a bite that required Ben's expertise."

I chewed on my lip to keep from laughing. Seymour was the bespelled Red Dragon flytrap I'd given him. He was meant to be a little ornery, but not deadly. My spell must have gone a bit awry, or Seymour had taken on a mind of his own.

"If he's biting you, he must feel threatened."

Caelan's withering look almost made me laugh out loud. "That thing is a menace," he muttered.

I pulled a few pots forward and reached for the flat of creeping thyme seedlings on the bottom shelf. These would leave the greenhouse in a couple more weeks to grow in my landscaping bed. I reached once more for the cascading petunia hybrids I created. Once they bloomed, they would provide a stunning riot of color outside the shop and my front door.

"You can give Seymour back if he's that much trouble."

He blinked. "No. He's fine."

I eyed him and spotted a telltale white bandage peeking from the underside of his forearm at the edge of his partially rolled-up sleeve. "Is that what he did?"

Caelan shoved his sleeve down. "It's a minor scratch."

I snorted. "You're a shifter. Wearing a bandage. The wound seems more than minor."

"Seymour is fine," he growled. "I'm not giving him back."

My hands stilled as a smile tugged at my mouth. "Aww. You have a soft spot for that deadly little plant."

Caelan rolled his eyes. "I like puzzles."

"How's the other one doing?"

His smile made my heart skip a beat. "The water to Seymour's fire. She's taken on quite the personality and has grown quite close to Simone."

I'd spelled the vine, too, but only in a way to give it more autonomy. The turtle vine had taken a shine to Caelan right away. "You're giving her the right conditions to grow?"

"Of course. I follow your instructions to the letter." But his brow furrowed.

"What? Is there something wrong with her?"

"No. Quite the opposite. Sometimes I find her in…different places."

I tilted my head and studied him. "I'm going to need a little more."

"She moves herself. I don't know how, but I'll have her on the window ledge one day, and the next I find her on my desk, or by Simone's favorite chair. One time, I found her in the conference room, sitting where Rowan always sits."

I blinked in surprise. "Err. Maybe I should take her back instead of Seymour."

Caelan shook his head. "No. She's harmless. I think she's curious, that's all."

"Would you like me to take a look when I come for your meeting?"

Caelan stiffened when I reminded him of his upcoming

wedding. Tension lined his frame. "I've been meaning to speak with you about this."

"This?" I laughed. "You mean your wedding."

"Yes," he said through gritted teeth.

I carefully added dirt to a large, decorative pot. "There's no need. You could have sent Simone with any message you had."

His fingers curled around my arm. "Evie."

Heat seeped through my sleeve, his touch electrifying. I stared at his tanned, elegant hand and pulled my arm away.

"I had no choice." His voice was low and harsh. "I—"

I went back to filling the pot. "We all have a choice. You made yours." Once that one was full, I pulled a matching pot over and started the process again.

Magic pulsed around me, reacting to all the plant life, but also to Caelan's presence. Very few people came into my sanctum, and my plants were unsure about him. The Shifter Lord was leashed violence, strength and power vibrating in his every motion.

"The other Lords have begun questioning my grip on my territory."

Once that pot was full, I pulled the flat of petunias over. "This is none of my concern, Caelan. And I don't want to be involved. It's always dangerous for me to know more than I should."

"You are involved," he snarled. "The other Lords recognize how powerful you are and…" He stopped himself and turned, swearing under his breath.

My magic reacted to his words. Petunias grew half an inch under my fingertips, and the butterflies on the pipe vines fluttered back through the greenhouse opening as the leaves shuddered. The greenhouse rumbled, stones shifting against each other as they reacted to my emotional turbulence.

"And what?" Power turned my voice deeper. "I made a mistake when I saved you that night."

Caelan stilled, his eyes flashing golden. "You would have left me to die, flower girl?"

No, but he didn't need to know that. "If I had, I would be

tending my greenhouse without the threat of destruction hanging over my head every time a Shifter Lord comes around."

He stepped closer, heat radiating from his body. A finger reached out and brushed my hair from my face. "No, Evie. If you'd left me to die in that forest, someone else would have taken my place, and it wouldn't have been your pretty flower-loving Rowan or gentle Ben."

"Hmm." I turned my body into his. "But would he be better than you?"

Caelan's hand dropped like I burned him. Our eyes locked, his blazing with fury. "In only a few weeks, I'd managed to forget how vicious your tongue is."

"And I'd forgotten how calm my life is without you in it."

Caelan snorted and took a step back, his heat retreating with him. I mourned it for a second before steeling myself against his presence. Being vicious-tongued was one of my few defenses against him.

"For what it's worth, I didn't want to hire you," he said.

I blinked. "Then why did you?"

He inhaled a heavy breath. "Simone made me."

"Simone? Why in the world would she do that?"

"For some reason I've yet to fathom, she likes you."

"Or it could be that I'm the best florist in the state," I snapped.

Caelan grinned. "Regardless, you and I are stuck together."

I lifted a shoulder. "I have a kill clause in the contract. All you have to do is say the word. You'll forfeit your deposit, but I'm sure that's a drop of water in a rainstorm for you."

"It *would* be easier if I canceled," Caelan mused.

For both of us. I could go back to my normal life and pretend I'd never met him, and he could continue being our fearless leader with a brand-new bride by his side. That would be for the best.

"Have Simone send a request in writing to the shop email. As soon as I receive it, I'll stop the supply order from being filled." I paused and forced the rest of the words out. "Best of luck on your upcoming nuptials."

Caelan's low chuckle walked down my spine. "I said if."

I started placing petunias around the inner edges of the pot. "You just said you didn't want to hire me. Simone isn't the Shifter Lord. You are." I patted the soil down on the first. "So fire me already. It's best for everyone."

"Evie."

I dug another small hole in the pot and placed another petunia, leaving the middle open for another plant, maybe a grass. I needed something taller in that spot and in the small area left around whatever I put. Planting gorgeous pots had three simple rules: thriller, filler, and spiller.

You need something to draw the eye, something tall and showy in the middle. I tucked a pretty ornamental grass in the spot. The next layer needed to be a filler. I looked around and spotted some salvia that would stay on the shorter side. Grabbing those, I dug small holes and planted them around the thriller.

"Evie," Caelan said again.

"I don't think there's anything left to say. If you don't want to fire me, I'll be at the scheduled meeting."

His heavy sigh made me still. "Does it have to be like this?"

I slammed the empty grass pot down. "You are not a normal man, Caelan! You're a Lord, and I am a florist. A Floromancer. We could never have a normal friendship." An annoyed growl rumbled from my throat. Around me, plants grew several inches. Caelan's eyes flicked around the greenhouse, cataloguing threats. "But I'm not sure if that's what you're even asking, and if it's the other thing, that's even worse!"

Caelan rubbed a hand over his chin. "We can have a friendship. If you want."

I laughed and pulled the next pot over, repeating the process, but switching out the grass for a small palm. "For the love of the gods, just fire me. Make it easy on yourself and me for once."

A hand on my waist and a gentle shove, and my back was to the work table, Caelan pressed against me, his hard chest against mine, and one of his thighs between my legs. My heart raced as he placed both hands opposite my body and leaned in.

He pressed his nose in the vulnerable spot between my neck and shoulder and inhaled. I froze even as my insides turned to liquid heat. When his tongue flicked out and laved the same spot, a soft moan escaped me. Caelan's grip tightened, his massive hand curving over my hip.

"I don't want to be friends with you, flower girl," he murmured against my neck.

"I knew it," I breathed.

He raised his head, grey eyes burning into mine. "I didn't come here for…this."

"I'd hope not. Your fiancée is going to be big mad." He was still pressed against me, and my fingers itched to pull him closer, to take his scent into my body and hold it there forever.

This was madness.

He snorted and stepped away, his hand sliding down my hip and giving it a rough squeeze before it dropped.

"My fiancée and I do not have that sort of relationship."

My brow furrowed. "You mean the kind where you care if your husband is putting his hands on another woman?"

Caelan shoved his hands into his pockets and watched me.

"Oh," I said softly, yearning to reach out to him. I stayed where I was, the wooden work table digging into the skin of my back. "For what it's worth, I'm sorry. You deserve someone to lose their mind over something like that."

One side of his mouth curved up. "And you would care?"

"I'd rip that bitch's hair right out of her head and stab my husband if he dared touch another woman." Not that it would ever happen for me. I had far too many secrets to dive into a relationship. Speaking of…I had to do something about Ben. My heart was softening toward him, and I was dangerous to be around. For many reasons.

Caelan's eyes widened before he barked a laugh. "The man you choose will be very lucky, Evie."

I snorted. "Doubtful, but thank you."

He didn't say anything for a long moment. But then, a strange look crossed his face.

A look I did not like.

"What?"

"I'm not going to fire you, Evie. The opposite, in fact."

My heart stopped. "Err. What's the opposite? I'm already hired."

A slow shit-eating grin formed on his face. "We'll address your new role at the meeting."

I took a step forward. "Caelan."

He took a step back, that disturbing grin never leaving his face. "Have a good evening, flower girl."

"Caelan!"

His low chuckle sent a chill down my spine. I hurried after him, but Caelan was too fast. In the blink of an eye, his car was peeling out of my driveway, gravel spraying behind the bumper.

Well, shit.

Early the next morning, I arrived at the shop only to see Moira had gotten there before me. Not a rare occurrence, but not too common, either. I came in through the back to see her staring at the ward.

A horrific scent blasted me right in the face. "Ugh. What is that?"

Moira pointed at the bouquet. "I'd wager a guess it's that thing."

I handed her an Earl Grey latte I'd picked up. Her eyes lit up when she saw it. "Thanks. I just got here, but the smell was so bad I didn't want to start a pot." She grimaced. "Just in case that smell seeped into the tea."

The smell was hard to describe. Like hot, rotting garbage, with a sinister beat of magic pulsing at its heart. I had to get this thing out of my shop before it started running customers off. I took a step closer and peered through the ward.

"The preservation spell failed. Again." I swore as I straightened. "This bouquet might not be salvageable."

"Who'd want to keep that thing, anyway?" Moira shook her head and started toward the main shop doors.

"The bride might be human. Maybe she can't sense the same

thing we can." I dropped the ward and reached for the magic dampening sack. "I'm going to stick this back in the fridge." Hazel would be here soon, but if the preservation spells kept fading, there was no reason to keep the thing warded. The pouch would suppress its power long enough for Hazel to get here.

Ash pushed through the doors, yawning and immediately regretting it when the scent hit him. "Oh, gods. That is rank!"

Moira pointed to the pouch. "Blame the cursed bouquet."

Tess came in right after Ash and gagged. "We should chuck that in the bin."

I zipped the pouch shut and held it at arm's length. Even through the material, I could feel the sinister beat of its power.

"We can't. It's sentimental." They followed me to the walk-in and watched as I deposited the bundle in the very back.

Careful not to touch anything, I held both hands up and waited for Ash to open the door for me. "I need to wash my hands."

"We all need decon baths," Moira said.

"Maybe we should light a candle," Tess added. "Everywhere."

"Good idea." I hurried to the office and carried a couple of well-loved candles out, setting them at opposite sides of the room. "Everything should be back to normal by the time we open."

"What about opening the doors to let some air in?" Moira mused.

Everyone let out a vocal protest that made the vampire laugh. We might be getting close to autumn, but it was still hot as hell outside. The mornings were somewhat cool, but air conditioning was cooler.

"Candles it is," Moira said, stepping away from the door.

Through the banter, a thought occurred to me. "Moira, can you bring all the info about the bouquet over, including the intake form the mom signed?"

Moira gave me a curious look but went to the box where we kept most of our important ledgers. I motioned her over to the worktable and pushed a stool over to her. We both sat and Moira unlocked the box, pulling everything out. Ash and Tess lingered by the register, murmuring in quiet conversation.

A few minutes later, the scent of a strong dark roast filled the shop air and a steaming mug appeared before both of us, courtesy of Ash. I gave him a grateful smile and took a sip of the brew, glad caffeine didn't give me the jitters like it did humans sometimes.

"Are we sure the woman who brought the bouquet in was actually her mother?" I asked as I examined the ledger one more time.

Moira's mouth opened, then snapped shut. "I guess not. I had no reason to doubt her."

"And we're sure there was a wedding?"

Moira's jaw tightened. "Do you think the bouquet is meant for you?"

The thought had niggled at me for a while, but it made no sense. There were dozens of easier ways to get to me, and if anyone knew even a little about my power, they'd know I'd sense the magic clinging to the petals.

"If someone wanted to take me out, there are tons of easier ways to get the job done," I said.

Moira blew out a breath. "I hate when you talk like that."

"It's true, though." Tapping my fingers on the shiny wood, I flipped through the rest of the papers, trying to see if I'd missed anything. But it wasn't until the intake form that I spotted it. "There."

Moira leaned closer. At the bottom of the form was a space that asked for the wedding planner's information. We rarely used that box because most people these days don't use the services of a planner. More brides than ever preferred DIYing certain parts of the wedding to save money, and planners were becoming a dying breed.

"I suspected it was her."

Moira snorted. "Caroline Merritt. Queen of the soulless mood board wedding."

Caroline had a knack for copying something down to the

errant string, but her weddings came off as cookie cutter copies rather than anything filled with joy or heart. For humans, that didn't matter so much. But for paranorms, weddings were rare and precious. Immortals did not take weddings or joinings lightly. Thus, Caroline had fallen out of favor with many in Joy Springs.

But this bride was human and might not have realized or… she'd been encouraged to use Caroline for some nefarious reason.

But something about this bothered me. "Caroline usually checks for nefarious magic," I murmured. "Why wouldn't she do so this time?"

Ash leaned over to freshen our coffees. "Maybe she never met the groom. It's not outside the realm of possibility, especially if he traveled a lot or wasn't involved in planning."

"Maybe," Moira acknowledged.

But it didn't feel right.

"You think they threw money at her?" I asked at Moira's thoughtful look.

"Possible, but Caroline comes from money."

Ash snorted. "Rich people stay rich because they don't turn their nose up at more money."

"Not all of them," Tess said as she floated over. "The smart ones invest wisely and don't buy a new Porsche every few years."

My nose wrinkled. "Those things seem like death traps."

"Death is a lot more fun when you're going 190 miles per hour," Ash murmured.

"What about some kind of magical influence?" I asked. "Could someone have spelled her into silence?"

"Maybe," Moira said. "Or compelled silence from her."

"Interesting. Did you hear back from the mother?"

"Nothing as of this morning, but the email was delivered, so it wasn't a fake address."

I grimaced. "The person might know we're onto them."

Moira shook her head. "All the questions were pretty innocent. But I don't think we should ask her again. Or whoever it is who owns the email address."

"Should we pay Caroline a visit?" Ash asked.

I nodded. "After the meeting at the Keep."

Once I drained my coffee, I stood. "I'm going to try to see if I can get anything from the blooms."

"You haven't tried already?" Moira asked, surprise in her tone.

"Only the preservation spells. I try not to read the memories from anything our customers bring us. Doing so could degrade the plant."

"I guess it wouldn't hurt too much now since it's beginning to fall apart." Moira rose. "I'll walk with you."

"Thanks. It should be fine, but the magic is unfamiliar to me, so better safe than sorry."

"How can something so pretty be so vile?" Moira whispered, standing slightly behind me and peering at the bouquet over my shoulder.

"Everything we touch holds a resonance of our energy. For it to hold this much, the groom must have either spent a lot of time around the bouquet or handled it for more than a few minutes at a time."

"Weird." Moira stepped up beside me, rubbing her hands over her arms. "Grooms usually care little for the nuts and bolts of a wedding."

"Right. Which is why this is so strange."

We stared at the thing for a while.

"Are you going to touch it or stand there all day?" Moira said, amusement coloring her voice.

"Haven't decided yet."

"I don't blame you."

Finally ready, I reached out and touched one finger to the middle bloom, the blush rose still in perfect condition.

Normally, when I focused my magic on memory retrieval, I'd get a flash or two back, a hint of a larger memory. Sometimes, I'd get a full memory. Today, I got way more than I bargained for.

A stunning bride with mahogany-colored hair, dressed in her wedding finery, standing in a tastefully decorated room, crying. "He's different!" she screamed. "He's not the same man I'm supposed to marry!"

The back of a shifter, hunched over, fur crawling down powerful arms, groaning in pain. His nails were curved into lethal claws, blood soaking his hands all the way to his wrists.

A small chapel with stained glass windows, burnished oak pews, and a flower strewn aisle with a white runner, smiling family and friends in attendance, but one individual snagged her attention.

Finn, his eyes burning with malice, sat toward the back, a small smile on his lips.

I jerked out of the vision with a harsh gasp, magic punching me in the stomach.

Moira caught me as I sagged. "Evie!"

"Finn," I breathed. "He was at their wedding."

Moira's low curse and my harsh breathing were the only sounds in the fridge. She helped me to the floor and sat down beside me. "He's one of Caelan's then?"

I shook my head. "No way to tell. It's possible. Finn posed as Halvar for months, maybe years. But there was no sign of Caelan in the chapel."

"What else?"

"The bride said the groom wasn't the same person she was supposed to marry. I saw him, but his back was turned to me. He'd partially shifted, and there was blood all over his hands and wrists."

Moira's expression turned grim. "We're supposed to go to the Keep tomorrow. It might be a good time to ask."

I hadn't told Moira about Caelan showing up at my house. "Right," I said. "If I can get him alone."

Moira's eyebrows wiggled. "If you get him alone, I'm sure you won't be talking about rogue shifters."

I shoved her shoulder, making her laugh. "Perv."

"Please," Moira said as she stood and held her hand out to

help me. "You haven't had a real date in years. That thing might be a dried-up old prune if it's still there."

"It's my prune," I said primly as I got to my feet. "They last way longer than fresh plums, anyway."

"Because prunes are for old people," Moira retorted, her snickering laugh following her out of the walk-in.

"Jerk," I muttered.

Once I'd put the evil bouquet back into the bag, I locked the walk-in and headed back to the front, going straight to the sink to scrub my hands.

"What did you get?" Ash called from his bonsai table.

The dryad was hunched over a small red maple. He held a pair of tiny scissors in one hand and used the other to slowly turn the lazy Susan that held the ceramic pot holding the tree. His bonsais were revered and rare, each taking months, sometimes years, before they were ready to go to a new home.

I'd begged him for one for years, and all he would say was that he had one for me, but it wasn't ready yet. Knowing Ash was set in his ways, I never asked again. If he said he had one, I believed him.

Patience was a virtue, especially when it came to dealing with a living, breathing, talking tree.

I repeated the story, telling him we would go see Caroline once the shop closed unless someone wanted to stay behind. Tess raised her hand.

"I'll stay. Investigating doesn't appeal to me."

Moira snorted and ruffled the banshee's hair. "I love how uncurious you are. It's refreshing."

Tess lifted a shoulder, her orange cardigan sliding to reveal pale skin. "Human motives have never been something I'm curious about. Only the immortal world piques my curiosity."

Everyone fell silent before Moira let out a dry, "Good to know, ghostie."

Ash chuckled.

"Banshee," Tess insisted. "We are far more evolved than our ghost counterparts."

"Regardless," I interrupted before their banter could turn into bickering, "we may not be back before closing time. Can you handle it on your own?"

Tess looked offended. "I've been with you for years. Of course I can handle things on my own. Closing is a simplistic act. I merely must remember to clean up and lock the doors."

That wasn't quite everything, but if she managed to do both of those things, it was good enough.

"Alright. Let's eat lunch and head out. Any preferences?"

And so began the inevitable lunch argument. A smile tugged at my lips. Sometimes things that never changed were a comfort.

We were just about to head out the door to visit Caroline's office when the bell jingled and Simone breezed in, looking smart in a pair of black trousers and a patterned blouse. She held a large black box in one hand and her trusty tablet in the other.

"Oh!" She stopped abruptly. "Going somewhere?"

No one said a word. "Team building exercise," I blurted when the silence got awkward.

Simone's eyes went to Tess who was hunched on the stool behind the register. She offered the shifter a lazy hand gesture. "I do not care for team building since everyone will die soon enough."

I put my hand over my mouth to keep from laughing.

Simone's jaw dropped and her brow furrowed. I watched as a dozen thoughts crossed her face, before shaking her head and letting out a small, frustrated sigh. Everyone felt like that around Tess at one time or another.

"Do you have time to finalize the details for tomorrow?" she asked.

"Details? Don't we just show up prepared to take notes?" I asked.

Simone's eyes flickered. "Not quite." She juggled the things in her hands before leaning the box against the wall by the door and fished in her purse. A moment later, she produced a scroll and handed it over.

"A scroll?" Moira said. "For real?"

Simone rolled her eyes. "He's the Shifter Lord. Appearance is everything."

"If you're in a video game," Moira said. "An email usually suffices in the twenty-first century."

Simone gave her a flat look.

I loosened Caelan's formal seal and unrolled the scroll, skimming the contents.

It was an agenda of sorts written in a scrawling, feminine hand. Most of it was normal except for one note:

Bride: TBD

My eyebrows lifted. "I thought the wedding already had a bride. Isn't that the usual order of things?"

Simone's nostrils flared. "Someone's idea of a joke."

"But not yours?" Moira asked.

The shifter ignored her, stooping to pick up the box. "Evie, this is for you."

I didn't take the box. "What is it?"

"From the Shifter Lord. The occasion is formal."

I sighed. "Seriously. No one wears ballgowns to meetings. Is that what this is? Another gown?"

Simone let out a pained sigh. "I'm only the messenger. Can you please just take the box and address it with Caelan at another time?"

"Fine," I growled, taking the box from her outstretched hands. "But he'll hear about this later."

Her lips twitched. "Of that, I have no doubt."

"Dammit," Moira said. "How come I never get a dress?"

Everyone ignored her. Getting a dress from the Shifter Lord could only bring trouble, and Moira was refreshingly free of that.

Simone turned to go but paused at the door. "Evie."

I hitched my purse higher on my shoulder and moved the sack

holding the bouquet to the other hand. "I know. Please don't antagonize the Shifter Lord tomorrow."

Sadness flashed across her face. "No. That wasn't what I was going to say at all."

Surprised, I blinked and fell silent.

A small smile played over the shifter's lips. "I was going to say be yourself. Caelan needs that right now."

Moira's delighted chuckle sent my hackles up.

"I'm not sure how to take that."

Ash snorted as Simone sailed through the door without answering.

"I think she's implying our beloved Shifter Lord might be going through it and some normalcy would be nice."

I glared at the dryad. "Trust me when I say there is nothing normal about our dynamic."

"Maybe not, but it's normal to him. Caelan seems like the kind of shifter who likes a little violence with his romance." Moira winked and held the door open.

"There is no romance," I growled under my breath. "He's getting married."

"Mm-hmm," Moira said, winking at me as I passed.

I let out a huff of annoyance which sent Ash into a fit of laughter.

I didn't say anything else until we were situated in the car and on the road.

"Can we please try to behave ourselves at Caroline's?"

Moira grinned, her bright white teeth shining in the sunlight. No fangs present. She wasn't like a lot of vamps who chose to flash them all the time, a fact I appreciated about her. "No promises, but we'll try."

That was about the best I could hope for with this motley crew of friends.

CHAPTER
Five

Caroline's office was in one of the few "high-rises" Joy Springs had, which wasn't saying much. We pulled up to a six-story building and parked. I never had any need to visit this part of town, so I wasn't very familiar with the area. From the look of it, this part of town held little natural appeal. Most of the trees had been destroyed to make room for office buildings, retail space, and wide-open parking lots, something that hurt my heart every time I passed by the place.

Caroline's office was on the third floor, a small space with a decorative wood sign that read, "Caroline Merritt Weddings." Her office hours were posted on another more sedate sign to the right of the door, along with another note that said walk-ins were welcome.

Good thing because we went in, regardless. The waiting area looked straight out of an interior design magazine, everything situated just so to produce a farmhouse chic vibe, but I felt nothing. Even though it looked appealing and like it cost a lot of money, every product here was made or produced in another land, most of it plastic or mass produced.

Even the furniture was particle board or that new "lumber" that had always puzzled me—poly lumber, I think it was called.

Made from a mix of recycled plastic and wood fiber, the material was resistant to weather and wear but possessed zero soul. Whatever life the wood had once possessed had slowly drowned under the tight grip of the plastic encasing it. A faint chemical smell tingled my nose as I walked up to the reception area.

A woman who resembled the lifeless poly lumber greeted me. She was slim and possessed the same nose I'd seen across every influencer's social media channel showing up on my algorithm. Puffed lips courtesy of a local beautician witch (or so she called herself), and the kind of brows that looked frightening when you got too close framed a face with too much cheek filler and a heavy layer of foundation and bronzer.

My magic always itched when I ventured too close to a human like this. I never pitied humans if I could help it. They lived their lives like a burning star, knowing they were close to death and embracing every second they could. But when someone messed with nature and injected substances into their face, my fingers itched to reach for them and extract every bit.

Not because I judged them for it, but because when those humans closed their eyes for the last time and someone they loved put them into the ground, those substances would leak into the ground, poisoning our water systems and earth with toxic chemicals.

This was an odd quirk of my magic, and something I never mentioned to anyone, but with the explosion of social media and corporations continued advertisements preying on women's insecurities and ridiculous societal expectations, the amount of people who had procedures like this had skyrocketed over the last several years.

I don't think I could survive in Los Angeles or New York.

The woman's brow barely crinkled. Magic sparked at my fingertips, itching to pull out that neurotoxin and dissolve it harmlessly into the atmosphere. As body pollutants went, that one metabolized inside the body and was technically a natural substance—specifically a bacterium called Clostridium botulinum. "May I help you?"

I realized I'd been staring at her for way longer than was polite. "Yes. Sorry. I'm here to see Caroline Merritt."

"Do you have an appointment?"

"No. But she'll want to see me. My name is Evie Quinn."

Her eyes said, *we'll see about that,* but the woman reached for her phone and pressed a button.

You okay? Moira mouthed.

I nodded, realizing she'd seen me acting weird. It'd been a while since Caroline and I had spoken. I could only hope she stayed off the procedure train.

And honestly, don't even get me started about the funeral business and their blatant disregard for the environment. Decomposing bodies trashed the environment. Humans were filled with microplastics and heavy metals, all of it leeching into the earth, but throw in conventional burial practices and how they affected the earth while funeral homes lined their pockets…well, if things didn't change soon, we were all screwed.

The women made some affirmative noises, then hung up the phone. "Go right in, Miss Quinn."

Ash and Moira rose to follow. We entered a lavishly decorated office with a large tinted window allowing filtered light to come in. Caroline sat in an executive leather chair behind a burnished cherrywood desk, a credenza littered with awards and trophies behind her.

She wore a lavender suit with gold jewelry at her throat and ears. Her makeup was perfectly applied and…there it was.

Lip filler and Botox.

I stifled a sigh and squashed my rebelling magic, offering her a friendly smile. "Hello, Caroline. Long time, no talk."

She gave me a blinding white smile and rose from behind the desk to extend a hand with perfectly manicured nails. We shook, the moment our hands met, the feeling of wrongness brushing against my senses.

Her magic didn't feel the same anymore. I didn't react and resisted the urge to wipe my hand against my thigh to rub the feeling away.

"What a surprise!" Her gaze landed on Moira and flicked to Ash, a subtle appreciative curve to her lips as her eyes raked over him. "I didn't realize you had a dryad on your team."

Ash didn't usually go out with us, but he'd loosened up over the years.

"This is Ash and Moira."

Caroline didn't shake their hands, instead inclining her head regally. She perched on the edge of her desk, her bare, shiny legs crossed demurely.

Her office had the same false feel as the outside, though her desk and credenza were made of real wood. The stain and polyurethane coating had diminished the wood's natural energy, but I could breathe easier in here. Somewhat.

A glass and chrome table topped with a wooden vase filled with white roses sat by the window, wedding magazines scattered purposely across the surface. There was a seating area at the back of the opposite wall, a long, emerald green couch with a matching loveseat on the other side. A glass table separated them, the centerpiece another hastily put together wedding bouquet.

I hated it here.

"What brings you in today?" Caroline's eyes glittered. "I've heard some rumors about you and a certain Shifter Lord."

The woman practically vibrated with greed. Nailing down a Lord's wedding would be the scoop of the century. "If you're here for my services, I'm happy to oblige."

Ash coughed to cover up a laugh.

"Sorry," I said. "I hope to be single forever."

Moira snorted.

Caroline's lips thinned. "I see. If you aren't here for my services, please explain why you're here. I have a busy schedule and do not have time for social calls."

"We both know I wouldn't come here for a social call," I said dryly.

She rose and went back around to her chair, putting the desk between us. A power move I didn't give a shit about.

"A bouquet has come into our possession recently. The mother requested we preserve it."

Caroline flicked a hand. "Normal business for you, I assume. What does it have to do with me?"

She'd done nothing to trigger my inner alarm yet, but Caroline and I would never be friends simply because she was terrible. "You're correct in that the practice is common. We preserve a few bouquets per month, but this one is different."

Caroline stilled.

Now we were getting somewhere. "There's some residual magic making it difficult to preserve. I was curious because I know you're well versed in magic types, and I believe you don't take cases where you believe the marriage won't last. Is that correct?"

She crossed her arms. "I'm not omnipotent," she said, her tone clipped. "I can't always predict whether a marriage will be successful."

"But you have a good track record, correct?"

Caroline shrugged, the compliment pleasing her based on the curve to her lip. "Upwards of ninety-eight percent. Which wedding are we speaking of?"

I rattled off the last name. Caroline froze before plastering a smile on her face. "Ah yes. I remember that one! She was such a lovely bride. The wedding went off without a hitch."

From the earlier vision, that was a lie.

I walked over to the glass table by the window and pulled the bouquet from the sack. Malevolent magic filled the room. I grimaced and stepped away.

Caroline paled.

"What was the bride's name?" I asked.

She lifted a tanned hand to her head and rubbed her temples.

"I—I don't remember. She wasn't from here but said she was moving after the wedding. I remember she was sweet. Quiet. Forgettable."

Moira rose and walked over to Caroline's desk, leaning over it. She made it easy to forget how deadly she was usually, but today, with her dark hair swinging forward and hypnotic magic swirling around her, Moira looked every inch the predator.

The audible noise of Caroline swallowing made Moira smile. "Who dropped it off the day of the wedding?"

Caroline flinched. "I can't remember." Her voice quivered. "That's not normal. What is happening to me?" She exhaled heavily. "A woman? A man?" Caroline shook her head. "I'm sorry. I don't know."

Moira and I exchanged a grim look. Caroline was showing classic signs of memory tampering. The most likely culprit?

Finn.

Dammit.

I came closer to Moira, guilt eating at me. "Try harder, Caroline. Remember."

Caroline blinked, tears filling her eyes. She squeezed them shut. The room shuddered. I turned toward the door only to see the rose petals dampen with blood, the liquid dripping onto the pristine glass table.

I blinked, and they were normal again. The room had stopped moving, but Caroline was weeping. "I'm not supposed to remember him. He said he'd make me like the groom if I talked."

The flap of wings sounding made me turn once more to the window. A huge black bird with burning red eyes landed on the sill.

Not Poe. Not a raven at all. Something different, a modified crow perhaps.

The thing watched us with an unnerving intensity, but there was something familiar...

Shit.

I turned to where Caroline couldn't see my face and mouthed, "Fuck you," to the window.

The bird let out an unholy shriek and pecked at the glass. A hole the size of a bullet appeared, sending spider-webbed cracks spiraling throughout the glass.

I turned away, trusting Moira to take care of the problem if the bird that was not a bird managed to get inside. The vampire's eyes flashed with violence as she sauntered closer to the window.

"What happened to the groom?" I asked Caroline.

"I don't know!" Caroline's hands trembled. A broken sob escaped her. "I can't remember. I'm so sorry." She put her head down on her desk and cried.

The bird let out another ear-splitting shriek and flapped away.

We'd gotten all we could out of her. Ash, who'd sat quietly through the entire ordeal, said nothing as we walked out, past the receptionist staring at us with judgment in her eyes, and into the elevator.

"That bird," he said at last. "Was it Finn?"

I nodded. "I'm afraid so."

"Does he always have the red eyes?" Moira asked. "If he does, that will help us identify him."

"I don't think so. At least not while he's in human form. Maybe only when he's in animal form?" The memories of my attack were hazy at best, prone to showing up in my dreams, but try as I might, I couldn't remember Finn's eyes when he shifted.

"Caelan might know," Moira mused. "There's no way he didn't shift into wolf form while the Lords were gathered."

As loathe as I was to talk to Caelan about anything, we'd already be at the Keep tomorrow, and I had other things to discuss with him. "I'll ask," I said begrudgingly.

Right after I bitched at him about the dress.

Once we were safely in the car and a few miles down the road, we spoke about Caroline.

"I don't think she's lying," Moira said.

"Agreed. She's too scared to lie convincingly."

The bouquet lay in the back seat, as far away from Ash as he could get it.

"And Finn was involved. Somehow," I said, surprised that I was actually surprised. He'd shown himself to be a despicable male, so it wasn't a stretch for him to curse a symbol of love and hope to get his way. But what did he want?

That was the million-dollar question.

Later, when we returned to the shop, I opened the box Simone had given me and pulled out a shimmering emerald silk floor length sheath dress pulsing with magic. It was similar to the other gown he'd given me for the formal dinner where Finn had attacked, but this one was slinkier with cleaner lines. The other dress had embroidered flowers all over the skirt, hundreds of tiny flowers brimming with plant life. This one only had embroidery across the bodice, primed with deadly seeds and vines.

I wanted to hate it but smiled despite myself. The dress was gorgeous and deadly. Like Caelan.

Maybe like me, too.

Ash whistled under his breath. "You're going to look like a knockout in that, Evie."

I turned, holding the dress up to the golden light. The silk shimmered like a jewel, magic glinting from the bodice. Ash moved closer, peering at the bodice with narrowed eyes.

"Do you know who's creating these dresses?"

I shook my head. "No idea. They're stunning, but I could never afford something like this on my own."

Ash chuckled. "Keep antagonizing Caelan and you might find yourself a rich woman." He winked and walked out of the office.

I shook my head and carefully folded the dress, placing it back into the mountain of tissue paper inside the box. A faint floral scent and Caelan's lingering magic pulsed against my palm.

How had a man I didn't trust come to know me so deeply? Discomfited, I put the lid on the box and carried it to the car.

I hadn't decided whether to wear it yet, but as I walked out, a delivery man holding another box walked in.

"Is there a Moira Devlin here?" he asked.

The vampire's brows rose. "Here." She took the offered clipboard and scrawled her signature before the man handed her the box. "Who's it from?"

The man's brow furrowed. "The Shifter Lord, ma'am." He dipped his head and left the shop.

We stared at the box like it was a snake.

"Should we set it on fire?" Moira asked.

I wanted to laugh, but her question was serious. "No," I said after a moment. "Caelan knows you're my bestie and how I might react if anything were to happen to you."

She frowned. "I don't sense a heartbeat inside. Can you take a look, too?"

I bent and pressed my palm against the top of the box, trying to sense if there was anything alive or sentient inside. Rising, I shook my head. "All I sense is Caelan's magic."

Moira sighed and reached for a pair of scissors lying on the worktable. "If this bites me, I'm going to bite you."

"You can try." I gave her a smile with all teeth.

Moira unsealed the box, keeping it at an arm's distance, as if she expected whatever was inside to reach up and bite her as soon as she opened the flaps. Instead, a hint of vampiric magic mixed with Caelan's floated up, and Moira gasped with delight.

"Oh," she breathed, reaching in to pull out a shimmering garment of crimson silk. "Mama like."

Moira held up a calf-length silk dress, with a scandalous neckline and a slit cut all the way to the upper thigh. She pressed the garment against her, swaying left and right.

I gaped. That was quite the dress. A slip of paper fell as she moved.

"There's a note." I picked it up and unfolded the parchment.

Miss Devlin,

Only the best for my favorite Floromancer's best friend. Be careful, my dear. On the right person, this dress might tame a Lord.

It was signed Caelan.

Moira's eyes glittered with amusement. "I like your Lord, Evie. He's a troublemaker."

"He's a menace," I muttered. "From his note, it seems like there might be another Lord there?"

Moira wiggled her eyebrows. "I hope it's that delicious Soren." She closed her eyes. "He is yummy."

"And an unrepentant womanizer."

Moira rolled her eyes. "All the Shifter Lords are womanizers. Just think. If I managed to tame Soren, we could still live right next door. He's the Lord of the South, so…just a hop, skip, and a jump back here." She grinned.

"Absolutely not. You're not leaving the shop. Ever." My words were gruff, but we both knew I'd never stop her from following her heart. Even if it was for Soren. I eyed her. "You're not seriously going to pursue him, are you?"

She snorted. "Soren? Absolutely not." Moira's eyes glittered with laughter. "Haven't you heard? He's an unrepentant womanizer."

CHAPTER

Six

The shop's air felt stale, heavy with an unfamiliar tang of magic. I stilled just outside my office door, a chill running down my spine. Setting my purse down, I crept through the back on silent feet, keeping my eyes peeled for anything strange or anyone who wasn't supposed to be here.

I sent out a soft pulse of magic, but the plants were alert, not alarmed. Seconds later, I discovered the door to the walk-in fridge wide open. A sound of dismay escaped me as I walked inside.

The preservation pouch holding the bouquet pulsed a faint crimson color, malicious magic beating at me. I grimaced and inspected everything inside. The rot hadn't penetrated anything else yet, but I needed to get this thing out of my shop before it did. Every display or arrangement I built had a protective shield and preservation spell woven into the plant's life force, something I did for my own peace of mind.

And thank goodness I had. If I'd left everything unprotected, I might have lost thousands in inventory.

The front shop door opened, Moira and Ash's laughter floating through the space.

"Guys, can you come back here?" I called.

Their conversation stopped abruptly, and moments later, three faces appeared. Ash recoiled, his handsome face paling. "What happened?"

"The walk-in's door was ajar this morning. Something happened to the bouquet, but I haven't opened the pouch yet."

"No one went near that awful thing once we put it back last night," Moira confirmed.

Ash nodded. "I double-checked the latch before I left. Everything was sealed tight."

"Dammit." I put my hands on my hips and glared at the thing that was fast becoming the bane of my existence. "I need to check the flowers."

Ash grimaced. "Are you sure? I say we set the thing on fire."

"I'm inclined to agree, but maybe that's what it wants." I reached out and grabbed the pouch, magic soaking into my fingers.

"The table is clear," Moira said.

Tess let out a moan of dismay and floated behind Ash as I hurried over to the table and set the bouquet down. With trembling fingers, I opened the pouch and pulled the bouquet out.

No one said a word for a long moment.

Tess broke the silence. "It's dead but not dead." A note of awe trickled through her voice. "Cool."

"Not cool," I said with a shake of my head. The once vibrant green leaves had turned brown and were curling up. All the blush-colored flowers were leaking a strange, dark-colored sap. "I'm going to lift it. Bring over a pan or something we don't need so the thing doesn't ruin my table."

Ash hurried back with one of those disposable foil pans, sliding it under as I lifted the flowers. Once it was situated away from my table, I slumped onto a stool. "Maybe we *should* set it on fire."

"I'm game," Moira said.

"I plan to speak to Hazel tonight. If she's not here in twenty-four hours, I may just do that." I pulled the pouch over. "Mind staying here while I wrangle this thing back into the pouch, just in case something goes awry?"

"We got you," Ash said, though everyone put some distance between them and the bouquet.

I snorted before reaching for the heavy gloves I kept in one of the table drawers, reserved for working with thorny vines. This one was metaphorically thorny, and I no longer wanted to touch it with bare skin.

As soon as I made contact, the pouch pulled away of its own volition, as if it didn't want to touch the thing any more than she did. I tried again. Same thing.

"Crap."

Moira came up.

"Gloves," I barked.

She rifled through the drawer before coming up with another pair.

"Hold the pouch. I'll take the bouquet."

Moira held both sides of it open, though the thing did everything short of biting her in an effort to get away. But it was no match for vampiric strength, and as I lifted the bouquet and placed it inside, I could have sworn the pouch made a sad sigh.

Creeped out, I took it from Moira and resealed everything, double-checking to make sure nothing could escape.

"Did that thing sigh?" Ash asked, horror in his voice.

"I thought I was imagining it," Moira muttered, grimacing as she stripped her gloves off.

"Don't put them back in the drawer," I cautioned as I stripped mine off. "Hand them over, and I'll cleanse them later." Moira handed her gloves over, and I tossed both pairs into a resealable bucket.

"I think I might go into the greenhouse if anyone wants to go before we open. There are a bunch of peonies ready for cutting. I thought we could use some of them in Hattie's bouquet."

Everyone was game, so we piled into the car, with the bouquet stashed in the trunk, and stopped for coffee on the way back to my house.

Sufficiently caffeinated, and after I'd stuffed the bouquet in the garage fridge, we all piled into the greenhouse. Tess sank down onto the stone floor and sighed. "I love it here, Evie."

Surprised, I smiled at Tess. "Really? I sometimes wonder how much you like working in the shop with all the green things."

Tess appeared to think about this for a moment. "Life and death are not so different from each other. Every breath you take could be your last. Someone like me straddles the line between warm breath and cold, eternal silence. Plants and greenery remind me that I still walk among the living and that I should stay in solid form when I'm around you."

Damn, I loved Tess, but she was creepy as hell sometimes. "Well." My head spun with the millions of responses I could give her, finally settling on, "I'm glad you remember you're still alive, Tess."

"Me too." She placed both palms flat on the floor and closed her eyes. When she said nothing else, I shrugged, figuring she'd gone to wherever banshees went when they were being super weird that day.

Ash came up beside me. "She meditates sometimes so deeply, even I can't reach her."

"Does she ever say where she goes?"

He shook his head, mossy eyes trained on the banshee. "No, but she's quiet most of the day when she finishes. I think it's a dark place full of fog and death."

"How would you know?"

He smiled sadly and reached for one of the tiny fronds on one of my ferns, stroking it with a finger the color of tree bark. "Because those same shadows are in her eyes when she awakens."

I fell silent, wondering when my team had grown so maudlin. When Ash made to walk away, I stopped him. "Ash?"

He turned. "Hmm?"

"Are you happy?"

His eyes widened in surprise. "Happy right now? Or in general?"

I thought about it. "I don't really know. At the shop, with me, I guess. And in general." Moira had made a joking crack about running away with Soren, and Ash seemed so sad that it was making me wonder if my team was beginning to fray around the edges.

But the serene smile he gave me made me breathe easier. "If there is ever a time when I wish to move on, Evie, you will be the first to know. Tess is happy in the shop, and so am I." He reached for me, rubbing a rough thumb across my cheek. "There is so much more in store for you that none of us can predict. Even if I weren't happy, I'd stick around to see what happens."

My brows drew together. "Thanks?"

He laughed. "Stop worrying so much. We all love you, and we're all here for the long term."

"He's right," Moira called from across the greenhouse. "Stop worrying!"

Relief filled me. "Fine!" I snapped halfheartedly. "Now go clip those peonies."

A piece of mulch thumped me in the forehead, Moira's laughter echoing through the greenhouse.

Chuckling under my breath, I gathered supplies to start more seedlings and worked for at least half an hour sowing seeds and tending the younger plants. Everything was fine for at least an hour. Moira and Ash's quiet conversation acted as background noise as I worked. Tess still sat motionless on the floor, her eyes closed and a blank expression on her face.

I pulled the flats of creeping thyme I'd just planted over in front of me and quietly gathered my magic, just a small amount to encourage growth, and pressed my index finger into the soil.

Earth magic ripped from my body, a tearing pain that stripped me of breath. Glass shattered as vines exploded from the back of the greenhouse, thick, pulsing tendrils of life coming up from the ground. Moira and Ash's alarmed shouts rang through the structure, but I couldn't pull my magic back. The thistle tattoo on my arm burned, agony sizzling on my bicep. My knees went out from under me, and I sagged to the ground. Plant life surrounded me, covering me with vines and leaves. I opened my mouth to scream, but nothing came out.

Pain bled through my body, my skin on fire. And just when I thought I might pass out from the pain, cool magic touched my skin, a fine mist of water blanketing my body, and the pain began to recede.

"Evie!" Tess shouted. "What were you thinking?"

Ash and Moira skidded to a halt, looming over my prone form. Moira went to reach for me, but Tess stopped her. "Not yet," she warned. "Her magic is still volatile."

A whimper escaped me.

"Oh, Evie," Moira whispered, tears shining in her eyes. Her gaze dragged from my face to my arm, and her eyes widened. "Your thistle…it's glowing."

My eyes fluttered shut. The only time I ever had difficulty with my Floromancy was when my Chimera magic acted up. Hazel had placed the tattoo on my arm and spelled it to hide the truth of my blood from prying eyes, but it served a dual purpose to keep the Chimera magic suppressed, though it wasn't completely foolproof.

As evidenced by all the broken windows and the mutant vines hanging above my head.

"Shit," I whispered.

"I'll say," Moira said, deadpan.

Ash's eyes glowed as he beat back the overgrowth. "I can't help with the windows, but I can put the vines back."

I closed my eyes and let out a slow, shaky breath. "Thank you."

It took several minutes, but Tess finally nodded. "She should be good. You can help her up."

Moira reached for me, helping me up. My legs felt wobbly, and my tattoo felt off, but other than that, I was unscathed.

"Close call," Moira said as her eyes raked me from head to toe. "You alright?"

"A little shaky, but I'm okay."

Moira tugged me closer. "Liar."

Tess's eyes glowed silver. "Your Chimera magic is growing, Evie. Every day you refuse to tame it is another day you might cause irreparable damage."

My first instinct was to snap at Tess. She was a subordinate employee and far younger than I, but when I opened my mouth to do just that, I pressed my lips together. Since when had that mattered to me?

Right was right, and Tess had just saved all our asses. "I know," I said, my voice hoarse.

Ash's eyes narrowed as if he knew how I had almost reacted. "Use your mirror and contact Hazel tonight. She needs to be here soon."

I nodded. "After the Keep meeting."

"Right after," Moira said, still holding onto my arm—a fact I was grateful for because I wasn't sure I could stand on my own yet.

I rubbed my breastbone, the area sore for some reason. Moira frowned and moved my hand to peer at the area.

"It's purple," she murmured. "Like a bruise."

"Evie had a ton of magic circulating through her body," Ash said. "She's lucky a bruise is all she ended up with."

Tess's nostrils flared. "Evie. I hate to ask this, but do you think you should talk to your mother?"

A bark of raspy laughter broke from me. "Absolutely not. I'd never summon her when I'm weak." Plus, she was acting weird these days and seemed to have something to do with those rogue magic pockets from several weeks ago. They were divine in nature, and no other gods had suddenly popped into town. Cliona was the most likely suspect.

"She might be the only one who can help you," Moira said quietly.

"Cliona is not a Floromancer or a Chimera," I said, slowly testing my strength as I straightened. "I'd never trust her with any information about how my powers work."

"But she's your mother," Tess said, her voice trailing off when she saw my expression. She dropped her gaze. "Sorry," she whispered.

I could never invite my mother into my life. She'd be the death of me and everyone I loved.

"Evie," Ash barked. "Your eyes."

Moira dropped my arms, her mouth open in an oh of surprise. "They're crimson," she whispered. "Just like that freaky bird."

I squeezed my eyes shut and waited for the rising Chimera magic to subside. Once I felt the power settle, I opened them to see my friends gathered around wearing identical expressions of concern. Better than horror, I guess.

"I think I should take the rest of the day off. Should we close up the shop?"

Ash shook his head. "No. Tess and I've got it. You were taking off early anyway because of the meeting. Stay here and get some rest so you're ready to face the Shifter Lord this evening."

I smiled gratefully and pushed the thyme away, so I wasn't tempted to work on it anymore. "Guess I'll find someone who can fix that glass, too."

"Did you get Caelan's handyman's number?" Moira asked.

I frowned. "No, but I think I remember the name on his truck. Good idea, Moira."

"That's why they pay me the big bucks." She winked and tugged on a lock of my hair. "I'll swing by and grab you at six. Good?"

I nodded. "Do you mind grabbing the binder I put together? It's under the register."

"The one labeled Foxy?" Ash said, his lips twitching.

"That's the one." The automatons I made for one of Caelan's

meetings with the Lords went down in infamy. I'd made several as table centerpieces, each depicting a scene from an old fairytale called The Wolf and the Fox. The moral of the story was basically don't be a dick, which didn't sit well with Caelan, and he ended up destroying most of my shop as a result.

Good times.

To his credit, he was genuinely remorseful and paid for the repairs, but the dude was seriously scary when he wanted to be.

As a private joke, Rowan, my favorite Shifter Lord, had started calling me Foxy in our texts.

"I'll bring it," Moira said, "but I'd suggest you cover up the binder's title. We're trying to be professionals here."

I stared at her. "Are you serious?"

She snorted. "No. You should make the font bigger and label it that way on both sides."

"There you are. I thought you might have a fever."

Moira grinned and waved as she exited the greenhouse. Tess floated after her, but Ash lingered, concern brimming in his mossy green eyes.

"Are you sure you're okay?"

I nodded. "Sorry to scare everyone. I've been doing a decent job of suppressing the newer power from whatever Finn did to me at that dinner, but the fluctuations are getting worse."

"You really think Hazel can help?"

"She helped me last time and gave me several years of peace. If she can't, I bet she'll know who can."

Ash nodded, though he didn't look convinced. "Knock 'em dead tonight, Evie."

"How about I succeed in not ruining our business or killing anyone?"

He laughed. "Acceptable."

I waved and told them to be careful. When the greenhouse door shut, I sagged against the worktable and put my head in my hands.

Holding back the Chimera shift was becoming impossible. I

was doing a good job of hiding it at work, but every night when I got home, I fought a grueling battle between myself and the beast.

A battle I was losing.

CHAPTER
Seven

I wore the dress. How could I not? Caelan, or whoever helped him, had excellent taste in clothing. The dress fit like a glove but wasn't so tight I had trouble moving. Comforting magic slid over my skin, the awaiting life in the bodice of my dress pulsing against my collarbone. I traced my fingers over the embroidery and wondered how I could incorporate such magic into my daily wardrobe.

Sewing wasn't one of my talents, but maybe I could find a local seamstress to help. A sharp knock on the door interrupted my thoughts and announced Moira's presence. The front door opened with a creak, and Moira poked her head in.

"I'm here!" she called. "If you're covered in baby oil and rolling around on plastic, yell 'Kris Kringle!' I won't peek!"

"No baby oil, I'm afraid."

"For shame." Moira came into the bedroom grinning, but when she saw me, her eyes widened, and she whistled low. "Damn. If I liked women, I'd eat you like a lollipop."

"First of all, gross." I fastened a pair of gold teardrop stud earrings into my ears but kept my neck bare. The embroidery around the bodice was stunning, and adding jewelry would take away from the overall effect. Our eyes locked in the mirror. "Second of all, thank you."

Moira winked. "You got it, babe."

"Third," I said when I turned, "you look vicious, deadly, and hot, hot, hot."

And she did. Moira was lean and slinky, the dress skimming over all her dangerous curves. She wore her hair half up and half down, a pair of diamond earrings twinkling in her earlobes. A solitaire pendant lay in the hollow of her throat, and a thin, golden bracelet was clasped at her wrist. Her heels were sky-high, showcasing leanly muscled legs.

Moira was a stunning woman, but she was also deadly, and that fact was difficult to ignore in that dress.

The vampire did a pirouette, and I had to admire her ability to do that in those heels.

"If Soren is there, he won't stand a chance."

"That's what I'm hoping for." She wiggled her eyebrows. "You ready to go?"

I held up a finger. "Let me get my shoes on."

Moira clicked her tongue when she saw my much more reasonable kitten heels. "Uh-uh. You got anything higher?"

"Nope. Only certain women can wear heels that high. Vampires named Moira, and other women not named Evie." I slid my feet into my sedate heels and stood, grabbing my small purse from the bed.

"No matter. Caelan will like anything you wear."

I tossed a makeup brush at her. Moira dodged, swift as a viper, and laughed. "Let's go see a Lord about a wedding."

To my surprise, Caelan had changed nothing I'd done to his property. The Jacaranda tree stood in front of his home, still blooming despite the late season, and a riot of wildflowers dotted the entire landscape. A chuckle escaped me when we pulled in, turning into a full-on bellow of laughter when we parked.

Moira snorted. "I bet when guests show up here, they have no idea what to think."

"Maybe I should cultivate it a little more." The place looked like something straight out of a fairytale. I loved it, but few people loved that much flora with that many colors right outside their front door.

"If Caelan hasn't done anything yet, I don't think he plans to."

"He's a busy Lord. Maybe he hasn't had the time."

Moira gave me the side-eye. "Caelan gets things done, Evie. If he wanted to change up his landscaping, he would have done it weeks ago."

I squashed the warm and fuzzy feeling down. Maybe he hadn't changed it because his new fiancée liked it.

"I'm going to punch you right in the pizza pocket if you don't wipe those thoughts right out of your head. Caelan has the hots for you, and he likes your weird pollute-the-place-with-flowers love language."

"As we pull up at his house to ask him about his wedding." I eyed the front of the house, my heartbeat picking up.

"Yeah, well. Even the best love stories don't start out perfect." Moira put the vehicle in park and slid out, handing her keys to the valet. My door opened, a handsome young man offering a hand to help me out. I obliged him and held on to my skirt for decency's sake as I got out.

Simone waited for us on the steps, a clipboard in her hand and a serious look on her face. "Hello." Her eyes skimmed over both of us. "Glad to see you accepted the Lord's gifts."

"I do not turn down fabulous clothing," Moira said.

"I didn't have anything else to wear." Not a lie, but I too had a weakness for pretty dresses.

Simone's lips twitched at my comment. "Come on in. We'll head straight to the dining room."

The wards buzzed against my skin, more powerful than they were the last time. A smile tugged my lips upward. The Shifter

Lord still couldn't keep me out, but maybe he and his security had learned a little since I'd broken in with little effort.

I steeled myself, schooling my expression into cool indifference. Caelan's fiancée would be here tonight, and I was here in a professional capacity. Being the florist on record would put Little Shop of Florals on the map. The shop was already popular around the state, but pulling this wedding off could open up more doors than I ever dreamed possible.

I had to keep my shit together, no matter what Caelan did to antagonize me.

The doors opened, our heels clicking on the stone floor. Simone led us through the entryway and down the long hall. My skin prickled.

We were being watched.

Moira sidled up beside me. "You creeped out?"

Simone's shoulders stiffened. "Be on your best behavior tonight, ladies," she hissed. "This meeting is important."

"We know," Moira and I said at the same time.

No one came to greet us, and there were no people in the hallways. "How many people are here tonight?" I asked.

"Only the necessary ones," Simone remarked, the cryptic answer making me roll my eyes.

"Then was this dress necessary?" The silky fabric buzzed against my skin, its magic alert. Aware.

Moira snorted. "I'd wear this dress to take out the garbage."

"Everything a Shifter Lord does or does not do draws scrutiny." Simone stopped before the large double doors. "There are eyes everywhere, and this wedding is the event of the century. If you showed up wearing blue jeans, your faces would be splashed across the front page of the Joy Springs newspaper in the morning, and by the afternoon, your business would be ruined."

"That's extreme," Moira murmured.

Simone looked over her shoulder. "That is what it means to be a Lord."

I grimaced. "Sorry."

Simone sighed, both hands raised to push open the doors. "It is difficult for someone who is not exposed to this life to understand what it means to be under such intense scrutiny twenty-four hours per day."

"Privacy is the most underrated asset we have," I said. "We never realize how valuable it is until it's gone."

Simone's eyes glittered with approval before she turned away. "Exactly. So try to wear those dresses with a smile." She grunted and pushed the doors open, revealing a massive dining room bustling with activity.

But before we could walk in, the feminine sound of a throat clearing sounded in the hall. I was staring right at Simone's shoulders when they tensed just slightly. Someone who wasn't right next to her might have missed it.

"Hello," a purring voice said. "You must be our little florist."

Moira stiffened. From the woman's tone, I knew this must be Caelan's fiancée.

Simone stepped in front of us. "Gianna. You look splendid, as always."

Gianna wore a slinky dress in magenta pink, her cool blonde hair done in a perfect chignon. Her makeup was flawless, accentuating high cheekbones and startling green eyes. She was tall and lean and dripped with diamonds. "Thank you, Simone. You look adequate."

Anger spooled through my veins. Simone was shorter and had more honey in her blonde hair, but she looked hot tonight. The Omega was dressed in a stylish black, one-shoulder jumpsuit, a pair of diamond drops in her ears. She wore her hair loose, curls spilling down her back, and had chosen diamond-encrusted, flat sandals, probably because she was constantly on the move. Nothing worse than heels that pinch when you have business to attend to.

Gianna was old New York money, and Simone was Southern lady class.

Moira reached out and ran a finger down Simone's arm. "Are you kidding? My girl looks smoking tonight."

Simone blinked, color turning her tanned cheeks pink. "Er. Thank you, Moira."

The vampire winked. "No need to thank me. My eyes should thank you."

I hid my smile. One thing about Moira, she never discriminated when it came to beauty.

Gianna's eyes flickered with fury. "We can head inside. The caterers should be finished setting up in a little while."

She breezed past us, leaving behind the scent of a deep, musky perfume I didn't care for.

"Patchouli heavy," Moira whispered, grinning when she saw Gianna's steps hitch.

"Be good," I warned in a voice so low Gianna couldn't hear me. "We need this job."

"We really don't. The shop is doing fine."

"Yes, but we don't have 401ks. If we get this job, I might be able to swing them for everyone."

Moira fell quiet.

"Exactly," I murmured. "Immortals especially need financial security."

"I hate it when you're reasonable. That hasn't happened in a while, so I'm not sure if I like this Evie or the crazy one who gets chased through the streets by pissed off shifters."

"The reasonable one keeps us all out of trouble."

Moira sighed. "Some trouble is good for the soul."

"Will you two shut up?" Simone hissed.

"And we liked you better when you were nicer," Moira murmured.

Simone rolled her eyes. "As you can see, things have changed." She glared daggers at Gianna's back.

Caelan's fiancée didn't appear to be popular around here. Interesting.

Caterers and decorators ran around, everyone keeping one eye on Gianna as she crossed the room. A single long table was set up by the large bay windows, multiple stainless containers steaming with fresh food. Flower arrangements littered the room, soulless and white.

I hadn't done those arrangements, and I could tell by the look of them that a Floromancer wasn't involved. A human had done these.

A stab of hurt speared me.

Gianna led us to a large round table. She gestured with a perfectly manicured hand. "Please have a seat. My fiancé and his counterpart will be here soon."

Simone made no move to join us. "You aren't staying for dinner?" I asked.

Gianna snorted. "The help doesn't eat at our table."

I stiffened. Simone's jaw clenched, but she said nothing. She took a couple of steps away from the table and held her iPad at her waist, the device like a piece of armor.

There's no way Caelan knew how Gianna was treating his most loyal shifter. He wouldn't stand for it, and if he could, then I wanted nothing to do with him.

Moira's lips tightened. An almost imperceptible shake of Simone's head told us to drop it. I reached over and touched Moira's knee. We'd drop it.

For now.

But Gianna better have a full shifter escort next time she goes out, because if we got a hold of her, it won't matter who she belonged to.

In the middle of the table sat a stack of laminated pages and a binder. "We'll wait until Caelan gets here before we officially begin. Would you like some wine?"

"I would," Moira said.

"None for me, thanks." There was already water on the table, and that was the strongest substance I planned to imbibe this evening.

Gianna gestured and a quivering server came over, holding a

bottle of red wine. "Mistress," she said, pouring the woman a large glass.

"For the vampire, too," Gianna said, her emphasis on the word pissing me off.

Moira moved her glass for easier access.

"I wasn't aware vampires could imbibe other substances," Gianna said.

Moira offered her a tight smile. "I'm full of surprises." And she was. Moira could eat and drink like a normal person, which wasn't completely unheard of among certain vampirekind, but she could also day walk and had other specific powers, some of which she had yet to show me.

Moira couldn't be 100% vampire. I suspected she either had a witch or fae somewhere in her maternal bloodline, but Moira always claimed she hadn't known her parents.

The doors opened again, revealing two Shifter Lords.

Moira let out a satisfied chuckle. "I hoped it would be him."

Gianna sent her a curious look but returned her eyes to the Lords.

Soren and Caelan entered the room, their power a punch to the gut. Simone remained in place, eyes watchful. Moira and I rose. Gianna stayed seated for longer than she should have. She might be Caelan's fiancée, but even family members were required to show proper deference to the Lords.

Simone's teeth pulled away from her lips at the insult, but she held her tongue.

Soren was a stunning male. Like most Shifter Lords, he was taller than average, standing at least six foot four. His chestnut hair was wavy and a touch too long, and his eyes were the color of the Aegean Sea. Cruelty edged his face, and his eyes held the knowledge of too much pain. Power crackled over his skin as he walked, but when his gaze skimmed the room, they stopped and stayed on Moira.

Uh oh.

Where Soren was traditionally handsome, Caelan was a

storm-tossed sea on a cold winter's night. He was power and pain and sorrow mixed up in a devastating package. Our eyes clashed. He stopped dead in his tracks, his gaze raking down my form. The dress reacted, humming against my skin. A flower, bright yellow with an aromatic scent, bloomed against my bodice.

Helichrysum, the flower of immortality.

Another curled from the embroidery, rising from the bodice, and brushed against my skin. Lupine.

His gaze rested on those flowers, and one side of his mouth kicked up for a small second—a heartbeat, before he wiped his face completely free of expression and sauntered after Soren.

"Miss Quinn," Caelan said. "Miss Devlin."

Moira inclined her head. All I could do was gawk at him like a moron. He wore a charcoal-colored suit with a deep blue tie. As he came closer, I spotted a tiny pin on his tie.

It was in the shape of a helichrysum flower.

Woof.

Evie Quinn, you are in danger.

Gianna finally rose from her seat, a slow graceful glide. She came around the table and smiled, a perfect, emotionless thing on her face.

"Darling," she breathed, both hands outstretched as she cupped his chin, "you look so handsome." She snapped her fingers, and a server scurried over holding a small clear box. With deft fingers, she extricated a small boutonniere and pinned it to the lapel of Caelan's jacket.

I hated it. A boutonniere like that would have never left my shop. It looked like one of those cheap things you bought from the discount fridge at the local florist.

His posture went stiff before he smiled, a small flash of teeth. "Gianna. You look beautiful as always."

A tiny crack appeared in my heart, but I kept my emotions off my face.

Soren's gaze tore away from Moira and landed on Gianna,

disgust flickering over his expression, there and gone in the blink of an eye as she turned to him. "And you, handsome as always."

Soren gave a small bow to Gianna. "Always the stunning, consummate hostess, Gianna. Thank you for your hospitality this evening."

She preened under his attention. "It's always a pleasure to welcome any of Caelan's allies to our home."

Caelan pulled Gianna's seat out for her. She settled once more, smoothing her hands over her skirt. Caelan sat beside her, and Soren at Caelan's left, the Lord's eyes lingering on Moira.

With silent choreography, the servers came over and presented salads, a small pile of spring greens with candied walnuts, sliced apples and pears, and a poppyseed dressing. They refilled my water and everyone else's wine and faded into the background like they'd never been there.

Whatever this was, it wasn't my cup of tea. I was sitting with people who weren't my friends, except Moira who was here mainly for moral support, while being forced to eat with people I didn't trust.

Moira and I exchanged looks. She wasn't keen on this either.

"Dig in, ladies," Gianna said. "We have three more courses to go."

I gave her a tight smile. "What time are we discussing the arrangements?"

Soren smirked. "We don't discuss business during dinner, Miss Quinn."

Moira speared a slice of apple with her fork. "Oh?" Her voice was low and sultry. "What do all important Lords and their Ladies discuss during fancy dress-up dinners?"

Caelan hadn't taken his eyes off me since he sat down, and it was making me fidget like a hooker in church. The man didn't just stare. He bored a hole in my soul with the way he was looking at me.

A slow grin curved Soren's lips. "What would you like to speak about, Miss Devlin?"

Moira chuckled. "Flower arrangements would be nice. Evie turns into a pumpkin soon."

"There are certain ways a Lord conducts his business, Miss Quinn," Gianna said in a no-nonsense tone. "Pressing a Lord to hurry simply isn't done."

Caelan's low laugh tightened things inside me. "Evie works on her own schedule."

Gianna gave him a sharp look. "She is our employee now. Miss Quinn will work on our schedule."

I blinked. "I do not work for you," I said archly. "Our contract is temporary, and you are not entitled to any more time than is allotted by our agreement." I set my fork down. "Tonight was a personal favor to Simone and the Shifter Lord, a way to keep open relations as I've worked for him before on a contract basis." Anger simmered within me.

"I can see now this was a mistake." I rose from my seat.

"Evie." Caelan rose.

My teeth gnashed. Without thinking, I reached toward him and squeezed my fist. The hideous boutonniere turned into fine ash, grey dust falling down his jacket. "If you need something like this in the future, I would rather make it for free than see you wear something so ugly."

One of his eyebrows rose. Using the back of his hand, he brushed the rest of the dust off, eyes glittering with heated amusement. "Gianna's taste offends you, Miss Quinn?"

"Danger," Moira said under her breath.

"I believe a florist over-exaggerated their talent, Lord. White roses and baby's breath are cheap and do not befit the status of a Lord."

Gianna scoffed. "Miss Quinn, you are out—"

Caelan lifted his hand. "Let Evie speak."

Gianna blinked, her eyes widening. She clamped her lips shut, the edges of her mouth going white.

"And what befits my status?" Caelan asked.

Soren watched us like we were playing tennis.

"A black orchid on a simple stick pin. But there are no true black orchids. I'd choose one so dark it looks red in certain light." My gaze flicked to his lapel. "It would suit your attire this evening." I cocked my head. "Or maybe purple."

Caelan's lips twitched.

A vine snaked from the bodice of my gown, twining out to lift Caelan's lapel.

Moira sucked in a breath. Soren's eyes glimmered with amusement.

"Charcoal grey is considered neutral. You could wear a white flower, but it would look gauche."

Soren barked a laugh, quickly covering it with a cough.

"Are you calling me gauche?" Caelan asked, leaning to brace both palms on the table.

He was enjoying this. And heaven help me, so was I.

"Only your boutonniere." I smiled sweetly, stroking the wool fabric of his suit with the vine. "But I think I would do something more dramatic. More befitting a Lord."

"And what would that be?" A low, dangerous, interested tone.

"An Anastasia Chrysanthemum," I mused. "It looks a little like a spider, with all its spindly petals, but it's showy. Like all the Lords."

"Hey," Soren protested.

"Shh," Moira whispered. "Evie and Caelan are being interesting."

"And what else?"

"That's all. On a silver pin."

His face curved into a grin. "Dangerous. I like it."

We stared at each other across the table. "Anyway. I'm leaving. Perhaps we can discuss your wedding arrangements at another time." I glanced down at myself and frowned. "And when I'm wearing fewer fancy clothes."

"We will do this now," Gianna snapped.

I finally looked at her. Gianna's slender frame bristled with rage. "Again, I am not your employee, and I am not being paid. So I bid you adieu."

"I'll pay you," Caelan said.

Moira's low chuckle made my lips twitch.

"Are we doing this again?" I said.

"Double time?" Caelan tilted his head.

"Are they always like this?" Soren whispered to Moira.

"Yup."

"Nice. Maybe I'll come around more."

"You should. It's been pretty fun since those two met."

"I am right here," Gianna snapped.

"Yeah," Moira acknowledged. "Things won't be so fun after the wedding."

Caelan and I were locked in a staring contest. "Quadruple, and you stop trying to force your hand."

Caelan's eyes narrowed. "You know I won't stop."

I huffed out an annoyed breath. "Quadruple anyway."

"Done." He gestured with his hand. "Please. Sit down."

My eyes narrowed.

"Just for dinner and flower arrangement discussion. That's all."

I slowly sat back down, adjusting my skirt. The servers swept in and cleared our plates, but I didn't have a chance to mourn the salad I didn't eat because another wave of servants swept in with the second course.

No one said anything for a long moment. Caelan picked up his fork. "Please. Let's continue as if nothing happened."

Moira snorted.

Soren grinned. "Must say, Caelan, this is the most fun I've had in ages."

I rolled my eyes. "I have some ideas."

"Eat first, then discuss," Caelan said, gesturing with his fork. "You missed the first course. Once the second is done, we'll discuss the arrangements."

Gianna leaned over and whispered something in Caelan's ear.

His jaw tightened as he turned, murmuring something low in her ear. I picked up my fork and cut into the next course, a piece of prosciutto-wrapped asparagus, topped with crab meat and a lemon butter sauce.

It was delicious, so I stopped paying attention to Caelan and turned my focus to the plate before me. Once I finished, I set my fork down and looked up.

Caelan pushed the binder in the middle of the table toward me. "Gianna has some ideas."

I opened the binder.

"Since we're joining two royal houses, I'd like a court theme using red and white florals. I was thinking Phoenix lilies to begin."

I stared at her for a few seconds and wondered if maybe I should turn this job down and pretend I'd never met the Shifter Lord. "Are you speaking of Alstroemeria?"

Gianna blinked. "The Phoenix lily. That's the one I want."

"There's only one Phoenix lily that I'm aware of."

"Then that must be it." She made a disgusted face as if I were an idiot and she was the plant expert.

I kept my tone measured. "The Phoenix lily is pink. If you want to use a red lily, we have numerous options I can show you once I'm back at the shop."

Color appeared high on her cheekbones. "Surely you must be mistaken."

I wasn't. "I'm happy to double check my records, but I've been involved in the florist industry my entire life."

A tense silence settled over the table, so I made it a little worse. "As such, I'd like to make a suggestion. If there's no compelling reason to use red and white, I think softer, creamier colors would put a more elegant spin on the day. Things like cream and navy or emerald and navy. Deep jewel tones and soft, creamier neutrals. I'm happy to show you some examples."

Gianna's mouth pinched. I opened my binder and pushed it over. "I took the liberty of putting some quick arrangements together. You're more than welcome to keep this. I have another copy at home."

Caelan pulled the binder over and flipped through the pages.

And so it went. A torturous hour of back-and-forth suggestions, with Gianna disagreeing with everything. Finally, I cried uncle.

"I'm always happy to accommodate any suggestions the happy couple brings. I don't want you to feel like I'm resisting your feedback. If you want red and white, I'm happy to oblige. I'll have to go back to the drawing board and make up some new examples, but I can have those back to you in a few days." I pushed the last plate away, wishing there'd been a larger portion. The dish was some kind of hazelnut tiramisu or something with a feather light cake and a cream filling.

"What color are your bridesmaid dresses?" I meant to ask earlier and had gotten distracted by Caelan fingering the Helichrysum tie pin.

"Blue," Gianna said as she picked up her wine glasses.

Moira choked on her wine and turned her head to cough. I almost laughed before I realized Gianna was serious. That movie came to mind where the busty blonde remarks about how her friend looks like July 4th, and it makes her crave a hot dog.

"If she bends and snaps, I'm going to die," Moira whispered.

I nudged her under the table. That poor wedding is going to look like America threw up all over it. "Of course," I said. "I'll get you some new concepts in a day or so."

I couldn't wait one more moment to get out of here. "If that's all, we will get out of your hair."

Moira and Soren were whispering something to each other. Their chairs had gotten much closer without me noticing, and I had a weird feeling, whatever this was, wouldn't stop at tonight.

I kicked her calf gently.

Moira jerked. "Oh. Yes. Right. Let's go."

Caelan rose. "I will walk you out."

"It's not necessary. We know where the front door is, and I'm sure you're very tired."

One of his dark eyebrows rose. "I insist."

"And I will escort Moira," Soren chimed in. "There is something I'd like to discuss with her."

I sent Moira a beseeching look, but she was locked onto her prey. I reluctantly rose, Caelan leading us out of the dining room. Gianna gave us a regal head incline and sailed away, her high heels clicking on the stone floor. Simone was right behind her, but not before she shot me an exasperated but amused look on her way out.

Moira and Soren walked ahead of us, leaving Caelan and me alone.

"You hate the vision," he said after a moment.

I thought about my words. "It's not up to me to hate anything. All I can do is guide and suggest, and when none of those are taken, I am required by contract to go ahead with whatever the couple wants."

Caelan sighed. "It's going to look like the fourth of July."

I pressed my lips together to keep from laughing.

He held out his arm. I hesitated before curling my fingers around the crook of his elbow.

"Your fiancée is beautiful."

"She is," Caelan agreed.

"I'm sorry about tonight. My behavior was appalling." And it was. I'd touched him when I shouldn't have, destroyed his property even if that boutonniere deserved a fiery death, and had a smart mouth most of the night. I don't know what got into me when it came to the Shifter Lord, but normally I knew when to keep my mouth shut.

"You really hated my boutonniere that much?" His words held a touch of amusement.

"With the fire of a thousand suns," I said vehemently.

Caelan laughed, the sound bright and free. He rarely laughed or smiled, and I felt like I held a gift in my palms when he did.

"Do you want to marry her?" I asked softly.

Caelan's posture stiffened. "It is not up to me."

I blinked. "Of course it is. You're a Shifter Lord."

He sighed. "If it were only that simple, Evie. I might be a Lord, but I answer to the Council. They felt it was time to take a bride, and Gianna was chosen."

I eyed him. "You can't choose your own bride?"

He glanced down at me, sparkling gold glowing in his eyes. "Are you offering?"

His words made my stomach lurch. And not with horror. But there was so much I couldn't tell him. He'd never forgive me once he knew what I was. My mouth opened and snapped shut. I glared at him. "Not funny."

"I'm not trying to be funny." He grinned. "But it is fun to needle you."

"There are women out there who would love you, Caelan." I believed that one hundred percent.

We rounded a corner, and I found myself jerked off my feet and tucked into a stone corner, Caelan's hard body pressed to mine. "There are no cameras here," he whispered, one hand pressed to the curve of my hip.

My heart thundered in my chest. "Even so," I said, my voice unsteady, "you have a fiancée not too far away. I'm sure she won't approve."

He dipped his head, his mouth close to my ear. "Gianna doesn't give a shit what I do. She only wants power."

I pressed against his chest. "I won't be anyone's mistress."

"I'm not here to ask you anything of the sort. I'm here to warn you. The Council is watching you. They think you're dangerous, Evie." His hand tightened. "And so do I."

"Then why do you keep hiring me for shit?" I hissed. "Just leave me alone and I'll leave you alone!"

"We both know that won't happen." He bent closer, his teeth closing over my ear lobe gently.

My breath caught as my neck arched, seeking more of him.

"You are in my blood so deep I can't even burn you out," he whispered.

His words set a fire deep in my soul. "Caelan. This is madness." I pushed him off as anger settled inside me. "If we're to work together, I need you to stop antagonizing me."

His eyebrows went up. "Antagonizing, Evie? You offered me your throat in surrender. You did not seem antagonized at all."

Color burned on my cheeks. "Ass," I hissed. I smoothed down my dress, only to notice two more flowers had bloomed on the bodice. *Traitor*, I thought. "Tell me how I'm in danger."

"The Council believes you are more than you claim. And they still think you're tangled in the rogue magic attacks."

I sighed. "I thought we were past that. Those were divine in nature." Notice I said nothing about the belief concerning my bloodline. I wasn't touching that with a ten-foot pole. The less everyone knew, the better.

"The Lords have good instincts." He took a step back, outside of the alcove and waited for me. "And so do I."

A chill ran down my spine as I rejoined him in the hall, glancing in both directions. "Even though there aren't cameras in that alcove, won't it seem suspicious we both walked out of the same place at the same time?"

"Simone will take care of it."

I winced. "I don't think your Omega is my biggest fan right now."

Caelan's eyes grew stormy. "Simone is not a fan of my situation. If things were different, I suspect you'd be...what do the humans call it?"

"Uh. Besties?"

He snapped his fingers. "Yes! Besties. You'd be besties."

"I already have one of those, but she can be a second bestie."

We started for the door again. "Simone doesn't like second place."

I laughed. "We can settle the bestie semantics once your situation is settled. Two months and you'll be a married man."

"Two months," he agreed, a strange note in his voice.

"And afterward, I'll never get hired for another Keep event again." I snickered.

Caelan's lips turned up. We stopped at the front door. "Thank you for coming this evening, Evie. Isn't it better to walk through the front door than sneak in?"

I stepped outside. "Not necessarily. Flying is always better than riding in a car."

A beat of silence. "I adjusted the wards after your stunt. Breaking in won't be so easy next time."

I winked. "I looked forward to trying."

Caelan's wicked chuckle slid over my shoulders. I turned and hurried down the steps toward Moira, patiently waiting for me by the car.

CHAPTER
Eight

CAELAN

vie's vehicle disappeared around the bend. I rolled my neck, working out the tense knots. My jaw ached from holding my tongue most of the evening, and my palm burned from where I'd held Evie's hip.

Her flowers bloomed for me. Satisfaction burned in my chest at her reaction. And when she burned away that terrible boutonniere and I felt her claim on my body…my fists clenched.

What was I doing? My fiancée stood behind me, disapproval simmering in the surrounding air. Our behavior tonight was inappropriate and disrespectful. It didn't matter that I didn't want Gianna. Nor did it matter that she didn't want me. We had an image to uphold, that of a united Shifter Lord and his Lady. And it couldn't happen with Evie in the picture.

"You're awfully quiet for someone who slunk off with another woman who was not his fiancée tonight."

I closed my eyes and exhaled. When I turned it was to see Gianna lounging against the doorway, her arms crossed over her chest, a cool expression on her face. Tall and deadly, she was the picture of grace.

"Did you think I wouldn't notice how your eyes never left

her?" she said, fury quivering in her voice. "You chose a dress for her."

I had and didn't regret it. "Evie is a valued member of the Joy Springs community and has the potential to become a magical powerhouse." She already was, but Gianna didn't need to know that. The woman wasn't dumb and had probably figured out there was more to Evie than met the eye. And if she hadn't, it wasn't my place to tell her, not when I still wasn't sure how things would shake out in the future.

Marriage wasn't the issue. It never had been. Marriage to Gianna was the issue.

Gianna's delicate snort set my teeth on edge. "Fuck whoever you want to, Caelan, but remember our agreement. If the florist stands in my way, she will pay the price."

"Touch Evie Quinn and know my wrath." My words were soft, deadly, and true.

Her eyes glittered with realization. "You sentimental fool," she murmured.

"Enough," I barked. "Evie is a useful political tool, but there is no emotional bond."

Gianna's laughter was genuine this time. "You've always been a terrible liar, Lord. Emotion burns between you two." She took a few steps closer. "Though I'm curious why your Council chose me as your bride. Why not her?"

That was the question, wasn't it? All Lords were ruled by the Council, their behavior and rule under a constant microscope. Marriage was rarely pushed, but Evie had upset the apple cart in more ways than one. She'd broken my wards, destabilized my rule, shown a disturbing amount of power, and gathered the attention of every Shifter Lord in the country.

"The Lords like their bloodlines pure." Which, honestly, was the biggest bunch of bullshit I'd ever heard.

Gianna's eyebrows rose. "I am not a wolf Shifter."

"But you are of royal blood."

"Ah. And your Evie is a mutt."

"Watch your tone," I growled, the animal inside me pacing restlessly, itching to burst from my skin. "My decision was made to keep the peace in my territory. It's not a personal choice."

"Your florist is dangerous and unstable." She came closer, one sharp nail pressed into my chest. "That is why the Council chose me over her. Remember that when you pant after her like a dog."

My nostrils flared, magic pulsing around me. Claws itched their way to the forefront of my knuckles. "Tread carefully, Gianna."

She laughed, a wicked sound in the quiet room. "My family is powerful. Our influence is felt throughout the entire country. If you or your florist embarrass me or try to discredit my family's name, we will wipe your line off the map."

I pressed my chest into her nail, feeling the skin split under the sharp point. "This is the second time you've threatened me tonight. Do it one more time, and I don't care who your family is."

Fear flickered in her eyes. I slapped her hand away. "Leave me."

Gianna stepped away, her lips pressed tight. "Our agreement stands. Do not disappoint me. Lord." With that, she turned on her heel and exited the room.

My fists clenched at my sides. Evie was an innocent in all of this, and I'd made her a pawn in a game I wasn't sure I could win.

She wasn't safe, and it was my fault.

The realization threatened to send me into a rage. Whatever happened, I would ensure Evie remained unscathed. But knowing Evie, she wouldn't let me fall alone.

CHAPTER

Nine

After a restless night, I showed up at the shop ten minutes late the next morning. Ash, Tess, and Moira were already there, the smell of fresh coffee ripe in the air.

"Thank goodness," I grunted, heading straight to the pot.

"Late night?" Ash asked, good humor twinkling in his eyes.

"Not the kind of night you're thinking of." I took a sip of the life-giving brew, sighing as the warmth hit my body.

Moira winked. "Our little prude is still wearing her crown."

"Shut it," I muttered. "And you? Soren seemed enamored with our friendly vampire last night."

Ash and Tess made wooing sounds. Moira laughed. "Woo all you want. Everyone here knows I have no shame." She wiggled her eyebrows.

"Be careful. You should know dating a Lord is dangerous."

"Dating your local Lord is dangerous. Soren isn't in our region and has no plans to make a move on Caelan's territory." She sipped her tea. "I'm not planning on marrying the guy, Evie. There's no need to worry."

"You little vixen." I shook my head and laughed. "I wish I was more like you."

"You wouldn't be our lovable Evie if you were." Moira held up a piece of paper and waved it. "Got an email this morning from the supposed mom. She relinquished the name of the wedding planner, but not much else."

"A dead end, then."

"Looks that way, unless we can ask Caelan."

I shook my head. "No. Not with Gianna in the picture. I'm not going back to the Keep until I have to."

Ash let out a low whistle. "Would you go if Gianna wasn't there?" he asked.

Ugh. Why did everyone pay attention to everything I said? "Dammit. No. I wouldn't go either way."

"Lies," Moira teased. "Evie can't resist the Shifter Lord."

"I can resist him just fine." I topped off my coffee. "It's Gianna we need to worry about."

"You're right. Those penciled in eyebrows are terrifying," Moira said. "Anyone as elegant as she is definitely has something to hide."

"True," Ash said. "Do you know anything about her?"

Moira tapped a pencil on the desk. "She's from a royal line. Swan shifter."

"Ugh. Of course she's a swan shifter."

Three pairs of eyes turned my way. Moira's lips twitched. "We should have tagged her as one when we first saw her. That neck. Dead giveaway."

True. Gianna's neck was long and graceful, and her bones were slender and delicate. Simone was smaller but sturdier.

"Swans are mean as hell," Ash said. "And territorial. If she thinks you're making a move on Caelan, Gianna will get territorial."

"I'm not making moves on anyone."

The doorbell rang.

"Except for him," Moira said under her breath.

Ben walked in, his soothing magic sweeping across the store. I closed my eyes and smiled. Every time he came around, all I felt was peace.

He smiled when he spotted me. "Morning. I hope it's not too early."

"Nah. We just opened, but almost everything is still closed, so we won't get any customers for a while." I headed to the coffee pot and poured him a mug.

"Here you go." Black and hot, the way he liked it.

Ben took the mug and curled his large hands around it. "Thank you."

"What brings you in," Moira said. "Searching for anything in particular?"

Ben grinned. "Just your lovely Floromancer."

My cheeks colored. Ben and I hadn't gone on a single date, and he hadn't asked me out yet, but there was something between us —a spark we had yet to explore.

"You found her," Moira said.

"Can I steal her for breakfast?" Ben sipped his coffee.

"Please," Ash said. "She can take the entire day off. We have it under control."

"That's not necessary," I said.

"I won't take you away from the shop for the entire day. Breakfast is good for now." He glanced at me. "Ready to go?"

I downed the rest of my coffee. "Sure am."

He slung an arm over my shoulders, pulling me into the warmth of his body. "My treat."

"Bye, Evie!" My team said in unison. "Either be good or be good at it!"

Ben chuckled as he held the door open for me.

The shifter had me back at the shop by 10:30, leaving me with a small charm he said was good for grounding. Comforting magic pulsed from the small stone I'd tucked into my pocket. He left me at the door, one finger tugging on a loose strand of hair, saying he'd come by in the next day or so. His blue eyes crinkled at the edges as he bent to brush a kiss over my cheek, the spot tingling when he rose.

Catcalls greeted me when I walked into the shop.

Moira plopped her head onto her hands. "How's our hot little healer?"

"So hot," Tess said dreamily.

Moira grinned. "Tess! You little minx."

Ash chuckled. "Even I can admit Ben is hot. I'd have to be blind not to see it."

Most shifters had something about them that made them hard to resist. Ben was traditionally handsome, and he had a gentle way about him. Despite that gentleness, Ben's magic was an inferno. He wasn't a wolf, but he'd never disclosed what type he was. Not that it mattered. Caelan had warned me away from his healer, and I had heeded that warning.

Somewhat.

I wouldn't tell Ben no if he asked me out again, but we could never have a serious relationship.

Not with all the secrets I held.

"Yeah, yeah," I said, waving their words away. "How's business this morning?"

"Here and there. There's time to finish some projects and get the new bouquets done for your other lover boy." Moira winked.

"Please stop," I begged.

Tess moaned, louder than she normally did. We all froze. "Tess?"

"She approaches," the banshee said and popped out of existence a second later.

There was only one *she* Tess would sense that well.

"Shit," I swore. "My mother is here."

Moira's eyes widened. "She can't get in. Right?"

"Right. But not letting her in is disrespectful."

"And if she destroys everything?" Ash said, his features paler than normal.

"I'll allow her in under fae hospitality rules. If she touches anything, even us, we can appeal to Cernunnos." Who'd been suspiciously silent lately.

On that note, a phantom wind blew the door open, revealing a woman wearing a dress of bright blue silk.

All goddesses are beautiful. Those are basically the rules of the fae. But my mother? She was on a different level. Her hair was dark as night and flowers were carefully braided through the strands, her skin pale as cream. Long considered one of the most beautiful of the fae, my mother could stop traffic if she ever dropped her glamour among the humans. Right now, any tourists milling around would see a dark-haired woman, girl next door pretty, holding a basket of flowers.

We had the same azure-colored eyes, though my mother's held a chill no matter how warmly she spoke.

Cliona, Goddess of beauty, love, and passion, Queen of the Banshees, Queen of the seas…I could go on and on with her titles, but the one that mattered most to me was the one I called her.

Mother.

"Hello," I said politely.

One of her dark eyebrows went up. "Daughter, I always enjoy your warm greetings."

"This is the second time I've seen you in only a few weeks. Is something wrong?"

She rolled her eyes, the gesture one of the most human I'd ever seen on her. "Does there have to be something wrong for me to visit my daughter?"

My eyes narrowed. "No, but I rarely see you. This is the first time I've seen you this much since I moved away."

"Then maybe we should change that."

No. We absolutely should not change our situation.

"You haven't answered my question. What's wrong?"

She scoffed, a delicate sound. "Aren't you going to invite me in?"

"If you agree to hosting rules, yes."

Anger rolled over her face. Her jaw tightened with annoyance. "And what would you have me agree to?"

"Once you step onto the premises of my shop, you are a guest. No harm shall come to you as long as you agree to bring no harm to any living things inside. Mammal, paranormal, animal, plant, anything that has any sentience must be left alone. You also agree to leave everything inside alone. Anything inside is my property and is to be left alone. You'll have twenty minutes inside, and then you must leave. You are to cast no spells, murmur no incantation, take nothing even if you consider it yours, or try to coerce anyone or anything inside to join you or come work for you."

Mom sighed. "Honestly, Evie. You make me sound like a common thief."

She wasn't, but I can remember a few times where she got sticky fingers, and a couple of those were at my house. She'd stolen a couple of my treasures, nothing I couldn't replace, but annoying, nonetheless.

"Do you agree?"

"Fine," she snapped. "I agree to your rules. Do you have good tea at least?"

"I keep your favorite blend in the fridge." With a mental nudge, I loosened the wards to allow my mother inside.

She stepped over the threshold and brushed past, her familiar scent of fresh sea and florals washing over me, bringing with it an aching wave of sadness.

Ash and Moira hadn't retreated, much to my surprise. The dryad already had a cup of tea prepared for my mother and held it out. "Would you like cream and sugar?" he asked.

My mother's lips curved in approval. "Ash. I'd forgotten what a gentleman you are. Thank you. I would love both, please."

Ash inclined his head and went back to the fridge. Mom settled onto one of the seats, smoothing her skirts out.

"Moira," she said when her eyes found the vampire. "Always a pleasure."

"Cliona." Moira hated my mother. With good reason, but it

always made me afraid for her whenever Cliona deigned to show her face. Though the vampire knew when to hold her tongue, Moira loved me like family, and I wondered if there would come a day when she lost her temper with my mother.

That day might mean Moira's death.

While Mom was under guest rules, she'd be on her best behavior, but she'd try to push my buttons and get me to violate them first. That way, anything that happens would be on me.

I had a lot more to lose than I used to.

And…we had a magical bird roosting in the office, one who'd shown up unexpectedly and threatened to upend my life.

It started with an egg and ended with a Phoenix hatching in the middle of my office, delighting my raven, Poe, and horrifying the rest of us. Mom had three magical birds capable of resurrecting the dead, and one of them was the mom of our brand-new baby bird.

If Cliona found out we had her baby, she'd lose her everloving mind.

Tess had placed a magical damper on the bird's presence, but I hadn't asked her if she'd refreshed the spell lately. In my defense, I hadn't expected my mother to show up so soon after her last visit.

Mom sniffed. "I smell the banshee. Where is she?"

"Tess is off today. I'll tell her you stopped by."

Mom gave me a tight smile. "Must it always be so antagonistic between us?"

Ash pressed a cup of coffee in my hand. Goddess bless the dryad. I sent him a thankful look and focused on my mother. "Why don't we get to the point? You never visit just to visit, Mom. You're obviously here for something." I checked the clock on the wall. "You have seventeen minutes left."

"Evie, honestly," Mom said with a huff. "I am your mother."

I set my mug down and crossed my arms. "Sixteen minutes."

"Fine." Mom exhaled. "There's someone in town you should know about."

"Alright." I waited. Mom liked to draw things out. Our relationship was nothing but antagonistic. I thought sometimes I'd crawled out of the womb with the urge to argue with my mother.

"A god walks this town, Evie. A dangerous one."

"All gods are dangerous. Especially the one sitting right in front of me."

"This is not a joke, Evangeline!"

Silence fell in the shop. Magic crackled around Mom's form. Her hair lifted in a phantom wind.

"Mom? What's wrong?"

"Neit is here," she said softly. "I cannot protect you from him."

Numbness settled in my bones. "Neit, your ex-boyfriend?"

"Evie, I swear to the gods, you are infuriating! He is the god of war. And he hates me. You are a target for him."

I studied my mother. She seemed genuinely bothered, but her ability to lie with a straight face could win awards if she were in Hollywood. "Neit and I had a decent relationship. Why would he want to come after me?"

"Because you belong to me!" She blew out a breath and picked her teacup back up. "I recommend you vacate this place for a while."

Ah. Now we were getting somewhere. "This is my place of business. I can't just vacate it temporarily."

She waved her hand at Ash and Moira. "You have people to take care of things while you're gone."

"And where would I go that Neit would not find me? If he's so adamant about getting to me?"

"Home, of course."

"To Seattle?" I asked, deliberately playing dumb. My mother wasn't as devious as she thought. I knew exactly what she'd suggest, but the question was why?

"No, Evie. Our home is the Otherworld."

"Your home," I corrected. "I've never been there."

"You lived there for a period."

"Mother. No. I lived with humans and then in Seattle. With you. Don't you remember?"

My mother's face turned crafty. "I'd forgotten why you don't remember."

The fingers of the grave walked down my spine. "Why would I not remember such a large part of my life?" If she were telling the truth, that meant she'd done something to me, somehow manipulated my memories. And if she had, again, the question was why?

The fae had always been manipulative and fickle, even if I were one of them.

"You'll return with me to the Otherworld." She drank the rest of her tea and rose. "I'll be back to collect you soon."

I gawked at her while I gathered my thoughts. She'd ignored my question and assumed I'd do whatever she wanted. In the past, I would have, but that was before… everything. I was no longer Evie. My body and mind were not my own, not completely. And there was no way I'd divulge those secrets to the woman who would do nothing but use them against me for the rest of my life.

"Thank you for the tea. I'll see you in twenty-four hours."

Ash, Moira, and Tess wore similar looks of horror.

"No," I said, the words clear in the quiet shop.

Mom's eyebrows went up. "Excuse me?"

I rose. "I said no. I'm not coming with you. If Neit wants to come after me, he can. I'll be ready for him."

A muscle ticked in my mother's cheek. "I am your mother," she gritted out.

"And I am a grown woman. This is my home and my shop, and I don't plan to run every time someone wants to come after me."

From my peripheral, Ash and Moira high-fived.

The shop trembled, glass vases clinking against each other as my mother's magic rose.

"Remember, you are here on guest rules," I said softly.

"You cannot beat me," she said confidently.

"You're right. But my wards will expel you before I have to."

The bell over the door jingled. I stilled, cursing myself that I'd forgotten to lock it with such a dangerous guest inside.

But familiar magic slid over my shoulders, curling around me sinuously.

"Am I interrupting something?" Caelan's rumbly voice asked, his stormy eyes landing on my mother.

Shit. Fuck. Damn.

He would sense what she was immediately.

"My guest was just leaving," I said, keeping my eyes on Cliona.

My mother's eyes narrowed. "You are the Shifter Lord."

Caelan inclined his head. "I am. And you are…"

She held out a graceful hand. "My name is Cliona."

The only surprise Caelan showed was a slow blink. He took her hand, palm down, and brushed a kiss over the back of her palm. "To what does Joy Springs owe the pleasure of hosting a goddess in our midst?"

My mother smiled prettily, her fae glow so bright she was almost painful to look at. "I've always heard you were a charmer. I'm here to visit—"

Oh gods, please don't.

"My daughter."

Caelan's brows flicked up, his gaze going to me for a split second. I could almost see his furiously spinning thoughts. "Our Evie has been keeping secrets," he murmured.

Mother's laugh sounded like hundreds of tinkling bells. "She's quite good at her secrecy," she agreed.

"And the purpose of your visit?"

"Stop being nosy, Lord," I snapped.

Caelan's grin made me want to stab him in the kidney.

But my mother, pretending to be vapid and guileless, kept spilling our business. "I'm trying to convince Evie to return home."

Caelan's eyes flickered. "Oh? And where would home be?"

"She's half-fae, Lord. Evie belongs in the Otherworld, even if she's temporarily chosen this place as a waypoint."

"Mother, your time runs out in less than a minute."

Caelan glanced at me, his brow furrowing.

"I demand an extension," Cliona snapped.

"No," I snapped back.

"Evangeline." Her voice turned deadly.

"Forty seconds," I said.

"You are being a terrible host," Cliona said.

"I never claimed to be a good one. Thirty seconds."

"This is not over. I will return in twenty-four hours."

"And my answer will be the same. No. Fifteen seconds."

Our gazes clashed, magic swirling in the fathomless depths of my mother's eyes.

"Five seconds," I said with a smile.

Cliona disappeared in a puff of golden smoke.

No one breathed for the next several seconds until we were sure she was gone. I sagged back to the couch and exhaled.

"Fuck me," Ash breathed.

"Your mom is a fucking bitch," Moira said, making me laugh.

Caelan stared at all of us, a curious expression on his face. "So...half goddess, Evie?"

I didn't like the way he was looking at me, part possessive and part cunning.

"It doesn't matter."

Caelan sauntered uninvited over to the coffee pot and made himself a cup, but just as I was about to bitch at him about it, he poured two cups and brought one over to me. I'd drunk far too much caffeine today, but I accepted it gratefully and curled my freezing fingers around the warm mug.

"I assure you, it matters very much."

Ash and Moira scattered to the back as Caelan sat opposite me in the same spot my mother had just vacated.

"Does anyone else know?" he asked as he sipped his coffee.

Ben knew the gods had visited me, but he didn't know of our relationship.

"Not that I'm aware of." I studied him. "So tell me, Lord. How will you use this against me?"

A flicker of a smile. "You assume the worst of me."

"Am I wrong?"

He didn't deny it, and I didn't expect him to. "The other Lords would pay dearly for this information."

"And will you sell it to them?"

He took far too long to answer. And just when I wondered if I should go to the Otherworld to see what my mother was hiding, Caelan shook his head. "No. The secrets of your heritage are safe with me."

"What do you want in return?"

Caelan laughed. "Have we always been this transactional, Evie?"

A dumbfounded snort escaped me. "Have you forgotten about our short history, Lord?"

"Caelan," he growled. "We are in private."

"Fine, Caelan. Our entire relationship is transactional." My gaze skimmed down the slate blue suit he wore, snagging on another boutonniere. Disgust made my upper lip curl. Before I could stop myself, I slashed my hand downward turning the carnation and rose monstrosity into ash.

Caelan looked down at himself, sighed, then burst into delighted laughter. "My dear Evie, how will I explain this when I get home?"

I held up a finger. "Wait here."

Stomping back to the fridge, I wrenched the door open and gathered a few things before heading to my work table. In less than five minutes, I'd put together a small, stunning boutonniere made with the Anastasia Chrysanthemum and a deep black orchid, topping it off with a small spray of eucalyptus, and tying it with a deep black ribbon and a silver wax impression with the initial C. A small touch of my magic boosted the life force of the cut flowers, ensuring it would last for weeks if properly cared for.

When it was finished, I double checked my work and stomped back over to him, anger at myself and my possessive behavior simmering in my chest. "Stand up," I snapped.

Caelan's slow grin made my heart turn over, but he rose.

I unhooked the cheap safety pin and tossed it into the closest trash can and fastened the new one to his lapel, brushing away the residual ash as I worked. When I finished, I stepped back and inspected it before taking him by the arm and leading him over to the mirror behind my work desk.

"This is something befitting of a Lord," I growled. "But no one should be wearing a boutonniere unless you're going to a formal dinner or prom. It's not something you wear during the day."

Caelan's lips twitched, his tan fingers brushing over the fresh flowers. "It's stunning."

"I know."

His chuckle made me want to smack him. "The arrangement will last for weeks if you store it in the refrigerator after you wear it."

"Why?" he asked, our gazes catching and holding in the mirror.

I wasn't sure why, but I'd felt the need to mark him. And how could a Floromancer do that better than with flowers? "If I'm to be the florist for your wedding, I want my work advertised properly, not with cheap discount store boutonnieres."

"Ah. Of course," Caelan said, though I could tell he didn't believe me.

I shook my head. "Why did you come by today?" If there was a purpose, it was completely derailed by now.

"Gianna sent me with more photos."

"She could have emailed them."

"I know." His fingers brushed over the flowers once more, eyes sparking gold. "I like wearing a piece of you."

I swallowed hard and took a step back, turning away from

him. "You can leave the photos on the couch. I'll add them to your file."

"Evie."

I stilled but didn't turn around.

"I will keep your secrets. You can trust me."

I scoffed. "You are a Shifter Lord. Every one of you deals in secrets. Mine are safe until you need something from me."

Caelan fell silent. I went to the register and opened up the shop email. A few moments later, the bell jingled, and the Shifter Lord was gone.

CHAPTER
Ten

Moira insisted on driving me home later that night, telling me it wasn't safe to keep riding the bicycle with everything going on, especially with my mother in town. I grumbled a little but acquiesced, mostly because every muscle in my body hurt.

All the tension over the last few days was starting to get to me.

Moira waved as she started the car, then urged me to sleep with a weapon under my pillow. After a lame joke about my two fists being weapons, she rolled her eyes and spun out of the driveway, leaving me sitting on the front steps contemplating the chaos that was my life.

The weather had taken a sharp turn toward the cooler, a blessing in this part of the country. I relaxed on the front steps for a little while before dusting my pants off and going inside to drop my purse and keys off. It had been a while since I last walked the property. With the new wards I'd put up, it was more important than ever to ensure there were no weak areas in the magic.

I'd left the wards open to Ben and Caelan, but now I wondered if that was a mistake. Shaking my head, I changed into a pair of joggers, a tank, and a soft cardigan before sliding my feet into a flexible pair of sneakers.

The weight of everything followed me onto the property, so many decisions and forks in the road swirling through my mind. But soon enough, the fresh air and the wild flora and fauna on the land began to relax me, my Floromancy a humming, living thing inside my veins. I walked the acreage, siphoning my too full magic into plants who needed it, patchy areas of grass, trees lacking in nutrients, vines and other wildflowers I thought could use a boost, and soon enough, happiness and contentment had settled into my soul once again.

I rarely took my magic for granted, but I'd been far too busy and stressed lately to use my Floromancy like I should. Siphoning the magic helped immensely, and my shoulders felt loose for the first time in a couple of weeks.

My land had flourished under my touch, a wild space in a town controlled by powerful Lords. Much of Joy Springs had become commercialized under Caelan's hands, but there were still wild spaces on the outskirts. Places I needed to visit to really siphon my magic. My land could only take so much, and letting my magic out in one wild burst would be a mistake. Collateral damage was real, and there'd be far too many questions if the entire town suddenly looked like a garden.

I visited the greenhouse next, wincing when the broken windows came into view. Making a mental note to contact Caelan's handyman, I pulled the tray of thyme over, hoping this time I could boost their growth without my magic going haywire.

Nervous but hopeful, I sent a tendril in, and my magic responded with no issues. Siphoning had helped. Letting out a sigh of relief, I spent the next hour inside working on all the plant life.

When dusk fell, I stretched out the stiff muscles in my back and left the greenhouse. But the second I stepped onto the grass, I sensed a disturbance on the land. Heart thumping, I turned toward the new fencing at the back of the house. The fertile soil had taken on a brittle feeling in my mind, and some of the flowers were wilting, impossible since I'd just boosted them less than two hours ago.

Frowning, I got closer, only to sense a familiar hot prickling of magic. A cloaked figure stood by the fence, but I recognized Finn right away. Swearing, I gathered my magic, but it came too hard, too fast, reacting to the Chimera's presence. An oversized Thistle grew in my palm and shot out toward Finn, embedding itself into the oak fence with a sharp thwacking sound.

My tattoo flared with heat, a scream tearing from my throat as my skin burned from within. Finn's mocking chuckle sounded through the air, his silent message clear as day.

I can find you anywhere.

He disappeared with a mocking wave.

I stood there for several minutes, waiting for my land to settle once more. Disturbed, I turned back to head inside, but not before reinforcing my wards once more.

Later that evening, I burned a blend of sage and lavender, protective herbs, but when I lit the charcoal briquette, the flames burned green and too high. Cursing, I extinguished the blaze, but it had lit the charcoal, still allowing me to burn the herbs. As I walked through the house, coating the rooms in protective smoke, I watched the charcoal carefully and extinguished it using water when I was finished.

Back in my bedroom, I glanced at my cell and suppressed the urge to contact Ben or Caelan. Neither of them could help me in the way I needed it, so I put the cell on the charger and grabbed a dagger for under my pillow.

Sleep was a long time coming, but when it finally did, my dreams were disturbed and confusing.

CHAPTER
Eleven

CAELAN

I sat at my desk reviewing Council reports from across the country. Halvar still had not been found, a fact that had begun to press on the Lords. If there was no sign of him in the next thirty days, the Council would be forced to elect another Shifter Lord.

Every time an election happened, things would destabilize while all the older Lords got used to a new personality. Sighing, I tossed my pen down.

The pockets of rogue attacks were building, expanding to other Lords' borders. In a way, it was good news. The rogues were testing others' borders now, not just mine. But it would require a response sooner or later.

Simone sat in a chair across the room, studying something intently on her tablet. Her presence was soothing, as I hated being alone. Garrett was off trying to track down the missing Lord, and Ben…Well, things weren't the best with him since he was trying to steal Evie right out from under my nose.

And how could I be mad? I had a fiancée waiting for me in the other room.

A shift of wind before I could react, and a feisty flytrap had chomped onto my forearm.

"Shit!" I hissed, extricating Seymour from my sleeve and righting his pot, relief flooding me that the damn thing hadn't broken the skin. Evie had boosted the plant by making its bite poisonous. Or venomous. Hell. No idea, but Seymour held a dangerous paralytic in his teeth, one that had gotten more than once of us before. The Red Dragon flytrap announced his displeasure by chomping at me.

Amusement filled me, but I couldn't let the little bastard know I liked his violent tendencies. "I know you like those special worms your mistress sends you, so if you don't behave, I'm going to feed you houseflies."

Seymour dramatically keeled over, the edge of his sharp teeth catching on part of my report. He chomped down, leaving several perfectly spaced holes at the top of the paper. I folded up a tissue paper and wiped the glistening poison from the edges.

"Last warning, Seymour."

The plant went still. I reached for the base of the pot once more and righted it, careful not to position my arm where he could grab it. At first, the plant had amused me, but once he'd bitten me, I almost turned it into ash, but how could I destroy a piece of Evie?

The grumpy, dangerous flytrap was like having a piece of the Floromancer with me. Even if it still didn't know whether to like me or try to kill me yet.

What pissed me off the most, though, was that Seymour adored Ben, the Keep Healer, allowing the shifter to gently stroke the top of its head when he visited.

I tried and spent the next two hours unable to move my legs.

What an asshole.

An amused snort made my shoulders tense. "You're early," I said to the other Shifter Lord. Rowan pulled up a chair at the opposite end of the table. "Seems like your plant has better instincts than most of the other Lords."

I gave him a quelling look. "Seymour has trust issues."

"Seymour knows how fixated you are on his mistress and has opinions about it."

"Why are you ruining my peace, Rowan?"

Out of all the Lords, I liked him best. Rowan was as good as his word, but lately, he'd gotten closer to Evie than I was comfortable with. And even though she wasn't my property, and we were technically nothing to each other, the thought of her being with another Shifter Lord, or hell, anyone, made me grit my teeth and suppress the urge to gut the guilty party.

Unfortunately, the unrepentant bastard knew it. Rowan kicked his legs up on the table, out of Seymour's reach (or so he thought) and grinned. "Caelan, you haven't had peace since Evie saved your sorry life."

I rubbed a hand over my face. Rowan wasn't wrong.

Simone spoke up from her corner. "Evie's volatile nature intrigues Caelan. Despite my repeated warnings."

I gnashed my teeth at her. "You like her, too, and you know it."

Simone scoffed but fell silent.

"I can't help it," I admitted quietly. "There's something about her that keeps drawing me in against my better judgment."

Rowan, one of the few Lords I trusted, studied me. "You need to decide. Are you going to protect her, or are you going to use her to further your goals?"

Magic flared in my eyes.

Rowan laughed and held a hand up. "Peace, Caelan. Evie and I are only friends. We respect each other. I've never met another person so in tune with nature."

I didn't believe him. "And if the other Lords try to force you into marriage?"

Rowan grinned, his eyes sparkling. "Hell, I'm not blind, man. I can learn to love the violent little Floromancer given enough time."

I sighed. "Seymour. He's the one you need to bite. Not me."

Seymour turned his freaky little head to study Rowan. The Lord stilled.

"Not cool," he hissed.

I laughed.

"She makes the Council nervous. We all know what happens when the Lords get itchy."

People died. I was no stranger to violence. Peace reigned in Joy Springs because of my power, and I hadn't had a viable challenger since I'd taken over.

"They either want her dead or neutralized," Rowan murmured.

"Through marriage," I growled.

Rowan's teeth flashed in a grin. "I see you're still pissed about why you weren't chosen for matrimonial bliss with favorite Floromancer."

"They'd be too powerful together," Simone observed. "The question remains, who are they saving her for?"

"Bite her, too," I muttered to Seymour.

"I'm only pointing out the obvious," Simone insisted.

"The same problem will occur if she marries another Lord," I said, pushing the reports away.

Rowan snorted. "You can't be that blind, man."

I looked up at the Lord.

"You're the most powerful Lord on record right now. That's the only reason they haven't shoved Evie at you. The only two Lords who aren't afraid of her are sitting in this room."

"Caelan is afraid of her sometimes."

I bared my teeth at my Omega.

Rowan barked a laugh. "The woman makes my balls shrivel occasionally, but the others are genuinely terrified of Evie. You and I both know she's not merely a Floromancer."

If only he knew. "As long as she continues presenting herself that way, we have to operate under the assumption that's what she is, otherwise we'd break our own laws."

"Forcing a woman to marry one of you is breaking about a dozen laws in this country," Simone groused.

"We fall under our own law," I said to her, "as you well know."

"Doesn't mean it doesn't piss me off," Simone grumbled.

Powerful magic pulsed from Seymour, a tourmaline-colored flash cracking in the room. The plant stilled, motionless for a long moment before it shivered, the magic gone as suddenly as it had risen.

Every hair on my body stood up. That was Evie's magic. Had something happened?

Rowan stared at Seymour. "What just happened?"

Simone was already tapping at her tablet. "I'll check on Evie, Lord," she said simply.

Dangerous things were moving around my Floromancer.

The gods help me. I should not have let that woman wiggle her way into my heart.

Twelve

At dawn the next morning, the shop doors blew open, the bells jangling a discordant tune, and a small, fearsome woman walked in, her strawberry-colored hair floating away from her shoulders even though the wind outside was still.

Her eyes were a freakish ultramarine blue color, her gaze sharp and intelligent. Hazel had an odd way of being able to read everyone in the room and their emotions to boot. She wasn't a Seer that I could tell, but I felt positive Hazel got flashes of the future sometimes.

She was way too observant not to.

Hazel carried a battered leather duffel that crackled with power. She tossed it down, blew her hair out of her face, and let her gaze sweep the shop before she turned, her sharp gaze landing on me.

"Tea," she demanded in her smoky, accented voice. "Hot, black, and fast."

Moira scrambled to get it for her. The vampire was scared of few things, but Hazel both fascinated and scared the shit out of her. She also held quite a lot of respect for the witch as Moira never would have met me if Hazel had left me to die in that Scottish field of thistles.

The witch studied me for a long moment, then nodded as if she'd convinced herself of something. She held her arms open, and I went to her as if hypnotized. Hazel wasn't the most demonstrative witch, but when she asked for a hug, you gave it to her, because usually Hazel wasn't the one who needed it.

She crushed me to her small frame, the hug smelling of a dozen different herbs and magic. Hazel stroked a firm hand down my hair and patted me on the back. "Your magic smells different, my dear. Is your tattoo acting up?"

I nodded, my face buried in her shoulder.

"Well then," she said decisively. "I'll get to work on that soon, then."

She stepped away just as Moira held her teacup out. Hazel took it with a thankful grunt and settled herself on the couch.

"Cream or sugar?" the vampire asked.

"Both, please."

As Hazel fixed her tea, Ash and Tess came out, the dryad giving me a curious glance.

"Hazel, this is Ash and Tess, friends of mine. They also work at the shop."

Hazel's startling eyes narrowed. "We used to have many dryads back home. They've all retreated to the deeper forested areas."

Ash smiled. "I have some family in Scotland, though I haven't seen them in years."

"If you ever decide to visit, my home is open to you." Before Ash could respond, Hazel's attention was on Tess. "Dangerous to have a banshee as a friend with your mother coming around, Evie."

Tess floated closer. "I sense the queen before she appears."

Hazel's lips quirked. "Allowing you to haul ass?"

Tess let out a little squeaky moan in agreement.

"And you," Hazel said, turning her attention to Moira, "sucking on many veins these days?"

Moira rolled her eyes. While she had a healthy fear of Hazel, she wasn't afraid to talk back. "I prefer it straight from the tap these days."

Hazel snorted. "Liar. I can smell O negative in that mug of yours."

Moira's brow furrowed as she looked down at her tea. "Seriously?"

Hazel tapped the side of her nose. "A hereditary witch has an excellent sense of smell. Though your donor was a touch anemic, my dear. Don't be surprised if you're hungry again in only a couple of hours."

Moira swore. "Dammit. I knew there was something up with this batch! I'm going to ask for a refund."

I stared at the vampire. "You couldn't tell?"

"That she was anemic?" Moira scoffed. "I'm not a doctor, Evie."

Her tone was exasperated, and it made me laugh. "Sorry. I wrongly assumed vamps could tell that sort of thing like a built-in survival instinct."

"Maybe in the past, but I've always taken bottled blood. Part of the way I was raised."

Hazel's eyes narrowed, but Moira ducked her head and turned away. Hmm. Maybe Moira hadn't always been a well-behaved vamp.

No judgment here. I hadn't been the best-behaved Floro-mancer lately, either.

"Let me finish this tea, and we'll take a look at that bouquet."

We chatted about her trip and the weather, all inane things, as Hazel sipped her tea. She'd always been a small thing, but power didn't always come in large packages. I didn't know much about witches because I'd never had many run-ins with them. Most wanted to be left alone, and they lived far from civilization. That wasn't always true, but Hazel had happened upon me because she was out foraging and had sensed a disturbance. Pure luck.

Or so she said.

When she finally set her teacup down and rose, I led her to the walk-in. Hazel grimaced and moved her fingers in an odd pattern. A moment later, a warm, comforting spell had settled over our shoulders.

"Something dark lives in that fridge," Hazel murmured. "Better safe than sorry."

Ash and the others took a few steps back. I opened the fridge and held the door open for Hazel.

The small witch stepped inside and let out a litany of curse words that made me blush.

Ash chuckled under his breath.

Hazel moved closer, reaching out a finger to touch the pouch. She shook her head. "That thing is dangerous. Its magic is familiar to me, but I can't place it. What I do know is there's some kind of binding on it as well as concealment magic."

The preservation spell holding the bouquet together flickered and died.

"Shit," I muttered. "There won't be much left if the preservation keeps failing."

"Let me try something," Hazel said. A faint emerald glow came from her fingertips as her magic rose, the scent of lavender and sage rising in the walk-in.

The bouquet thumped in its bag, retreating from Hazel's magic.

A shocked gasp escaped me. "It moved!"

"It doesn't like my magic," Hazel said, a curious look on her face. "Put one more preservation spell on it, if you don't mind. That will give me time to figure this one out."

I did as she asked, the spell taking only moments. Hazel nodded with approval. "Your Floromancy has grown. You've practiced quite a lot."

"Every day," I said. "It's easy enough to do with the shop and the greenhouse at home."

"Good. It will keep the Chimera magic at bay."

I wasn't so sure about that these days. The beast lay just under my skin, waiting for a moment of weakness.

We left the bouquet in the fridge and settled at the front once more. The shop would open in half an hour, but until then, we had time to figure things out.

"Tell me everything you remember about that thing. Leave nothing out," Hazel demanded.

Moira started at the beginning. Hazel listened intently, never interrupting even when I could tell she had a question. When she finished, Hazel nodded.

"When was it dropped off?"

Moira rattled off the date.

Hazel's eyes widened a hair. "By whom?"

"Someone who said she was the bride's mother, though we doubt that now."

"Are you aware of the laws governing supernatural weddings?" Hazel asked.

"Err. Should we be?" I never thought to ask about laws, assuming supernatural weddings were the same as humans, except with a much scarier guest list.

Hazel's look made me want to curl into the fetal position. "Any food or drink must be destroyed completely. Fire is the best way. Any flowers must be held in stasis for at least three weeks after the wedding, to allow any residual energies from the wedding party to fade."

I blinked. "Moira, see if you can get a copy of those laws from…"

I looked at Hazel, who gave a put-upon sigh. "The Shifter Lord's office usually has a copy."

Moira wiggled her eyebrows. "Sure you don't want to be the one to make that call?"

I shot her a dark look.

Hazel didn't miss the exchange. "You messing around with the local Lord, Evie? That doesn't sound like you."

"Because it isn't," I muttered. "He hired me to do his wedding flowers."

Hazel's penetrating stare made me squirm. "Did you try to say no?"

"No," Moira said, just as I said, "yes."

"Et tu, Brute?" I whispered.

Ash snickered.

"I couldn't refuse him," I grumbled. "He'd make my life difficult if I tried."

"Why would he do that?" Hazel asked, her sharp eyes missing nothing.

"You've missed quite a lot of shenanigans between our favorite Floromancer and the local Lord," Moira said, grinning at me when I turned to mouth, "shut up" to her.

Hazel grunted. "We'll address those shenanigans later. The priority remains that cursed bundle in your fridge. But..." her voice trailed off as she watched me with those hawk eyes, "it is the height of foolishness to get close to someone who has the potential to destroy your life so thoroughly. Chimeras are put to death on sight for a reason, Evie."

I swallowed hard. "I know."

Hazel was right. I was profoundly dumb for acting like Caelan was anything more than a deadly foe. Even if he made me feel special. The Lord had no idea who I truly was, so everything between us was built on a lie.

Trusting anyone except the people in this room could be a deadly mistake. Caelan already knew too much about me.

I thought about running, something I used to think about far more before I'd learned to control the dangerous flares of magic building inside me.

Somehow, I didn't think I could ever run far enough that Caelan wouldn't find me. The thought both lifted and sobered me.

Geez. I was cooked, wasn't I?

LATER THAT EVENING, I was working out my frustrations in the greenhouse when I noticed the new tray of thyme seedlings were struggling. Concerned, I pulled the tray closer, sending a tendril of tourmaline-colored magic out.

Several withered under my power. I gasped and extinguished my magic, grief welling inside me at the unnecessary death. Shaking the power from my fingers, I plucked the ruined seedlings from the tray and tossed them into the compost pile, whispering an apology as they disappeared into the darkness.

When I stepped outside sometime later, a voice whispered through the wind, Finn's voice.

"You'll come to me soon, Evie."

Unsettled, I hurried inside the house, double-checking all the locks and windows, knowing I'd never be safe if Finn really wanted to bring me to him.

Sleep was a long time coming that evening.

CHAPTER
Thirteen

A few days passed. Hazel continued working on the bouquet, and I occasionally caught her muttering obscenities to herself from the walk-in. She seemed fine without my help, so I left her to it and busied myself with the sample bouquets for Caelan's nuptials. When I'd finished all of them, I messaged Simone, who responded almost immediately with a request for a meeting the same evening at the Keep.

But this time, Moira was not invited. Odd, but if she wanted to come, I'd bring her with me anyway.

When I tried to refuse, Simone kept kicking back my refusals by changing the time in fifteen-minute increments until I got so annoyed I accepted the damn invite.

Three hours later, another decorated black box showed up at the shop, delivered by a quiet man wearing a sharp suit who said nothing and held out a clipboard for my signature.

I stared at it as if it were a snake. "What happens if I refuse delivery?"

The man's flat stare was so quelling, I almost screamed in frustration. "Fine," I snarled, scratching an angry signature on the paper and shoving the clipboard back at him.

He spun on his heel and left the shop, leaving the box against the side of the couch.

Moira came out from the back and gasped. "Dammit. Another one?" She looked around, and when she realized there was only one delivery, her lower lip jutted out. "I'm just the stepchild to your Lord. How disappointing."

"You can wear mine if you'd like."

Moira laughed. "I do not have a death wish. That one is all you." She jerked a thumb at it. "Open it up and let me see."

"Later." My gaze went to the double doors leading to the back.

"Ah," Moira lowered her voice. "Scared of mom's disapproval."

I snorted. "We've gotta get this box out of here before Hazel senses it."

Tess drifted over. "Want me to take it to your house?"

I sagged with relief. "Please. And take a longer lunch break since you're doing this for me."

Tess smiled and snatched the box before hurrying out, her purse and keys in her hand.

"She was already going somewhere, wasn't she?" I muttered.

Moira snorted. "Ash already snuck out about ten minutes ago."

I glanced at her, realization dawning. "Ack. Gross."

"Let's just hope she drops the dress off first."

"Moira! Eww." I loved both of them, but thinking about them making the beast with two backs was enough to make me want to stab my eyes out with spoons.

The vampire laughed and went behind the register. "Business is still slow. Think we should do some paid marketing?"

"No. I haven't announced our involvement in the Lord's wedding yet. Once we do, we won't be able to keep our heads above water for a while."

Moira's glance was curious. "And why haven't we announced it?"

"Because we might all get fired," I muttered. "If Caelan keeps sending me dresses, I'm afraid Gianna is going to booby-trap my car."

"True, but I'd guess she values her pretty hide, too."

"Depends on how badly she wants to murder me. She seems to have a strong sense of self-preservation, so let's hope she keeps to the occasional verbal riposte and away from explosive material."

"Hope is a fickle thing," Moira said with a twinkle in her eye.

"You're not going to laugh at my funeral when all that's left of me gets put into a tiny box."

"As long as the box is pretty," Moira said, laughing when I flipped her off.

Later that evening, when Hazel was out communing with the land or whatever weird Scottish witches did, I flipped open Caelan's box. My breath caught in my throat. A vivid amethyst-colored satin dress lay nestled in creamy tissue paper.

"Dammit," I muttered. How did he have such great taste?

Raised golden vines decorated the skirt, mid-length this time, magic humming against my fingers as I brushed over them. The bodice was etched with the same vine motif.

But to make it worse, a small box lay to the side, the same size jewelry came in. My hand trembled as I reached for it, hesitating over the top.

An envelope lay above it, so I reached for the parchment note first.

In case the first didn't suit the florist's taste.

A smile tugged at my lips. I reached for the small box, carefully tugging the lid off.

A pair of rose-cut, flawless amethysts in the shape of flowers winked up at me. "Caelan," I breathed.

I dug my cell phone out of my pocket.

I can't accept these.

Can't or won't, came his response.

This is too much. And inappropriate.

I have an ungodly amount of money.

I'd forgotten how terribly humble you are.
Amethyst is a cheap stone.
So you have an ungodly amount of money, but you're cheap?
I didn't say those particular amethysts are cheap.
Gianna will notice.
I don't care.
You should care.
Wear the dress. With the earrings.
No.
Please.

I didn't respond again, a heavy breath escaping me as I put the lid back on the box.

Caelan never said please. And they were gorgeous. Amethyst was one of my favorite stones.

"Evie. Shut up," I muttered to myself.

I lifted the dress up and hung it carefully, unable to stop myself from running my fingers over the exquisite, magical embroidery.

I picked my cell up again.

Who's making these dresses?
Wear the earrings and I'll tell you.

I snorted.

I'll ask Simone.
I've already instructed her not to tell you.
I'll ask the butler.
I don't have a butler, but if I did, he wouldn't tell you either.
Then I'll instruct Seymour to bite you. Repeatedly.
Don't threaten me with a good time, Evie.

I laughed out loud.

If I promise to wear the earrings, do you promise to tell me who made the dress?
As long as you wear the dress, too.
Dammit, Caelan. I'm not yours to dress up.
My two months aren't up yet.

I did not respond again, his words clanging inside my head like a bell.

Moira had elected to stay behind because Soren wouldn't be at the Keep. I thought about begging her to go, but I didn't want to make her uncomfortable.

After downing the soup Hazel had left on the stove, I got into my car and drove to the Keep.

Once I valeted and someone who was not the butler let me in, Simone greeted me and walked me to the same place as before, staying silent the entire time.

She looked more strained than the last time I'd seen her, and before we went in, I touched her elbow.

"Are you okay?" I whispered.

"Be careful, Evie," was all she said, her gaze snagging on the amethysts in my ears. She shook her head and stepped behind me.

The doors opened, and a scene that looked straight out of a Christmas movie greeted me. There was red and white every-where, and just as I felt my face tugging into an expression of horror, I caught myself and slapped an inane smile on my face.

"You've redecorated," I said.

Gianna stood at the same table as before, dressed in red this time, and I had an image of a mall elf sitting poor, hapless chil-dren on a drunk Santa's lap during the holidays. An almost hysterical giggle got trapped in my throat, and I coughed to try to get it out.

Rowan, my favorite Lord, stood at the table behind Gianna, grinning like a lunatic.

My lips twitched, just as my gaze snagged on the Shifter Lord. All the breath was sucked out of my lungs. He wore another suit, this time a cool dove grey. My boutonniere was attached to his lapel, fresh as the day I gave it to him. I had another in my bag I'd made for him earlier, but I hadn't decided yet if I should give it to him.

This felt like the strangest case of madness.

I tore my gaze away to see Gianna staring at me, her eyes flickering a strange silver color. "I thought it would be nice to see what the room looked like with the color palette I'd chosen."

"It's…festive," I said lamely.

Rowan coughed.

"Yes," Gianna agreed. "It is, isn't it? I had the red modeled after the color of blood. Quite an accurate depiction, isn't it?"

"My expertise lies in flowers, Gianna. Though I'm sure any decorator you hired would do their best to bring your vision to life."

Rowan's eyes widened.

Yes, you asshat. I can be as political as I need to be sometimes, even though I hate it.

Gianna's eyes narrowed, assuming I was being facetious. Which I was, but none of my words explicitly said so.

"Please," she said after a moment, "have a seat."

Rowan came around and took the box from my hands. "You look stunning," he murmured in my ear.

I gave him a grateful smile. Rowan winked and went back to the table, placing the box in the chair beside mine. I was by myself at the opposite end of the table, and it sort of felt like an inquisition.

"I've ordered refreshments and hors d'oeuvres tonight," Gianna said. "This should be a shorter meeting than last time, I hope."

Caelan shot her an annoyed look. "Thank you for meeting us this evening, Miss Quinn. I'm sure you have a busy schedule, so taking time away to assist us is always appreciated."

"As Gianna said, this meeting shouldn't take as long as the first."

The woman's razor-sharp gaze glided down my dress. "Your dress is stunning. My Caelan does have a type, doesn't he?"

I didn't visibly react, but I had the sense I was involved in a game where I didn't understand the rules. "Thank you. I do look good in war paint, if I do say so myself."

Rowan's eyes widened, even as Caelan's glimmered with approval.

The servers came over and filled our glasses with red wine before I could refuse. There was a glass of water beside the plate I could drink instead, though, so I scooted it a little closer.

"Are you not a drinker?" Gianna asked sweetly.

"I consider these meetings on the clock, and I don't drink during work hours."

"Oh? Caelan has agreed to pay you extra?" Her eyes flashed with annoyance.

Caelan had already dropped a disturbing amount of money into my bank account, far more than we'd agreed upon. "Based on our discussion last time we were here," I said.

"Oh. I thought you were joking." A brittle laugh, then, "Quadruple, really? We will discuss this later, Caelan."

The Shifter Lord's eyes went molten gold. I shifted uncomfortably and found my napkin to be of great interest.

He murmured something so low I was glad I didn't hear it, as the room temp dipped several degrees.

I finally lifted my head, my eyes finding Rowan's. "I'm pleased to see you again, Lord Rowan, but is there a reason both meetings have had the presence of different Lords?"

Rowan flashed a smile. "The Council wants reassurance that the festivities are staying on schedule."

"Two months is extremely fast for such a wedding," I remarked.

Rowan's eyes glittered with amusement. "We're all familiar with how quickly paranormals can end up shacking up. Marriage usually doesn't follow too long after."

Gianna twined her fingers into Caelan's. My stomach tightened with jealousy. The vines on my dress moved, sliding over the fabric with a soft susurrus of sound.

Gianna grinned. "We've already taken all the compatibility tests. Things look wonderful for any future offspring."

"Umm, congratulations." I think. Weird flex, but some women

did put a lot of stock in their fertility. It wasn't easy for certain types of shifters to conceive, so bully for her, I guess.

I reached for the box and pulled out the first sample, realizing as I did that the reds didn't match her candy cane hellscape.

"This is the first one I came up with based on the vision we spoke of last time. I can easily change the shades to match your preferred red."

The arrangement was pretty but had zero soul. The centerpiece was done with red lilies and white roses, complete with an opening for a small glass dome that held either a tea light or a battery-operated candle. None of my regular suppliers kept these flowers stocked because they were overly sprayed and over planted, so I had to use a wholesaler. All the life had been sucked from the blooms, and while they still looked fresh, even my Floromancer abilities weren't enough to bring them up to my standards.

Gianna's lips pursed. "Adequate."

I resisted the urge to roll my eyes. "I created this one, keeping the color scheme in mind somewhat."

This one had my stamp on it. I'd taken deep red anemones and placed them around the base of a creamy white vase and curved colorful Birds of Paradise around the top, resulting in a stunning abstract display.

Rowan's eyes widened. "Evie. That's stunning."

Gianna flicked a hand. "Too modern."

Caelan leaned forward and studied the display, reaching over to tug it closer. "This one would work, Gianna."

Her eyes blazed with anger. "We can set it aside."

And set it on fire, she said with her glare.

"I also have these," I said as I pulled a couple more. None were red, but they had gorgeous jewel tones. The one with deep purple orchids was my favorite, but the white anemone display with the Calathea leaves was a close second.

I'd boosted both arrangements with my magic, and the leaves

and buds slowly moved as if there was a phantom wind stirring the flora.

Caelan's eyes lit up. "Amazing."

Gianna's jaw dropped. "This is...beautiful," she grudgingly admitted. "But not what we're looking for."

As I expected. "Very well. The first one is more to your specifications?"

Gianna nodded. "Though the shade must match the rest of the room."

Blood red. Right. "I can change the color, though I'll need the hex code so I can make sure I get the shade correct."

Her head incline was regal. "Simone will get it to you."

"Then we're agreed," I said, just as the servers brought a round of meat and delicate cheeses.

"No," Caelan said, dashing my hopes for an early exit, "we are not."

Gianna froze. "Evie's ideas are too modern, Caelan. Our wedding must smack of tradition." A wheedling note in her voice made me grit my teeth.

"Must it?" He shook his head.

"Of course," Gianna snapped. "The Lords have a long history of sticking with traditional values within their kingdoms—"

"Joy Springs is not a kingdom. My reign is built on adapting to the current times. Perhaps that means our wedding must adopt, too."

Rowan glanced at Caelan, an odd look on his face.

"Rowan," Gianna demanded. "What is your opinion?"

The poor Lord looked like he'd swallowed an onion. "The Council does not attend these meetings to offer an opinion, only to ensure things are moving on schedule."

I stifled my grin. That was the perfect Lordly response from Rowan.

Gianna's eyes narrowed, almost like she knew Rowan was bullshitting her.

Which he definitely was. I'd never seen a Lord not offer an opinion, even when they weren't asked.

Strange magic rose in the room, the smell of it a frigid winter's wind, sharp and biting. Gianna's magic. Interesting. I'd never scented or been around a swan shifter before.

Though if I hadn't known what she was, I would have guessed bird of prey. The woman looked like she could swallow someone whole.

The vines on my dress shifted restlessly as I struggled to control my Floromancy, the rising Chimera magic in my blood flaring with it. It took a long moment, but I managed to get settled, keeping my breathing at a steady inhale and exhale.

My eyes met Gianna's across the table, and I read the warning in them. *Get in my way, and they'll never find your body.*

You can try it, I responded with my own eyes. *But you might not like what happens if you do.*

Gianna's mouth tightened.

Caelan interrupted our silent staring contest. "There's one more thing."

What now? Another automaton built to the size of a small car?

Rowan straightened and watched me. My brow furrowed.

"Whenever a Shifter Lord is set to marry, the old magic responds. A bonding ceremony is necessary to ensure our union is blessed."

A bonding ceremony? What the hell was that? I tried to stay in tune with current wedding trends and laws, but after Hazel's visit and now this, I realized I wasn't doing a great job at keeping up.

Gianna's perfect complexion went white. "Caelan."

My attention bounced back band forth between them. What was going on?

"A Floromancer is the perfect person to create the flowers for the bonding ceremony. Rowan will take care of the binding, and I've heard you have a powerful witch currently staying with you?"

I blinked. "Yes," I said slowly. Why was I surprised that he knew who was at my house?

"I plan to ask her if she will attend the ceremony for the essence blending."

My mouth fell open. "Uh. Essence blending. Right. Would you like her phone number?"

"Please leave it with Simone. I will call her first thing in the morning."

"Of course."

Gianna opened her mouth to protest. "Caelan, you can't ask a stranger to design this ceremony! It should be someone close to us."

"She's not designing the ceremony. Only the flowers. Rowan is one of my closest friends. The vows are his to create."

"And the witch?"

"I have no close witch friends. We would have had to hire a stranger, regardless."

Gianna's nostrils flared. Blood-red nails tapped against the table in agitation. "And what about me?"

"Evie has the skill level and magical instinct to ensure the ceremony is done right. Rowan and the witch will take care of the rest."

Caelan didn't trust Gianna. Interesting.

"Entrusting something so sacred to a Floromancer is madness, Caelan!" Gianna rose from the table and turned her back to us, hurrying out of the room, heels clicking a rapid beat against the stone floor. The door slammed behind her, plunging us into silence.

Rowan whistled low.

"She's right," I said. "Why in the world would you entrust something so sacred to me?"

The Shifter Lord poured himself another glass of wine from the carafe left on the table, refilling Rowan's glass while he was at it. "Because I have a feeling," he said.

Rowan's lips twitched.

"A feeling," I echoed. "That's it? A feeling? What kind of answer is that?"

A flat look. "My entire reign is based around my feelings, Miss Quinn."

"Evie," I snapped. "Stop calling me, Miss Quinn."

Rowan snickered.

"Shut up, you," I snapped, the words only serving to make Rowan laugh harder.

I pressed my index finger against the space between my brows, rubbing the rapidly forming headache away. "What's the deal with this ceremony? Why is it so important?"

"If I may," Rowan interjected.

Caelan shot him an exasperated glare. "By all means."

The other Lord took a sip of his wine and leaned forward, eagerness shining in his pretty eyes. "The bonding ceremony is the most important part of the wedding ceremony."

"Is it only for Lords?"

Rowan shook his head. "Not necessarily, but it is reserved for those with higher thresholds of power, beings like Lords and Ladies—"

"Wait, there are legit Ladies? Like female Lords?"

Rowan grinned. "There are. Though there are none in the U.S."

I scoffed. "Of course there aren't."

"Anyhow," he drawled after my interruption, "the old magic blesses their union. It's an ancient ceremony, one of our most sacred traditions."

"Does it always bless the couple?"

Caelan's eyes flickered, though he held his tongue.

Rowan sobered. "There have only been two times in our histories where the union has not been blessed."

"What does it mean when the couple doesn't receive a blessing?" I had to ask Hazel about this ceremony. What in the world was I getting myself into?

Caelan spoke this time. "Usually, one or both parties stops the ceremony."

My lips parted. "Even if they love each other?"

Sadness touched Rowan's handsome face, and I wondered who'd broken the tender Lord's heart. "Love doesn't make a union work. The gods' blessing is a precursor of what's to come."

I rubbed my hand over my face. "Why have I never heard of this?"

"It's not normal in regular ceremonies, even for other paranormals. If you've never attended once either, it makes sense you've never heard of it."

"Does every Lord hold this ceremony?"

Rowan's quick glance had my stomach tightening. "No. Several Lords have chosen to forgo the bonding ceremony."

"If the Lords want a marriage to happen and there is no blessing, what happens then?"

Rowan's eyes sparkled with an emotion I couldn't identify. "Then the Lord has an out, if you will."

I leaned back in my chair and studied both Lords who were projecting such an air of innocence I was immediately suspicious. Realization struck me like a truck a few seconds later. "Oh," I breathed. "You're playing a dangerous game, Lord."

Caelan's eyes glittered. "No games, Evie. The ceremony is sacred, and Gianna believes she is destined to be my bride." He tilted his glass up in a small salute. "We shall let the gods decide."

After that, there wasn't much more to say. I gathered the box up, leaving the last arrangement for Rowan when he asked if he could have it.

"I'll see you out," Caelan said.

My lips tightened. "No shenanigans."

"I make no promises."

Rowan's soft laugh made me shake my head. "Fine. But I need to get home. I have a house guest."

A question had been nagging at me for days now. I waited until we were almost at the door before I stopped, lowering my voice until it was barely a whisper. "Do you even like Gianna?"

Caelan stiffened. "Does it matter?"

I blinked. "I would think so. Hoping the gods will shun your bride on your wedding day is insane. What are you going to do if they bless your union with rainbows and butterflies?"

Caelan's stare was so intense my breath caught. "I've never been a man of unshakeable faith in beings who appear as fickle as humans sometimes."

"Better not let my mother hear you say that," I muttered.

The Lord grinned and took my elbow, gently guiding me outside. "What I do have faith in is myself. My beliefs. My rule. I've never failed in my duty, and I think Joy Springs deserves a strong Lady, someone who believes in the rule of law, fairness, and ethics."

"And Gianna doesn't?"

"Gianna is old blood, Evie. They make their own rules. I can't break my engagement without a political storm."

I took in a deep breath, inhaling the fresh scent of all the fresh flowers and greenery around Caelan's property. The man was batshit crazy. I had to appreciate madness like that. "Why'd you keep everything?"

"The new landscaping?" He chuckled. "I love plants, Evie. You should know that by now."

"But it's so wild," I whispered. "I thought it'd make you angry."

He turned and gripped me by the arms, looming above me like an ancient warrior. His eyes gleamed golden in the low light. "I like wild. I *am* wild. But more importantly, the woman who created it has a wild heart. How could I destroy something that came from the deepest parts of her?"

Gianna would destroy this the second she signed on the dotted line. "When you're married and your new wife begins making changes, remind me to give you the name of a good landscaper. He's much more sedate than me, but he uses only green methods for pest control."

Caelan's jaw ticked. "I bet my new wife won't change a thing."

I snorted. "Sure. The first thing that goes will be that mutant Jacaranda."

"The Jacaranda stays," Caelan growled.

I smiled and stepped away. "Take pictures if you don't mind. I'd like to remember it this way."

"The gods know, Evie."

I stilled. "Know what?"

"My heart." An invitation lingered on his face. If I took it, he'd take me inside and make me his, no matter the woman he was set to marry.

It was wrong. And terrible. And Gianna, as rude as she was to me, didn't deserve it.

But there was something between us, and if things were different, I'd go to him, Gianna be damned. But I wasn't just a woman, standing on a porch, begging Caelan not to cut his landscaping down. A beast prowled under my skin, wanting to consume me.

"I hope for your sake, they do." I waved and turned to go, just as the valet pulled up with my vehicle.

Caelan's eyes lingered on me until I turned the corner.

Fourteen

CAELAN SPEAKS TO THE FOREST

"Playing games with the gods is a fool's endeavor." The voice came from nowhere and everywhere all at once, from the wind and the trees and the ground at my feet.

I'd summoned the god with one simple bargain in mind and received a lecture in exchange. "Do I need to ask someone else?"

The being's laugh was aged and dry. Ancient. "You will die if you do. Consider me a curious god."

"Will you consider it?" Everything rode on my proposal.

"Why should I?"

I stood in a forest clearing, the full moon high above my head, and I knew I no longer stood on the earth. The moon at home was barely into the new phase, darkness lingering over Joy Springs for at least the next week. This place, wherever the god had brought me, dripped magic. My beast threatened to rip from my chest and run through the woods, a primal howl lingering in my throat. Lies, a Lord's currency, would get me nowhere this evening. "Because I have plans."

"The plans of a territory Lord do not concern me."

My shoulders tensed at the anger in the god's voice. "Because I am desperate."

"Better," the god mused, "but still not a complete answer."

I gritted my teeth. "Because I have met someone I…need."

"Need or want?"

"Both," I growled.

"And why do you need her?"

I couldn't answer him because how could I lay bare what was in my heart when even I didn't understand it?

When I didn't answer, the god tried another way. "Tell me about this woman."

"She is not a shifter."

"You'd sully your bloodline?" the god said, scorn dripping from its voice.

My nostrils flared, fists clenching at my sides.

A deep laugh as dry as summer leaves floated around me. "No need for anger. I ask due to your Council's stance on mixing non-shifter bloodlines."

I turned and tried to catch a glimpse of the god, to no avail. He was large but faster than me. A sense of unease crawled across my skin. "How would you know such things?"

"The gods know all," came the cryptic response.

"Then you should already know the answers to your questions."

"What is it you love about her?"

"I—" A Lord rarely thought about love. Was love what I felt for her? It didn't seem like it. My feelings were possessive. Primal.

Evie Quinn was mine. I wouldn't take her, not by force, but I would do everything in my power to lay open the path.

"And if she does not go to you of her own volition?" the voice said.

"She will."

Another dry laugh, this one deeply amused. "I fear you have much to learn, Lord."

"Will you consider it?"

A long pause before a fading voice spoke its last words. "So little amuses me these days. I will consider it."

It was all I wanted. Dipping my head in respect, the world turned upside down.

Seconds later, I stood in my office once more, the fading smell of loamy, ancient forest in my lungs.

CHAPTER
Fifteen

Hazel and I had a cup of tea once I'd returned from Caelan's, the witch raising her eyebrows when she spotted my dress but not commenting. Progress for Hazel, that's for sure.

When she retired with the promise we'd begin testing my magic the next day, I poured myself another cup of Earl Grey and curled up in the rocker on the porch, watching the night pass me by.

My thoughts were hectic and disturbed after the last meeting. It was obvious Caelan wanted me. Shifters were hungry, possessive creatures, and I was too smart to think he loved me. Wanting someone and loving them were two wildly different things.

As to how I felt about Caelan? Mixed. Some days I couldn't stand him, even as I craved his nearness. "Idiot," I mumbled to myself. If I were a smart woman, I'd pack my shit and set up shop somewhere else far from here. Ash, Moira, and Tess would come along if I asked.

Fresh starts were underrated.

Sighing, I sipped my tea and closed my eyes as a cool wind blew through the trees. Night-prowling creatures slithered and preyed on the property, tiny blips to my senses. Greenery and trees stretched toward the night sky, seeking the moon. Night-blooming flowers opened, their heady scents tantalizing and mysterious.

I smiled, pushing the rocking chair using the motion of the ball of my foot. As nights went, I'd call it somewhat of a success. Gianna wanted red, white, and blue, and she'd have it, even if it made my inner decorator shrivel up and die.

The wind died down, and with it the noise. My eyes opened abruptly, sensing the unnatural shift in the air. Every plant in the area turned away from the fence, seeking the safety of my wild magic.

Someone or something was out there.

A snapped branch caught my attention. I stood from the chair and went down the stairs, pressing my bare feet into the earth, just in case I needed to call on my power. A familiar scent made me freeze just as a man stepped right outside the property line.

A stranger rested against one of the fence posts, arms crossed over his chest. He smiled at me, a friendly smile if I didn't know better. The porch lights caught the crimson glow of his eyes.

"Finn."

"Hello, Evie. Nice night, isn't it?" His glamour flickered and fell away, revealing the too-handsome Chimera who'd come close to ruining my life.

"It was," I agreed.

Finn's smile widened. "You haven't made use of the gift I gave you. Why ever not?"

"You mean the curse? Why would I use anything you gave me?"

His eyes narrowed as he pushed away from the fence, stopping right at my new wards. Finn lifted a finger and touched the shimmering magic. My wards dropped like water from a bucket, gone as if they'd never existed.

Fuck. It had taken me a full week to create those! Note to self, make the damn things Chimera proof. How? No idea. I might have to zap myself a few times before I figured out how to keep him out.

"Nice try. Few things can keep me from a place I want to be," he said.

Finn possessed a devastating beauty, one that had gotten me into my current predicament. Night dark hair, wicked blue eyes, and lips made for sin, the man was beautiful, and he knew it. I'd met him on a trip after my divorce from the man I refused to think about, danced the night away, and met him in a field of thistle on a cold Scottish night.

I thought I might have been falling in love, but as soon as Finn and I were alone and he'd scented me, my life was over. He'd left me for dead in that field, broken and violated, and the only reason I was alive now was due to the kindness of a witch who'd taken me to her home and showed me my life still had worth.

"Stay back," I warned.

"Or what?" he asked as he drew ever closer. "Why do you push me away when I'm the only one who can help you become what you're meant to be? We are the last Chimeras alive, Evie. Together we can repopulate the world."

"Um." I stared at him in horror. "That's going to be a hard pass. Children are not in my future." Especially not with him.

"The Chimera gift is difficult to survive, it's true. You are not the first I've marked, but you're the only one who's survived." He stood about a foot away, his hands loose at his side, but I didn't trust his casual posture. I knew how fast the man could move.

Finn tilted his head and studied me. "I didn't mean to mark you." He closed his eyes and inhaled. "But your scent."

I took a step backward.

"What can I say? It drove me wild and kicked old instincts I thought I no longer possessed into overdrive."

The old fear and despair and disgust I felt when I thought about what happened to me on that field rose like a wave. My throat tightened and hot tears pricked the backs of my eyes. "Leave, Finn," I said hoarsely.

He ignored my command. Magic welled inside me, the property alert and waiting for my command.

Finn put his hands in his pockets, affecting a casual air, but I knew he was the most dangerous thing on my property tonight. "Acting as a florist for a Lord is beneath you. Why do you insist on menial jobs when you can be a queen?"

"Your queen."

"Who else's?" He clicked his tongue. "I've already touched the Lord's wedding in ways not even he will expect. Continue with your work. It won't matter soon, anyway. Those flowers you plot so meticulously won't be for a wedding when I'm finished." His smile hinted of madness.

I took another step backward and turned to run, aching for the safety of my house, but Finn darted out, his hand wrapping around my arm like a vise.

I lashed out with my magic, and the property rose to defend me. The earth rumbled beneath our feet, bucking us both off balance. A sharp pain ripped down my arm, and I tore away from his grip, throwing out a palm crackling with magic.

It collided with Finn. His bark of pain settled my resolve, but when I tried again, a tearing, horrific pain in my chest sent me to my knees.

Finn's bloody grin loomed above. Wild vines blooming with purple and crimson flowers rose from the ground, tangling around me. My bones cracked and shifted, the tips of my fingers turning to lethal claws. Every vein in my skin glowed golden, a low keening from my throat the only sound I could make. My hair lifted from my shoulders, floating around my head and neck, as power crackled through the air.

"Finn," I moaned, my voice a low, distorted moan of pain. Never-ending pain.

"Let it be, Evie," Finn urged. "Your transformation is almost complete."

I forced my innate power into my veins, but it couldn't compete with the Chimera's magic. The shift forced itself upon me, skin and bones morphing and shifting, flickering in and out of different forms, human, non-human, Magic poured into the ground, the sky, my body, burning me alive.

Finn's dark laughter echoed above until he popped out of existence, leaving me to die alone.

Again.

My eyes fluttered shut, the pain too much to bear. Darkness claimed me a moment later.

"Evangeline."

The voice was a wild forest in the tangles of my mind, a rumbling thunderstorm bringing me out of my pain.

My eyes opened.

Cernunnos, the fae king, crouched beside me, a glowing hand resting on my shoulder.

"Am I dead?" I croaked.

The god's mouth tightened. "Dying," he confirmed.

"Shit," I breathed.

"An understatement." Healing magic flowed through my body. "I cannot interfere more than to give you more time."

"I can't handle the magic," I whispered. "It's too much."

"You must. Or you die." Cernunnos wore simple brown pants and his chest was bare. His moss-covered antlers glowed with bioluminescent fungi, and his eyes glowed with ancient magic.

"Where's Hazel?"

"Inside. Trapped by my magic for now. She cannot help with this. You must accept the Chimera, Evangeline. You've gone far too long with dual magics. Your body is failing."

I hissed as I moved my arm, realizing with horror that Finn had damaged my thistle tattoo. Slapping a hand over it, I tried to sit up, unable to do so without assistance.

Cernunnos braced one muscular arm behind me, gently raising me until I could sit up on my own. Mostly.

"That is the least of your worries."

"Not true," I muttered. "If anyone scents what I am, I'll sign my death warrant."

"Won't matter if you die on the ground," Cernunnos said simply. "Choose. Death or rebirth."

My lower lip wobbled. "I don't want this."

"Few good people want power thrust upon them. Becoming Chimera is not a death sentence. It is…new. That is all."

Our eyes met. "I won't be like Finn."

His mixed color eyes swirled with power. "Finn was like this before he was changed. Power has only corrupted him over time. You are not like him and never will be." He lifted his hand, leaving behind a glowing, golden palm mark behind. "Dark days are coming, and you must be prepared to meet them at full strength."

"I don't want to give up my Floromancy," I whispered.

Cernunnos studied me for a moment before he tilted my chin up with his index finger. I shivered at the power crackling against my skin. "That was never a worry. Your Floromancy comes from the very heart of the world, a blessing from the oldest goddess herself."

A tear slipped down my face. "You promise."

Cernunnos smiled, the gesture one of terrible sadness. "Gods are not in the business of promises, daughter of the earth, but in this…" He laid a hand over his heart. "In this, I promise your Floromancy will remain. Perhaps changed, but forever there. The earth will still answer your call. This is not a death sentence unless you make it one. Change, Evie. Embrace who you are meant to be."

Fear, my ever-present companion, made my fingers tremble. "Stay with me?" I whispered.

"Always," Cernunnos promised.

The competing magics burned inside my body, snapping against each other, tearing my insides apart. I reached for the god's hand, not caring about showing weakness, and let my magic go.

I let go of everything. I let go of what it meant to be Evie Quinn, Floromancer and local florist, of what it meant to be confused and angry and hurt. I let go of past transgressions and mistakes and let the magic do with it what it would.

"Remake me," I whispered to the winds.

And the magic responded.

I sank into unconsciousness once again, the pain too much to bear, and awoke only at the barked sound of my name when Ben's familiar scent washed over me.

If I could shift, I would turn into a wren and fly away to avoid him seeing me like this, but I was as weak as a newborn kitten. Warm hands and blue healing light settled on my body.

The front door slammed open, Hazel's accented voice speaking rapidly.

"We need to get her inside," Ben murmured. "She's lost a lot of blood."

A scream tore from my throat as Ben lifted me.

"Shh, baby. I got you. I'm so sorry." His deep voice rumbled over me, concern thick in his tone.

Ben cradled me gently against his chest as he carried me. Every cell in my body screamed in agony. All I could do was whimper and wish for death.

When he laid me down, I gagged in pain.

Ben hissed. "I'm almost done. Hazel is getting something for the pain."

I opened my eyes to see Ben on his knees next to me, palms glowing with blue light. Hazel's herbal scent washed over me.

"A little stick and burn, Evie."

The needle went into my arm, blissful relief flowing through my body almost immediately. I moaned. "Hazel."

"Hush, child. Rest now. Let this healer work on you. We'll talk later."

My skin knitted under Ben's careful ministrations, the shifter's eyes glowing bright blue. I could barely keep my eyes open, but Ben and Hazel's murmured conversation kept me conscious. Barely.

"She was smoking," Ben murmured. "Covered in thorns and

blooms and magic I've never seen or sensed before, crimson magic all over her and soaking the ground."

Hazel sucked in a breath.

"What is she?" he asked.

"Some questions are never meant to be answered. If you're smart, you'll let this one lie."

A low growl sounded.

"Don't you growl at me," Hazel snapped. "I know how to neuter a dog just as well as a man."

A surprised snort from Ben.

And blissful unconsciousness.

CHAPTER

Sixteen

Hazel wasn't amused that I got up early and headed to work. After a blistering lecture, I hurried out the door and headed to the shop, leaving Hazel glaring at me from the porch.

Less than half an hour after I got to the shop, Hazel stomped in, cursing a blue streak.

"Do they know what happened to you last night?" she groused, giving the others the hairy eyeball.

"Yes, and they don't want me here, either," I said mildly. "I'm fine, Hazel."

A bald-faced lie, but I was fine enough to come into work today, so true enough.

Moira snorted.

I shot her a dark look. "I'm here. I'm standing, and I'm functional."

Hazel muttered something under her breath. "I'll be in the back looking at that damned bouquet. Call me if things go awry."

"That could mean a lot of things," Ash said.

Tess let out a soft moan and floated closer to me. "We'll keep an eye on her."

"See that you do, banshee," Hazel lectured, lifting her bag over shoulder and bustling past us.

When the doors closed behind her, everyone let out a collective sigh of relief.

"She's intense," Moira whispered.

"That's Hazel," I muttered.

Ash pushed a fresh mug of coffee my way. "Are you alright?"

I was exhausted, bruised internally and externally, and my magic felt fried. "I will be," I promised. Cernunnos' warning kept replaying in my head, the real threat of dying hanging over me like a scythe made all my muscles tense.

I felt different, every cell in my body snapping and alive. And I felt the desire to change.

I could be anything I wanted.

The thought scared the hell out of me.

EVERYONE HAD GONE off to run errands for the shop earlier, leaving me alone for a while. I enjoyed the silence, using the quiet time to think about my new body. Because that's what it was. Every piece of me felt different, alive in a way it never had before.

But in the mirror looking out was the same old Evie. All the new pieces of me lay deep inside.

The bell over the door jingled not long after, revealing Ben holding a large box of our favorite pastries. At the same time, banging, yelling, and eventually black smoke billowed from under the doors to the back. Hazel cursed up a blue streak before slamming open the doors. Her hair stood up on end and soot streaked half her face.

"That bouquet is a menace!" she barked.

Ben slid the box onto the counter. "Need any assistance?"

Hazel waved him away. "Bah. No. I'm going to crack that thing open like a coconut soon enough."

I came around the back of the desk and hugged Ben, but there was a hesitancy in his touch this time.

A small piece of my heart broke at that moment. I stepped away and smiled, but Ben had trouble meeting my eyes.

I'd been waiting for this day since that evening in the field, knowing someone would find out too much about me and turn away, unable to meet my eyes.

"Can I take your vitals?" Ben asked.

"I'm fine, Ben. Fit as a fiddle."

He met my eyes then, wariness that had never been there before all over his face. "I doubt that very much." Ben gestured to the couch. "Please. It will take only a moment."

Hazel motioned me away. "Go let the healer do his thing." She flipped open the pastry box, her eyes lighting up at the array of goodies. "I'll be right here, drowning my annoyance in chocolate donuts."

I settled myself on the couch. Ben sat on the coffee table facing me and held his hands out. "Take my hands."

I slid my palms over his. Gentle, calloused fingers closed over my hands. Ben's power brushed over my skin, his eyes turning an unholy blue. I felt his magic sweep through my body, gently touching every cell.

It was over in less than a minute. Ben extricated himself and rose.

"How's our patient?" Hazel asked, her mouth full of donut.

"Healthy as a horse," Ben said, lips turning up in a smile that didn't reach his eyes.

"Ben?" I said quietly.

"Step outside with me, Evie," he murmured.

My heart thudding, Ben said goodbye to Hazel, taking my elbow to lead me outside. It was still morning time in Joy Springs and there was a bite of cold in the air. A few shop owners had already arrived, waving as they unloaded their goods for the day.

"What's the verdict, doc?"

Ben sighed. "Evie, your entire body is different. Something is raging through your metabolism. If you haven't already felt it, your appetite will increase exponentially."

I'd already noticed the second Ben brought those donuts in. The urge to snatch the box out of his hands nearly overwhelmed me. I already had to restrain myself from gnawing on raw steak every time I went grocery shopping.

"Whether the change is permanent is unknown." He scrubbed a hand over his jaw. "Evie." Ben hesitated.

"Spit it out."

"You seem like a shifter. Sort of."

"But you've never examined a Floromancer before." I had to cut this off at the pass.

Ben's brow furrowed. "No, but—"

"Then there's no way to know what I was like before then, right?"

"Evie." Ben's voice was a growl. "You're hiding something."

"Someone came onto the property looking to rob me. That's all. He was some sort of magic practitioner." The lie came too easily, rolling off my tongue like water. "I'm fine, Ben. Really."

"A thief does not violate you like that, Evie!" Ben's nostrils flared. He held up a hand and stepped away. "You know what? Fine. Lie to me if that's what you want. But don't expect me to keep coming around hoping for a kernel of anything from you."

I reached out. "Ben. I'm sorry. I—I can't."

"You won't. Big difference."

We stared at each other for a long moment before Ben nodded and turned away.

My heart cracked as I watched him walk away. He didn't deserve this, my lies and deceit. Ben could never know me, not like he'd let me know him.

I did not go after him.

Ben deserved better than me.

When he disappeared from sight, I turned and pressed my hand against the door jamb, taking a moment before I went inside.

My hand flickered, briefly shifting from a claw-tipped paw to a scaled one. I gasped and clutched my hand to my shirt, hurrying inside before anyone noticed. When I was safely inside, I pressed my hand on the desk and stared, but it remained smooth and tanned, the hand I saw every single day.

Unnerved, I tried to will the shift again, but nothing happened. I hadn't tested my Floromancy yet. Even with Cernunnos' promise, I was terrified to find out if my innate magic had changed. If it had, I wasn't sure I'd be able to go on. Plants had been my life from the moment I could touch the earth. If the Chimera had ripped that away from me, I might lie down and die, letting myself be with the earth one final time.

So I couldn't try today. I was too emotionally fraught and still felt like crap.

Tomorrow I'd see how much my life had changed once more.

The bell rang again. Moira breezed in with a steaming to-go cup of tea. "That shop down the road ran out of that spiced blood! I wanted chai, and I had to get Earl Grey."

"Tragic," Hazel drawled.

Moira blinked. "I keep forgetting you're here." She waved a hand at the witch. "Don't you have some bats to play with or something?"

Hazel shoved another bite of donut in her mouth before she raised her middle finger.

Moira cracked a laugh and came behind the desk, gently nudging me with her hip.

Tess came in next, holding a massive bouquet of roses.

I gasped. "Do not tell me those are grocery store roses!"

Tess rolled her eyes. "I would never. These are for later. I'm planning a visit to the graveyard to see if I can lure out that other banshee I keep seeing. She might need a friend."

"You bring roses to the graveyard?" Hazel asked.

"Why wouldn't I?" Tess asked. "Banshees and ghosts deserve flowers, too."

Hazel opened her mouth, then closed it just as fast. "I suppose they do," she said in a musing tone.

I turned to hide my smile. Seeing Hazel speechless was a rarity.

Ash came in next, holding a massive box that clinked when he walked. Tess put her bouquet down and rushed over to hold the door open.

"Thanks." Ash brushed a kiss against her cheek making Tess blush furiously.

Moira and I exchanged low fives under the register desk.

He plopped the box on my work table. "I bought these from an estate sale at that haunted house down the road."

I peeked inside the box and gasped in delight. "That's real crystal!"

"Yup. I got the entire box for fifty bucks. Thought we could use some of them for the seasonal arrangements."

"Our customers will love them." I held a smaller one up to the light, marveling at the brilliant colors refracting as I turned it back and forth. "Reimburse yourself from the petty cash, okay?"

"Not worried about it." He plucked a smaller, single stem vase from the box. "I've been eyeing a few for myself."

"Take whatever you want," I said as I dug through the rest.

Tess spotted the donut box and floated over to take one. "Anyone else?"

My stomach let out an embarrassing growl.

"Evie first!" Moira announced, taking the box Tess passed, and opening it, displaying an array of goodies.

My stomach growled again. I was starving. Reaching in, I took a Bavarian cream filled and a cinnamon twist. Once I had my selections, the rest of my team fell on the box like a pack of ravenous wolves.

The first bite was so delicious, I had to stifle my moan. When I used magic more than normal, my appetite spiked, and I ate like a football player bulking up for the big game. On average, most magic users, no matter their flavor, ate more than a human.

Ben's words came back to me, sending a shiver down my spine. The Chimera had already changed my DNA, so it wasn't news, but to have it confirmed while knowing Finn did even more damage last night was enough to give me pause.

My hand shapeshifting of its own volition only added to my suspicions that I might have a rocky time ahead of me.

Just in time for Caelan's wedding.

I popped the last of the treats in my mouth and chewed, realizing everyone had stopped and was staring at me.

"What?" I said with my mouth full.

Tess slowly slid the box of remaining donuts back over. "There are three more."

Moira's eyes narrowed. "Evie. You alright?"

I nodded. "I skipped dinner."

True. Because I was comatose and near death.

Ash exhaled and leaned closer. "May I?"

I sighed and reached for another donut. "Go ahead."

Ash touched two fingers to my wrist and closed his eyes as he sent his magic through my body. His magic was different from Ben's but still gentle. Ash's felt like running through a forest on a crisp autumn day.

When he pulled away, he tried to give me a reassuring smile, but we'd all known him too long.

"Is she alright?" Moira asked, her voice sharp.

"She's not sick," Ash reassured her. "But the incident last night changed Evie's genetic makeup." His eyes narrowed. "Are you having issues controlling the shift?"

My pause was answer enough.

Moira swore. "Evie. Do you need to take some time off?"

"Nope," I said through a mouthful of donut. "Caelan's wedding is coming up. There's too much to do."

"We can handle it," Ash said.

"And so can I. This is a blip on the radar. I should be okay."

"Time will tell," Hazel said ominously.

"I will be," I insisted.

"We'll see what we're dealing with when we get back to your place this evening," she retorted.

As if I were something to deal with.

"And the tattoo?" I asked. Ben had fixed the cut across the thistle tattoo, but the magic had petered out, broadcasting my heritage to anyone with a sharp enough nose. Chimeras weren't common, but if anyone had ever had dealings with one, they would recognize me soon enough.

Even with my fae heritage mixed in.

"I slapped a magical patch on it," Hazel said. "It will hold until I can make a new one."

"Should we remove the old one?"

"Not until we're ready to put the new one on. Until then, I suggest you cancel any meetings with your Lord or anyone who might figure out what's happened."

"No meetings on the books," I promised. "Any update on the bouquet?"

Hazel gnashed her teeth like a fairytale goblin. "Nothing yet. I might take it back to the house tonight. Toting it around is dicey but leaving it here feels like a bad idea."

"I felt the same." Checking the clock, I clapped my hands. "Alright, team. People are starting to roam outside. Ready for the day?"

Nods all around. "I'll finish up Hattie's arrangement and get that delivered. Hazel will keep working on the bouquet. Ash, you good with ordering inventory today?"

"Got my list on my phone."

"Awesome. Let's get to it." I saluted them with my coffee mug and headed to my work table. As soon as I laid my palm against the table, the table pulsed. There was a usual hum every time I used it because a fae built it for me.

But it had never pulsed like this. Curious and a little concerned, I placed both palms against the table's top. Ash was walking past and stopped, watching me.

"Everything okay?"

"It's pulsing."

Ash frowned and came around beside me. "Take your hands off for a moment."

I obeyed, and Ash placed his palm on the top, in the same place mine had just been. His skin turned to bark and his eyes glowed.

A few moments later, he removed his hand, the roots slipping back into fingers. "Nothing to worry about. My uncle formulated the table for you, and it's confused." He snorted. "It recognizes you, but your blood has changed. Put your palms back on the table and wait. You'll know when it's ready."

"It won't bite, will it?"

Ash grinned. "There's no telling what failsafe my uncle put in that thing, so I can't promise anything."

"Great." With more trepidation after Ash's not so comforting words, I slowly put my palms back on the table and waited.

It took a while, and I felt a little violated when it was over, but eventually the table pulsed once more, flashing a bright green before it settled into its usual hum of comforting magic. I lifted my palms, waited a few seconds, and put them back down again.

The hum was still there.

Nice. One thing went right today.

Let's hope I was on a streak.

Hazel's shout of frustration made me laugh. As long as the bouquet wasn't actively trying to kill Hazel, she'd be fine.

Moira breezed back through the doors after popping out for another tea, this time at another shop. "I have hot goss," she sang. "About our resident Shifter Lord and one hot mess of a flytrap!"

I'd just put the finishing touches on Hattie's bouquet and gently moved it to the side.

Ash sailed to the front like he had wings. Hot goss was Ash's bread and butter. "Do tell!"

"Should we get Hazel?" Tess asked.

My eyes widened in horror. "No! She does not need to know what I sent to Caelan," I hissed.

"She'd get mad about a bloodthirsty, semi-sentient plant?" Moira said sweetly, batting her eyes at me.

"Spill before I animate another one of my plants and make it bite you every time you walk past."

Moira grinned. "Seymour ate the drapes in Caelan's office."

I choked. "What?"

Ash let out a low laugh. "All of them?"

"All of them," Moira said with wicked delight. "The entire Keep is talking about it."

A laugh bubbled from my lips. "How the hell?"

"Don't ask us," Ash said. "You're the one that created that freak of nature."

Moira held up her index finger. "I am not done."

I groaned. "No. The drapes are bad enough."

Tess bobbed up and down. She was spending less and less time on solid ground and preferred floating these days. All fine and dandy if we were the only ones in the shop, but a floating assistant would be hard to explain to any humans who walked in. "I think Seymour is psychic."

Three pairs of eyes snapped to Tess.

"I've heard of a plant psychic but never a psychic plant," Ash said, staring at her with wonder. No matter what weird shit Tess said, Ash never judged her.

"Why would you say that?" I asked. Seymour was partially sentient, but most of my plants were. Having a higher level of intelligence and autonomy was part of the deal with a Floromancer around.

"He sends me dreams sometimes." Tess floated over to the coffee station to make a new pot.

"Dreams," Moira echoed, sending me a bewildered look.

"Mm-hmm. He thinks Caelan needs to eat more vegetables."

I burst out laughing.

"We could all use a few more veggies," Ash said dryly.

"He's also concerned about Caelan's stress levels."

I stilled. "Oh? Any specifics?"

"Not really. Caelan keeps muttering about flowers and bondage."

My lips twitched. "Bonding maybe?"

Tess's brow furrowed. "That's it. Thought the bondage thing was weird, but I don't judge."

Ash's amused look turned to one of contemplation. I needed to shut this conversation down before things got weird.

Moira grinned. "I also heard Caelan tried to put Seymour back into your greenhouse, but the thing was back in his office the next day."

I slapped my hands over my mouth, horror rising inside me. What had I created? "Maybe I should go retrieve him next time I'm there."

Moira looked horrified. "Absolutely not! I am living for this ridiculousness."

The others wholeheartedly agreed. "Fine." I held my hands up. "I surrender. Seymour will stay at the Keep and continue being a chaos goblin."

Everyone cheered.

"Evie!" Hazel called from the back of the shop. The witch had taken the bouquet home last night with little to show for it. She'd gotten so busy with it, I'd been able to sneak out the back and walk my property for the rest of the evening.

This morning, she barely said a word and headed straight into the back with the thing.

"On my way!" Sounded like she found something. I opened the door and peeked in, making sure it was safe to enter.

Hazel stood a few feet away from the table, her eyes glowing with power. A wide smile creased her face. "Got it!"

She wiggled her fingers. "Told you I'd get you." Hazel's cackle made me grin.

The bouquet looked even worse today. Several of the flowers had turned black, and the bottom oozed a dark liquid. Gross.

"Come closer," Hazel urged. "I need to show you something."

Hesitantly, I edged around the table, coming up beside Hazel. She waved her hand, and the lights dimmed. A strange blend of magic floated above the bouquet.

"One layer is some form of shifter magic. The other is disguised as a blessing, meant to trigger when your magic reacts to it under stress." She tsked. "It's a good thing you haven't touched this in a few days."

I grimaced. The last few days had turned me into a complete stress ball. I hadn't used my Floromancy since Finn showed up. My muscles and magic still hurt, but I was much better today than yesterday. By tonight, I should be back to normal. Or whatever passed for normal these days.

"This was never about the bride. Whoever made this planned for it to be in your space. They knew you'd handle it and made the spell for you." Hazel blew out a breath. "Whoever planned this was smart. Several things had to fall into place for this to wind up in your hands."

Moira popped her head in, blinking several times as she stared at the bouquet. "Creepy."

Hazel waved her in. "It's safe."

"Ish," I said.

Moira came in, giving us a wide berth. "What's going on with that thing?"

"Magical trap," Hazel said. "Or a black magic spell. I can't tell which yet."

"Meant for Evie?"

"Looks that way," Hazel said.

"Bully for me," I muttered.

"We need to find out if the spells were planted before or after the wedding planner handled the flowers," Moira said. "Caroline doesn't seem like a criminal mastermind."

"Doesn't mean she doesn't have a deeper involvement than she's admitting to," I said.

"Maybe we should take another look at her," Hazel ventured.

My instincts nagged at me. "Maybe. But I think someone powerful orchestrated this. Not Caroline."

Hazel shook her head. "You really managed to step into it this time, child."

"I had nothing to do with this!" Shaking my head at her, I

shooed them both away. "Go get lunch or something. I'll close up the wards."

Hazel winked. "Troublemaker."

Moira laughed and held the door open for the witch.

If those two were getting along, things really were topsy-turvy.

Once they were gone, I stepped closer to the bouquet and peered down at the rapidly decomposing blooms. Sighing, I started to build the wards and was just about to close them up, when a bloom unfurled from the plant and snapped out at me.

I gasped and took a step back, magic ripping from my body in reaction.

Thorns burst from the stems, the other blooms unfurling and blackening over and over again. Gritting my teeth, I reached for my Floromancy, attempting to shut the surrounding wards, but the bouquet fought back, pushing against my magic.

It was no longer content with being contained.

I poured more magic out until the wards finally snapped closed with a loud pop.

I sagged against the stainless fridge, my breath coming in gasping heaves.

"What the hell are you?" I whispered.

The bouquet quivered in response.

Fiery pain bloomed over my damaged tattoo. A sharp cry escaped, and I slapped my hand over my mouth before I alerted the others, hissing through my teeth as the pain came to a crescendo and slowly faded, leaving behind a soft golden glow.

One more weird thing to contend with.

Awesome.

The rest of the day was mostly normal. Tourists filtered in and out of the shop, and we sold almost all the seasonal arrangements Ash and I had worked on for so long. By the end of it, I was dragging.

Hazel snatched up my keys. "You look dead on your feet. I'll drive us home."

"Careful, Hazel," Moira said, a wicked glint in her eyes. "Evie's car is far different from your broom."

Ash snorted.

Hazel's eyebrows went up. "Watch it, girl. I'll spike your blood with cyanide."

"Mm," Moira said. "Poison."

The witch rolled her eyes. "Come on, Evie. Let's get away from your terrible friends. I still need to take a look at your magic."

"We need to wrap up the bouquet first." I didn't volunteer. "Maybe Moira was right. Should we burn that thing to a crisp and tell the customer we lost it?"

"I'm game," Moira said.

"No." Hazel held up a finger. "This is a puzzle piece. We need to find out where it fits." She headed toward the back. "Give me five to wrestle with the damn thing, and we'll get out of here."

Lots of banging and cursing later, Hazel walked out with the magic dampening pouch, and we were on our way home.

Hazel handed me a glass of wine and pointed to the couch. "Sit."

"Ugh. Do I have to? How many people are going to put their fingers inside me today?"

A beat of silence before horror spiraled through me. "I could have said that better."

"Yep," Hazel agreed, mirth sparkling in her eyes. "But my fingers won't be any place fun."

"Thank the gods for that," I mumbled.

Hazel snickered. "Drink your wine and relax. This won't hurt."

Sighing, I settled back against the couch cushions and closed my eyes. Hazel's touch and magic were familiar. We'd spent months together in Scotland, Hazel acting as caregiver while I tried to survive the curse raging through my body.

Her magic was hard to explain. Ash's felt like ancient forests. Ben's was cool and gentle. Hazel's felt like walking into a circle filled with powerful women, thunderous and fierce, but completely painless.

Yet not relaxing, either.

When she finished, Hazel's touch lifted. I opened my eyes to see my former mentor's eyes glowing with concern. "Evie."

"If it's bad news, can I have another glass of wine first?"

Without responding, Hazel pulled the bottle over and topped me off. "Your body is acclimating to the Chimera magic. The first time we suppressed it." She shook her head. "It's far too late for that. Now we have to sit back and wait to see what happens."

"I love surprises," I said dryly.

Hazel patted my hand. "One more thing."

I eyed my wineglass and sighed.

"The suppression spell I put on the tattoo is fading. I'll spend tomorrow back here rebuilding the spell for another tattoo. Still want a thistle?"

"Might as well stay with the classics."

A knock on the door came and Moira poked her head in a moment later. "Thought I'd stop by and check on Evie." She came in holding a large bag of popcorn.

"Are you serious right now?" I asked.

She shook the bag at me. "You're always entertaining, but I like my movies with snacks."

"Ass."

She blew a kiss my way.

"On that note, I think you should practice shifting." Hazel rose and took the wine with her. She grabbed two more glasses and jerked her head toward the back door. "I noticed a wide-open space at the back of the greenhouse. Let's go out there."

We followed Hazel outside, and I was glad I'd brought a shawl. A chill had settled in the air this evening, and a strange wind blew through the trees, a moaning whine as it whistled through Joy Springs.

A precursor of things to come, I was sure.

And we hadn't even gotten to the warning from my mother about Neit.

There was a small pond at the back of the greenhouse, tucked behind a small alcove of trees. "Here," Hazel said. "Stand right there." She pointed to one of the few open spots by the pond.

Obeying, I turned and spread my arms out. "Command me, oh wise one."

Hazel reached over and tweaked my nose. "Don't sass your elders."

Moira perched atop a rock and munched on popcorn, giving me a little wave when she caught my eye. Then the jerk pulled out her cell and snapped a picture of me standing there looking like an idiot.

"You wait," I groused. "Revenge is a dish best served icy."

She flashed me a grin.

"Put your arms down at your sides. You aren't Jesus."

"If only," I muttered. "They'd never subject him to this nonsense."

Hazel shook her head. "No, my child. Only the horrible death via stoning."

Moira laughed.

"Now stop talking out of your ass, close your eyes, and think about what you would like to become."

I did and immediately cracked an eye open. "Anything?"

"Anything living," Hazel amended.

"Even a plant or a tree?"

Moira sucked in a breath. "You'd be the perfect spy. Imagine the possibilities. You could even break into the Keep and spy on Caelan!"

"Why ever would I want to do that? I like my head on my shoulders."

She lifted a slender shoulder in a shrug. "I dunno. Maybe to peek in on him in the shower?"

"Perv," I said affectionately, closing my eyes again. "I'll try a bird first."

"Not a wren. That's cheating," Hazel said.

"Nope. Something cool." I inhaled and thought of a bald eagle. Nothing happened.

"Focus," Hazel urged. "Clear your thoughts of everything except the animal or plant you want to be."

It took a while, but the first tingles of a shift pricked over my scalp. Not knowing what it would feel like, I waited, but when those tingles stopped, I opened my eyes to see Hazel staring at me in horror.

Moira choked on a piece of her popcorn and was bent over trying to exhale it from her lung.

"What?"

Hazel blinked. "Err. Whatever you were trying to do didn't work. All the way, at least."

I reached toward the top of my head only to feel silky, bony feathers. My face was still me.

A quick look down revealed the rest of me was still there, too. "Shoot."

Moira's laughter had died down to soft snickers.

"Try again," Hazel encouraged.

I tried to become an oak tree next, only for the wind to pick up and a great groaning sound to rocket through the forest. I opened my eyes to see all the trees bending toward me.

"Shit."

"Let go of the magic," Hazel urged.

As soon as I did, the trees straightened.

"That's a new one," Hazel murmured to herself. She stood before me and held me by the arms. "I'm going to guide you through a relaxation exercise. Think of nothing but my voice and the actions I tell you to take. Ready?

I nodded.

Hazel's accented voice guided me through a series of deep breathing until her words tuned out and all I could hear was the sound of my inhale and exhale.

"Try again," she urged.

This time, the tingles from last time were all over my body, and I felt my arms and legs lengthen. My back morphed until I was hunched over, and I knew something was happening.

When I opened my eyes, Hazel and Moira wore equally horrified expressions. I tried to speak, but my words came out garbled due to the mouthful of fangs. A quick look down revealed scaled skin, feathered wings, and a long tail, but when I tried to take a step, I promptly keeled over, right into the pond.

As soon as I touched the water, my form melted away, and I was myself again.

Soaking wet this time.

Hazel hauled me out of the water. "Not quite what I expected, but a good effort."

I spat out a mouthful of water. "Was it?"

The witch laughed. "Yes. You become something other than yourself. That's definite progress." She positioned me where she wanted me to be. "A few more times and we'll go inside."

"But it's cold," I whined.

A wave of her hand and a cheerful fire started, warming my backside but keeping my front chilled.

"Again," she demanded.

Sighing, I did as she asked.

CHAPTER
Eighteen
CAELAN

Most nights, I retired to my office as a way to soak up some quiet and contemplate the day. I found it relaxing, and the time alone often led to new ideas or revelations I hadn't considered during the day.

With Gianna in the Keep and the countdown to the wedding, this once-contemplative time became a time where I had to just sit down and take a breath because I was going out of my skin with stress and worry.

I tossed a piece of raw steak to Seymour, who promptly spit it out. The action made me chuckle because the thing was ravenous, so who or what had he eaten to make him not hungry now?

The flytrap hopped over—something I knew he could do, but he had never shown me before—using his pot to land flat on the table. Then he reached over to nip at my sleeve.

He bit every single person who came into my office, except for me. Even gentle Ben, whom he'd once liked. I didn't have the heart to ask Ben if something had happened, because I had to restrain myself from trying to rip his face off for even daring to pursue Evie.

Two kitchen staff had quit after Seymour's bite sent them into temporary paralysis, and Gianna had requested multiple times that I "dispose" of Seymour as if he were trash instead of a sentient being.

Seymour's teeth didn't break my skin, but I'd have to replace my shirt by the time he was finished. I'd never get rid of him, even if he were a bloodthirsty weirdo. He and the turtle vine were the only things I had of her, and Gianna didn't know where the other one had come from. I wouldn't tell her either, not trusting she wouldn't destroy it just because she knew Evie had given it to me.

Gianna wouldn't go near Seymour. The flytrap despised her and lunged at her every time she came inside.

Speaking of her, the door opened, a soft, mysterious perfume announcing her presence before she entered.

Seymour made a rumbling noise.

Gianna huffed. "You still haven't gotten rid of that thing," she sniffed.

"I already told you, Seymour stays."

My eyes roamed over Gianna as she closed the door behind her and sat down in one of the chairs facing the desk. Seymour started hopping toward her, but I grabbed his pot.

"Behave."

Seymour rumbled at me but made no move toward her again.

Gianna's gaze landed on the three additional samples Evie had sent over via courier earlier. "Those are the new choices?"

I nodded. All of them in Gianna's chosen red and white. I hated every one she sent but knew I wouldn't win this battle. Winning the war was more important.

"Better," Gianna acknowledged grudgingly. Her gaze flicked up to me. "Thoughts?"

Oh, I had so many thoughts. The woman before me had an icy beauty that turned many heads, but her heart was just as frozen. I liked my women to run hot and furious. A warrior didn't have to hold a sword to be terrifying. But Gianna preferred underhanded, manipulative tactics to win, not blunt, in your face war.

She was dressed to kill this evening, wearing a one-shoulder red cocktail dress and gold high heels. Her long hair was pinned in a perfect chignon, and her makeup was perfectly applied.

"Have plans this evening?"

Gianna scoffed and rolled her eyes. "Of course, I do. Unlike you, I don't prefer moping alone in my office during the evening."

Magic rose in the room, a physical manifestation of my anger. "I also like moping in the living room and the kitchen. Sometimes even the bedroom if I'm feeling really feisty."

Gianna sighed and rolled her eyes. "Honestly, Caelan. How do you expect me to be your wife if we're never seen together?"

"I don't expect anything, Gianna, dear. The Council expects it. All I'm required to do is marry you. Everything that comes after that is extra."

"And heirs?" Gianna snapped. "You must carry your bloodline on."

"Shifters have a notoriously low birth rate," I said mildly. "And who's to say any delay is due to me?"

Gianna sucked in a breath. Insulting a shifter's fertility, especially one of her impeccable pedigree, was one of the lowest insults one could offer. Her magic rose through the air, shifter cut with something I'd been trying to parse out from the moment I'd met her. Gianna wasn't one hundred percent shifter. I'd bet my territory on it. But my only suspicion had sent cold dread through my heart, so I hadn't said anything about it.

Only made a desperate deal with an unknown god as fickle as my fiancée.

"How dare you?" she seethed. "I am here trying to be a good wife to you, and all you do is insult me."

"I don't want you here," I snarled.

Gianna's eyes flickered. "My agreement is not with you, anyway. All I'm required to do is marry you, and my part will be complete." Her lips turned up in a cruel smile. "If you do not go forward with the bonding ceremony, your territory will be forfeited."

Rage carved a path through my bones with her words. If I could kill her right now, I would. Her smile widened. Gianna knew I would too.

She uncrossed one leanly muscled leg and rose, leaning across the desk. Seymour quivered in his pot.

"Remember who holds the power here, Lord. Do your duty."

I remained silent. She rose, her eyes flashing a strange violet as she left the room.

It took me a few minutes to contain my anger. When I had myself firmly under control once more, I rose and opened the hidden latch contained inside one of my bookshelves. When the device clicked, the shelf opened, and just as I was about to walk down, Seymour clanked his pot and lunged for me. I caught him with a surprised grunt and lifted him to stare.

"You want to come?"

Seymour quivered.

"Fine. But don't try to eat anything. If you do, I'll eat you myself."

Seymour didn't respond, so I took it as his agreement to behave.

I didn't come down here a lot, only when I needed answers I couldn't find on my own, but after I'd met Evie, I found myself down here much more often.

A strange smell of ash and oak burned my nose, and I stilled before I stepped off the last stair. Someone had been down here, and it hadn't been Simone.

I sent my magic out but sensed nothing else amiss and no other presences inside the library. With that, I headed straight to the scarred wooden desk and set Seymour down, only to see a scroll tied with a forest green ribbon.

I opened the parchment to reveal a handwritten note.

You will have your moment, Lord. I am still considering its price.

Relief and horror warred within me. I sank onto the old chair and leaned back, digging my fingers into the pocket of my shirt and brushing over one of the petals that had fallen from Evie's boutonniere. Her words about secrets came back to me.

Mine are safe until you need something from me.

If things were up to me, I'd burn the world down to keep her secrets.

CHAPTER

Nineteen

Hazel got more aggressive with her efforts to figure out the magic corrupting the bouquet, and a few days later, she hit pay dirt.

We all stood around the table, a safe distance away from the thing that had taken up so much of our time and effort.

"You may need to call the customer and tell them you can't salvage this thing," Hazel said. "I'm about to unravel it."

"I don't think they ever expected it back at all," Moira said. "They brought it here for Evie."

"I'm in agreement." Hazel stepped closer to the table, her hands held out. A ball of purple fire swirled between her palms.

The moment her magic touched the bouquet, powers rapidly fell from the main stem, decomposing into black goo. A foul smell poured forth. Moira gagged, and I breathed through my mouth, trying not to do the same.

Hazel touched each bloom, carefully moving toward the center. I watched in horror as she unveiled a small, glowing red orb in the heart of the bouquet. "Gotcha," Hazel said softly.

She dropped her magic and wiped her forehead with the back of her forearm. "Want the good news first?"

"Is there good news?" I asked, staring in horror at the poor, suffering plant.

Hazel snorted. "This thing wasn't meant to kill you."

"That feels almost miraculous these days," Moira said dryly, laughing when I nudged her with my elbow.

"Every time you've worked on it, the spell inside slowly siphoned your magic, destabilizing you even more than normal." Hazel eyed me. "Have you felt off lately?"

I stared.

Hazel let out a soft chuckle. "Right. The thing also has a tracker. Your Chimera has known where you are from the first time you've touched it."

That explained some things. "I'm not unpredictable with my whereabouts. Not really."

"True," Ash said. "If she's not at work, she's at home. The only anomaly is her deliveries."

"Finn could have gotten to you at any time," Moira said.

Tess stared at the bouquet, not saying anything, but her energy was off. Her slight frame quivered, and her eyes stayed fixed on the bouquet. Ash spotted me eyeing her and sidled closer.

"You okay?" he whispered.

"Bad," Tess said, her voice querulous. "Whoever made that is bad."

"Yes, child," Hazel agreed. "But we're going to find them and make sure this never happens again."

Tess didn't respond, only kept her eyes locked on the bouquet.

"If you're ready, I'm going to crack the spell," Hazel said.

"Should we leave?" Ash asked.

"Not necessary. Now that I know it a little better, I should have no trouble containing any magical backlash." Hazel sent out a simple spark of magic toward the center of the bouquet. A snap sounded in the air, followed by a violent crack, and a beam of magic sailed straight for me.

Before I could dodge, Hazel barked a command, and the red beam froze in mid-air.

Ash let out a low curse. My heart beat like a frightened rabbit. "Are you sure it's not trying to kill me?" I said hoarsely.

Hazel shook her head. "That one was meant to trigger a transformation. Naughty Chimera."

I moved out of its path just in case Hazel's spell broke. She snorted and slowly started dragging the magic in. "I've got the shifter's essence." Once Hazel had the spell contained, she pulled out a small vial and took just a touch of that red glow from the middle, carefully corking the vial and tucking it into her pocket.

"Is it safe to send that by courier?" I asked.

"As long as we don't get a curious one," Hazel said.

"I'll use one of our regulars. They know not to go poking around inside of our deliveries." Still unnerved, I headed to the door, with the others behind me. Hazel lingered back, still poking at the bouquet.

"One of Hattie's deliveries bit someone. That guy sweated blue for an entire week." Tess grinned. The banshee always loved when our flora got out of hand.

"Call the courier and have him here soon. The essence won't last very long."

"I'll do it now." Eager to get away from that thing, I retreated to the front of the shop to make the call.

The courier was eager to make a buck and agreed to come by within half an hour. I shot Caelan a text.

Courier on the way to you. A strange bouquet we received for preservation is linked to one of your shifters. Someone at the Keep was recently married, but there's been no sign of the bride that we can tell. Hazel extricated the shifter's signature. Take a look. I suspect something might be off with whomever this is. The magic feels off.

I said nothing about the bouquet being triggered to me or that Finn was entangled in the mess. My Chimera secret was still safe, and I'd do everything in my power to keep it that way.

His response, when it came, was short.

I'll have our Keep mage take a look. Anything else I need to know?

Be careful. The magic has an attitude problem.

Much like our resident Floromancer? I'll pass the warning along.

Funny wolf, I responded.

Caelan didn't text back. Oddly disappointed, I tucked my phone into my pocket. Ash and the others were gathered around the coffee pot, fortifying for the day.

My thistle tattoo still burned against my arm, but this morning it was worse. I ran my fingers over the raised area where Finn had cut me, hissing when I found a tender spot.

All three of my friends stopped what they were doing. "Evie?" Moira inquired. "You alright?"

"Tender area," I said with a smile. "I gotta stop poking things."

"Bears especially," Ash agreed.

"Evie has not met a bear she didn't want to poke," Tess added.

I laughed. "When did it become pick on Evie day?"

"Every day is pick on Evie day," Moira said, sliding a mug of hot coffee over.

I took it gratefully. "Thanks."

"We're going to the back to come up with some seasonal marketing campaigns," Ash said. "Things have been too busy, and our social media presence has suffered."

Part of that thanks to the Shifter Lord.

"Make sure you announce that we're working on an important wedding," I said absentmindedly. Caelan hadn't said anything about the most recent samples, so I don't know if they were a hit or miss. I'd wait until he came back with something about the shifter before I nudged him about those.

The wedding was fast approaching, and we had to crank it into high gear if we were going to get everything finished before the day. And I still had to do the bonding ceremony flowers.

I made a mental note to text him later about both.

And whispered a prayer he'd allow me a little more leeway with the bonding ceremony flowers because the red and white candy cane hellscape that was this wedding was living in my head rent-free right now.

The shop fell silent, still too early to welcome in many

customers. I sipped my coffee and enjoyed the silence, sending my senses through the shop to touch my plants and gently rouse them from rest.

It happened instinctively before I remembered everything that had gone wrong with my magic these last few weeks, and just as I jerked in remembrance, the plants responded, their gentle natures brushing against my mind.

Tears came to my eyes. My Floromancy was still there. Deeper yet unchanged.

My lips parted, and I exhaled, relief so profound it held me in a chokehold. If I had lost that part of my magic, I would have lost myself. Maybe forever.

I might be forever changed, but the most important thing was I was still me.

Still Evie.

I exhaled and whispered a thank you to the universe. Not the gods. Those guys were universally jerks, except perhaps for Cernunnos. The jury was still out on him. He was helpful, but no god was that helpful unless they had an ulterior motive.

But someone benign and maybe even good was out there listening. They had to be.

So I whispered my thank you to them.

Finn was playing the long game, and I wasn't sure what kind of ending he wanted. Whatever it was, I would not go gentle into that good night. He'd have a hell of a fight on his hands if he kept antagonizing me. Getting over my fear of him had to come first, though.

Otherwise, I'd keep freezing up every time he came around.

The wind had picked up outside, so I walked over to the window to check the sky. Our town hadn't had rain in several weeks now, and we were overdue for some moisture. But a chill ran down my spine as soon as I stepped outside to fix one of the signs that had gone wonky due to the wind.

Something was out there, and it was paying attention. The hairs on the back of my neck stood up. I turned.

A massive man stood across the street, and I knew right away he wasn't human. Nor could anyone else see him.

He stood at least six five. Dark hair, dark eyes glowing with violet power. He wore black leather armor threaded with crimson runes. His tanned forearms were exposed, glowing with some of the same runes.

Our eyes locked. His face held no emotion, only a disturbing blankness, but his eyes were a different story. They burned with curiosity and interest.

"You must be Neit."

A slow up-tilt of one side of his mouth, but he stayed silent.

I studied him, thinking Mom had great taste in men because damn, this guy was a looker, but he was dangerous. Deadly. Menace poured from his body as we watched each other. But he made no move to attack, only watched.

I jerked my arm over my shoulder. "I'm going back inside. It's cold, and I didn't put a cardigan on. If you're going to kill me, can you do it away from the shop? I have friends in here, and they really hate cleaning up messes."

No reaction from Neit's corner.

"Alright then. See ya around." I turned, my back prickling with his attention, and went inside, resisting the urge to lock the shop down like a military bunker.

"Second stalker. Cool." With a sigh, I turned to look one more time, but the god was gone, his appearance almost like a figment of my imagination.

When would I stop being hunted?

Honestly. This was giving me a complex.

CHAPTER

Twenty

CAELAN

Evie's text disturbed me. Though the furor over the rogue shifters had died down some, reports were still coming in every few days. This was one of the reasons the Council had stuck me with Gianna—the fear that I couldn't control my own territory, and Evie's disruption to the power structure.

If only they knew how much power she actually possessed. They'd lose their shit.

As it was, I expected one of those bastards to approach her soon for either marriage or binding.

A grin tugged at my mouth. I'd love to see the bastard who tried to force Evie to do anything.

Reports and maps were spread out all over my war table. I'd been examining them for weeks, and they all had one thing in common.

Or, one shifter, I should say.

Everyone who'd come into contact with Halvar, or the impostor who'd been posing as Halvar, had gone loup not long afterward. The Keep's head mage, a slight man named Kieran, had taken one look at the vial Evie had sent over and immediately paled.

175

"What is that?" he snapped.

Few dared to speak to me like that, but instead of reacting, I asked a question. "What's wrong with it?"

The mage, realizing his error, took an involuntary step back. "My apologies, Lord Caelan. I—I've never seen anything like that." He held out his hand. "May I?"

I handed it over. "Take care, Kieran."

He hurried away, the vial clutched tightly in his hand.

An hour later, he returned, pale and sweaty, and with the name of one of my shifters who'd gone missing several weeks ago. Lucas Veldt, a powerful and loyal Lieutenant, blessed in both looks and intelligence. He'd married a woman named Rebecca…

My hands stilled against the map. I hadn't seen Rebecca in weeks either. Closing my eyes, I stopped the rumble of magic coming to the surface of my skin. It'd do me no good to overreact. Answers first. Solutions second.

But there was one thing worse than the rogues and my impending wedding. The mage hadn't only come back with the shifter's signature. He'd been curious about the resonance of whatever that spell was in the vial and had done a deeper analysis.

My rogue lieutenant's essence was mixed up with Chimera essence.

We had no Chimeras in this country. They'd all been wiped out. As they should have been. They were deadly and vicious, and a natural enemy to most other shifters, my kind included.

The question was, how had Evie come into possession of something like this?

And what was I going to do about the potential fallout of a Chimera in my territory? I'd asked Kieran to double check his results, but he already had. All I could do was swear him to secrecy until I got to the bottom of things.

My fists clenched, rage swimming to the surface. Leaving the maps scattered on the table, I sailed from the office, punching a hole in the wall outside the door, plaster and sheetrock crumbling to the floor beneath me. The damage didn't make me feel any better.

I needed to run. Or scream. Or something. Anything to get this excess energy out.

Gianna and I rounded the corner at the same time. She was dressed casually today, as casual as someone like her ever looked.

Perfectly pressed and tailored chinos, flats, and a crisp white blouse, accented with a pink pearl necklace, Gianna looked the part of a Shifter Lord's fiancée. Her blonde hair was down today, not a single lock out of place.

"There you are!" Her delicate nostrils flared. "Why haven't you started the process for the bonding ceremony? I inquired, and that witch hasn't received a request yet. And the flowers haven't been booked either!"

"Evie's doing the flowers," I growled, in no mood to deal with her. "I'll send the letter out tomorrow."

"And your offering to the gods?"

Bonding ceremonies were more traditional than I liked, but even I avoided affronting the gods. They required a process. The flowers, the dagger, the words of the ritual, written by a powerful witch with Rowan's help, blessed water, and the presence of a god, brought by offerings and a humble request.

"I've already made it."

Gianna snorted. "Stop lying, Caelan. The altar is bare!"

The altar in the Keep chapel was rarely used unless there was a wedding, and since there were few shifter females, the chapel stayed dark most of the time, holidays notwithstanding.

"I made my offering elsewhere."

Gianna's eyes narrowed. "Where?"

My patience snapped. "Maybe the gods have decided not to come. Maybe they see right through your power games and your politics and these ridiculous performances and have decided not to bless our union."

Gianna sucked in a horrified breath. "Caelan."

"The gods don't care about us, and you're a fool for thinking this blessing is anything more than pomp and circumstance."

Her red lips curved into a cruel smile. "Donovan is going to have a field day when I tell him about this."

Claws shredded through my knuckles. I backed Gianna against the wall. Her heart sped up, pulse flickering rapidly against her throat. But this wasn't sexual, this was the fear prey felt when faced with a greater predator. I lifted a clawed finger, stroking it down her throat.

"Tell Donovan whatever pretty lies you like, Gianna, but know accidents happen all the time. And someone with your...delicate physique won't be as prone to survive as my other shifters."

I inhaled her scent, the deep, musky perfume that always tickled my nose, and the touch of rot at her core. Gianna might be a predator, but she'd never be dangerous to me. I ate creatures like her for a living. "Roast swan is my favorite," I whispered.

She swallowed hard, fear flaring in her eyes. The smell of acrid terror washed around us. I smiled and stepped away. "Begone and know if the gods refuse this binding, you will be out of my Keep immediately and banned from my territory." I straightened my shirt and allowed my claws to recede. "If there's any shopping you need done while you're here, I suggest you get it done immediately."

Gianna straightened, her lips pressed tight together. "You dare threaten me?" she hissed, but her bravado was gone, the scent of her fear lingering in the air.

I smiled, allowing a touch of power into my eyes. "I hear Donovan is at the popular cafe on Main Street. Don't be late, little bird."

Her eyes widened a fraction. I'd known the other Lord was on my territory the moment he'd stepped onto the land. Loyal people and clever spies are only one of the many tricks keeping me in power.

Gianna spun and hurried away, her spine rigid. I waited until she was out of sight before sending Simone a coded message.

Lucas has gone loup. Bring him back, dead or alive.

Simone's thumbs up response made me grin. The Omega was always up for a little bit of hunting.

I was about to head to the kitchens when I diverted back to the hidden library to check for any other messages, but there was nothing there. However, just as I was about to leave, the smell of oak and ash rose in the air, announcing a presence I couldn't see.

When the voice came, it was old, ancient. "What will you give, Lord?"

I was no longer afraid of the outcome. "Anything but her."

Wind ruffled my hair, the scent not of this world.

And what about you, the voice whispered in my mind.

"I will pay whatever you demand."

We'll see…

The wind stopped, the presence gone in an instant, leaving me disturbed but unshaken. I would pay the price, whatever the god demanded. My territory wouldn't survive someone as cruel as Gianna as its Lady. I might survive her, but I played a dangerous game.

I pulled out my phone again and texted Rowan.

Up for a bit of hunting?

In response, I got a picture of the Lord surrounded by a ton of plants and a pretty red-haired woman.

I laughed. *Fair enough. See you soon.*

Be careful. An inane warning from someone as powerful as Rowan but laced with meaning. Not many things could damage a Shifter Lord, but strange things stirred in Joy Springs.

Once I locked up the library, I passed by Seymour who lunged to get a hold of my sleeve. "Not today, Seymour. I have things to do. I'll be back later to feed you some of those worms your mistress sent."

The flytrap growled and shook my sleeve. I extricated him

gently and set him back on the desk, but Seymour was having none of it. He lunged again, catching my belt loop this time.

I again extricated him, but this time I held him at eye level. "Want to go hunting?"

Seymour quivered with anticipation.

I studied him for a moment. "Fuck it," I muttered. "You'll have to stay in the bag I wear. Cool?"

Seymour quivered again. "Alright. Let's go."

Once I was out of the Keep, I shifted, the bag I wore around my neck holding Seymour and a change of clothes if I needed it. The change immediately centered me. It had been too long since I'd changed forms, my inner beast stretching in my mind. I spent a few minutes sniffing around the property, checking the wards and potential weak points before padding down the driveway.

A few other shifters spotted me and waved, used to seeing me out and about. I ignored them and put my nose to the ground again, searching for the scent of rogue magic.

Nothing came to me until I hit close to the area around Evie's house. Odd.

I put my nose down and followed the strange scent wherever it led me. There were pockets of stronger scent laid around the area, places where the creature or person stayed for a while, waiting or watching.

The scent tugged on a thread of memory, but I couldn't unravel it yet. Its scent was odd, the smell of burning heather and cold winds, tinged with rot at its core. Whoever or whatever this was had performed much evil during their lives. No one was born inherently evil. I believed that down to my core.

Actions tainted one's body and mind, and eventually their magic.

Seymour sat in the pack still as a stone, and I chuffed a laugh. Six months ago, if anyone had told me I'd be hunting rogue magic users with a vicious flytrap sidekick, I would have laughed my ass off.

And now, here we were, held to some odd truce, hunting

down the source of magic that had resulted in me being forced into a wedding I never wanted.

Soon enough, the scent trail overwhelmed my thoughts, and all my focus went toward tracking it down. It took almost an hour, but I finally stopped, the scent strongest right at the edge of the fence line.

I lifted my head and stumbled, my back legs going out from underneath me.

We were at the edge of Evie's property.

I shifted to human form, Seymour's quiver of alarm his only movement.

Dusk had fallen some time ago, a sliver of moon visible in the sky. I investigated around the fence and area but found nothing strange. Why was the magic here? Did Evie have something to do with it?

I frowned and turned, a hint of a familiar scent in the air making me freeze.

"Hello, Lord," a male said with a deep, accented voice, his body hidden in shadow.

I inhaled, pulling the scent into my lungs.

This, whoever this was, he was the source.

"And you are?" I asked.

"You can call me Finn." The man stepped out of the shadows, his hands tucked into his pockets.

I smelled no gunpowder or metal. Surviving a gunshot was easy, but no one liked getting shot, so I was relieved to know he wasn't carrying any conventional weapons.

"Finn. Is there a reason you're around this Floromancer's property?"

The man grinned, his face full of good humor. "Easy to answer. She belongs to me."

I froze, rage cracking through my veins like ice. But I kept my expression neutral. I needed more information before I attacked without volition. Evie and I had never had many personal conversations. We were usually too busy antagonizing each other to worry about small talk. "Belongs is a strong word," I said. "Are you a friend of hers?"

"Did you know Evie was once married?" Finn asked.

I did. No one moved here without a thorough background check. "Does it matter?"

"She came to Scotland for a girl's trip. A getaway to help her heart heal."

I did not respond. I'd known the divorce was tough on her, as well as one could know who hadn't been there or experienced the same thing. Her friends were disturbed by the request for an interview but had consented once they knew Evie was okay and trying to find a place to land.

Evie had no idea how deeply we dug into her background when she applied to move here, but once I'd met her, I'd done an even deeper dive. Not that I unearthed all the skeletons in her closet. I'd missed the one standing before me.

"I'm not sure what this has to do with me," I said politely.

A strange, crimson haze rolled over Finn's eyes. His jaw tightened. "She ran from me, Lord. And I am here to claim her."

Right. Pretty sure I was going to have to kill this fucker and put his body in a hole so deep no one would ever find him. I inhaled again, holding his scent in my mind. He'd never be able to run from me again now that I had it.

Finn smiled. "Nice trick. But I have tricks of my own." His scent abruptly cut off, leaving only the crisp smell of wind and trees in my nose.

Not great, but even the most intelligent people screwed up. I'd still find him.

If he got away from me.

"Does Evie know you're here to claim her?"

Another manic grin, Finn's gaze moving to the back of Evie's house. "She's known for a while I'm here for her."

I chuckled. "And she's proven resistant to your charms?"

Finn's attention snapped back to me. "You fancy yourself her protector, Lord. I can smell it in the air." He shook his head. "I'll allow you a temporary dalliance before claiming her for good."

"I am a Lord. You allow me nothing." Power punched through the air, proof of my claim. Claws unsheathed and my fangs elongated.

Finn rolled his eyes. "Do we have to do this tonight?" He laid his hand on his chest. "I just bought this shirt."

I'd go for the jugular first, make it quick and easy. No need to stress Evie out too much if she walked out here. I removed the pack from my neck and laid it against a tree. Seymour lay still and silent.

If things went awry, maybe Seymour could bite him a few times.

"Evie is not yours to claim. Leave now, and I'll allow you free passage."

Another flash of crimson. "Don't you know what I am?" he asked.

"I don't give a shit what you are," I said mildly. "I care about the woman inside that house."

"You should care," Finn said quietly. "I am the thing that prowls the night, the creature your mother warned you about." Crimson magic pooled from his hand and spread over Evie's ward. A silencing spell.

Oh goodie.

"Yeah, yeah. I'm sure you're very dangerous."

Finn moved.

Pain flared in my left shoulder and collarbone. Stunned but not stupid, I hit the ground and rolled, barely avoiding decapitation. Memories slammed into me like a truck.

"You," I growled.

"Took you long enough. I almost had you that night. But our little Evie has such a soft heart, doesn't she? Poor timing on her part, but I've already forgiven her for healing you. How could she have known it was me after all her years of safety?"

"You like stalking women who don't want you, Finn?"

"Evie wants me. She just hasn't realized it yet."

"That's what all stalkers say."

When he lunged at me this time, I was ready.

Claws and teeth and magic and fire, Finn's power was crushing. I dodged and ducked and got several good licks in, but I was bleeding from a dozen places, and there was something in his claws preventing me from healing. I stumbled backward from an almost certain death blow, landing hard against a tree. The pack lay by my feet, and I watched as Seymour's pot rolled out.

Finn spotted it and snorted. "A gift from Evie? How very sentimental. She won't need her plant magic once I finish molding her into her destiny."

"You sound unhinged," I wheezed, the poison seeping into my veins.

His eyes went full crimson this time, a bark of laughter escaping me. "You don't like being called crazy." I clicked my tongue. "If the shoe fits."

Finn leapt, but Seymour was ready. The flytrap lunged for him, growing four times his regular size, and snapped down on Finn's thigh.

Finn let out a high-pitched squeal and went down, Seymour's special flavor of paralytic already working. I stumbled forward and snatched the flytrap up, tucking him against my chest.

Finn's mouth worked like a fish, his eyes wide with horror. He lay on his stomach, arms and fingers twitching, his legs completely still.

Just as I'd gotten close enough to end him, Finn's body disappeared in a flash of crimson light.

"Fuck," I muttered, swaying on my feet. There was no way I'd make it home. I climbed the fence, my limbs shaking like a newborn calf and forced myself onto Evie's back porch, but as I reached for the doorknob, the world twisted in a blurry haze and my knees hit the wood hard, barking in protest. "Hold on," I muttered to Seymour as I keeled over sideways with a loud thump.

A strange whine came from the flytrap as he tumbled from my hands.

I opened my mouth to yell for her, but I couldn't move anything. Not even my throat.

Wheezing, I clawed at my neck, but whatever poison Finn possessed in his body had overtaken my system.

Everything slowed to a crawl, my eyes slowly closing as my strength drained.

I was on the phone with Moira when a loud thump sounded from the back porch. Immediately on alert, I told the vampire I'd call her back.

"Soon," Moira said. "Or I'll come over and crash your party."

"Yes, my party of one. It's real wild around here." I made a kissing noise and disconnected.

Hazel was off somewhere in the woods gathering plants to take back to Scotland with her. I'd made my spin on Bolognese and was inhaling it on the couch, a glass of wine next to the bowl I'd set down when Moira called.

Curling my magic around me, I ventured to the back and cracked open the door.

My eyes widened. "Seymour?"

The flytrap thumped his pot several times in agitation. I looked over and saw a prone figure lying on my porch. Sucking in a breath, I hurried outside, Seymour thumping beside me.

I recognized him immediately. "Caelan?"

He was out cold. "Dammit." I rose and called vines from the earth to assist me, fresh, clean power roaring through me. They came at my beckoning, wrapping around Caelan's waist and arms. I directed them inside and had them rise high enough to put

Caelan on the couch. He was covered in blood and gore, his head lolling as I maneuvered him into the best position I could.

Maybe I'd send him the bill for the couch too.

First things first, though. I gently shook his shoulder. "Caelan."

Nothing. I had hoped all the blood wasn't all his, but his unresponsiveness sent worry spiraling through my veins. Throwing all decorum to the wind, I sat on my natural wooden floor, allowing my bare skin to touch the burnished mahogany.

When I bought the house, the floors had a polyurethane coating on the floor, the chemical smell long faded, but I felt the wood's suffering on my first visit. Once I had the keys in my hand, I removed every bit of that coating and refinished it with Tung oil. Tung required several more coatings and a lot more effort, but the end result was worth it. Everything in this house was as natural as I could make it because I needed to live in a space that breathed, but it was also excellent for emergencies.

Like right now. As soon as I touched the wood with my bare calf and connected to its energy, power roared through my blood. I placed a palm on Caelan's chest and sent a spark of magic through his skin.

"Oh, Caelan," I breathed, my power cataloguing his injuries. Several broken ribs, multiple lacerations, a few of them too deep, internal bleeding, a damaged spleen, a bruised kidney, and a collapsed lung.

Easy enough to fix, but why hadn't his body's natural healing process kicked in? I went deeper, my magic sweeping through his body.

There. My magic recoiled, pulling away from the source of Caelan's failure to heal. Poison raged through Caelan's body, a type I'd never seen before. It had overtaken almost his entire body. I forced my magic closer, even though the power tried to rebel. Whatever this was, it was the antithesis of life.

And it was trying to steal Caelan's.

If I was going to heal him, I had to purge the poison first.

Easier said than done with an unconscious Shifter Lord. An idea struck me. I pulled my magic from his body, opened my eyes, and called the vines back.

"Help me roll him onto his side," I said quietly. The vines slid under his form and wrapped around his back. I put a hand on his shoulder and one on his waist. "Roll toward me."

With a creak and a groan of the vinery, we managed to get him onto his side. I shoved pillows behind him to keep him in place and gently turned his head. Once he was as good as I could make him, I settled back onto the floor and put my palms back on his body, settling back in to find the poison.

Instead of attacking it, I moved it, pushing the thicker poison up, up, up until Caelan heaved, expelling the poison from his body.

I grimaced and held my breath, continuing to direct the poison out, not stopping until the last drop was gone.

Once that happened, I settled deeper into my power and began to heal the Shifter Lord's wounds.

Twenty~Two

CAELAN

I awoke with a jerk, my eyes scanning an unfamiliar room.

A toxic, foul odor hit my nose first. I grunted and gagged, slowly trying to orient myself.

Evie. I was in her house. How had I gotten here? And where was she?

And what the hell was I lying in? I slowly sat up, memories coming back to me.

Finn. My hands roamed my body, hitting something wet. I grimaced and pulled my hand away, wiping whatever the hell had gotten on me on the leg of my pants.

"Evie?" My throat felt like I'd gargled glass.

What the hell happened here? Once I sat all the way up, I swung my legs over, my feet landing in more liquid.

A large something lay to the left, covered in roots, vines, and leaves. Typical Evie. Whatever it was hadn't been there the first time I'd been here, and I assumed it was something she was growing until I stood and peered closer at it, only to see a feminine hand with long fingers sticking out of the side.

I swore and went to my knees, grimacing at the bark of pain as I landed. "Evie?"

Gently nudging a few of the roots away, I brushed Evie's hair from her face. Her eyes were closed, bright green leaves growing on the ends of her hair. A smile tugged at my lips. Even covered in roots and leaves, she was stunning.

I murmured her name again. Evie's eyes fluttered, opened, and went wide. "Caelan!"

Her nose wrinkled a few seconds later.

"Sorry," I said sheepishly. "I'm not quite sure what happened here."

"Poison," Evie croaked. "Give me a minute."

I took a few steps back and went to the kitchen to try to find some paper towels to sop up some of the mess. Her couch and floor were destroyed, and as more memories came back, I knew, once again, that it was my fault.

Would I never stop writing checks to Evie Quinn?

I found a roll of paper towels and went back to the scene of the crime, bending to clean up what I could while Evie extricated herself from her plant prison. Once I got what I could, I found a trash bag, stripped my shirt off, and tossed it inside. I had a second where I considered stripping my pants off, too, but I didn't want to scandalize the poor Floromancer.

It would be fun, though.

My thoughts sobered as recent events surfaced. I'd almost died. Again. In front of Evie Quinn.

Again.

Whoever that Finn guy was, he'd almost taken me out. Twice. I'd underestimated his strength and failed to use my full strength to take him out. He'd worn me down, using poison to worsen my condition, and almost had me.

I didn't remember the first attack. He'd gotten me from behind and quickly overwhelmed me. This time he'd attacked from the front, and I still almost lost.

Evie and I needed to have a conversation. She knew who Finn was. I washed quickly, scrubbing every bit of what I assumed was vomit away, and rinsed my mouth out multiple times until I felt somewhat human. By the time I finished, Evie was sitting up, a look of dismay on her face as she took in the carnage.

"Your place looks a bit like a frat house."

Evie turned to me, her eyes widening at my shirtless state. I didn't miss her gaze sliding from my face to my torso, her cheeks coloring when she snapped her eyes back up to my face.

"Where's your shirt?" she croaked.

"In the trash. Hopefully incinerated soon." The Floromancer looked disheveled and tired and gorgeous.

Her dark hair tumbled around her shoulders, covering the remnants of her ripped and scored tank top. She'd tucked her dirty bare feet under her body and sat cross-legged as she peered up at me with too bright eyes.

I loved her eyes. They looked like a crystal-clear sea on a sunny day.

I loved her hair and itched to run my fingers through it.

"Why are you staring at me like that?" Her voice sounded hoarse.

"You healed me again."

Evie nodded, her blue eyes wide in her pale face.

"Are you hungry?" I asked.

She nodded again.

"How about we clean this up and get something to eat?"

"I'll clean it up later. You should be fine to go home." Evie rose, wobbling as she stood.

I was by her side in an instant, my palm around her arm to steady her. "I'm not going home until I know you're okay. We also have some things we need to talk about."

She moved away, extricating herself from my grip. "There's nothing to talk about. Something with venom attacked you. I found you on my porch and pulled you inside."

My eyebrows went up. "Evie. I weigh over 250 pounds. There's no way you got me inside by yourself."

She scoffed, anger snapping in her eyes. "I might be smaller than you, but I am not helpless. I got you inside just fine."

I held both my hands up. "Alright. Let's say I believe you. Then what happened?"

Her jaw tightened. "Don't make me punch you."

My lips tugged in a smile. "And then what happened?"

She blew out an annoyed breath. "Then I catalogued your injuries and realized you weren't healing. So I tried to figure out why."

My gaze skimmed over the floor. "It was vomit then."

"Whoever attacked you poisoned you. I wasn't able to identify what it was, but it overrode your body's natural healing ability." Our eyes locked. "If I hadn't found you last night, you would have died on my porch."

Her somber tone sent a chill through my body. "This is the second time you've healed me."

Evie nodded. "And the second time you've managed to destroy my property."

I winced. "Apologies. I'll send a check over via courier."

"Don't worry about it. The floor is special. I'll have to find another source. The original is out of business. I don't want just anyone working on my place. It's…" Her voice trailed off.

"Special," I supplied. "Being in your home feels like being in the woods. I understand. But I still plan to pay for the damages." My gaze landed on the spot where she'd risen. "When you heal, you become one with the earth. How—" I paused.

A hesitant smile crossed her face. "It feels like I am unique and nothing, all at the same time. I can feel the heartbeat of the world when I'm cradled in Her arms."

I wanted her. Roots and all. "Her?"

"The earth holds feminine energy. Masculine too, but most of it is divinely feminine. Being one with her restores me." Evie blinked and looked down at her feet. "Sorry."

"Never apologize for the things you love." I glanced back at the kitchen. "Mind if I make a pot of coffee?"

"Not at all, but I don't mind making it. Give me a moment." She started toward the back.

"Evie."

She stilled. "I'll make the coffee. Go take a shower. I'll be here when you get back."

Evie swallowed hard, her cheeks delightfully pink. This was not like the feisty, violent woman I usually encountered. I liked this softer, rumpled side of her.

"I have some clothing if you want it. There's another shower in the second bathroom if you want to clean up."

The space between my ears sounded like a wind tunnel. "Clothing?" Why did she have male clothing? Who was he?

"Yes. They may be a little short and the shirt might be a little tight, but they'll get you home just fine. My ex-husband wasn't as large as you are."

The rage in my veins fizzled and died. Ex-husband I could work with. My nostrils flared as I scented the place, inhaling Evie's fresh, floral scent, and the smell of loam and greenery. I picked up another feminine scent, deep and herbal. That must be the witch who's staying with her.

"I'd appreciate anything you can spare."

Evie nodded and hurried to the back, returning in less than a minute with a pair of joggers and a black t-shirt. She also held out a pair of white socks and winced apologetically. "I don't have an extra toothbrush. I'm sorry." But she held out a small tube. "But I do have a sample tube of toothpaste if you want it."

I took everything she offered and waited until she'd gone to the back before I held the clothes up to my nose and smelled them. I wouldn't wear another male's clothes if they had any scent left on the fabric. But all my nose picked up was the scent of detergent and Evie's faint smell.

She'd washed these clothes several times. I wondered if she'd gone to sleep while wearing them after the divorce. The thought made my hands squeeze the clothing until I'd conquered the urge to tear them to shreds.

When my breath got under control, I turned and headed toward the second bathroom.

I needed to get it together. Otherwise, I was going to scare the shit out of Evie.

CHAPTER
Twenty~Three

By the time I'd clipped all the leaves from my skin and washed all the gunk from my body, Caelan was already in the kitchen, a fresh pot of coffee brewing. A skillet sat on the stove, the scent of sizzling butter and garlic a heady note in the air.

Caelan stood there, forearms flexing as he whisked together something in one of my vintage blue enamel bowls. My ex-husband's shirt stretched across the deep planes of Caelan's chest, and the joggers were a little too tight across his powerful thighs. A tug pulled low in my core, and I had to do everything in my power to hide my visceral reaction to seeing the Shifter Lord making breakfast in my kitchen.

"Hope you don't mind. You had everything to make French toast, so I thought I'd whip up something to eat. Do you eat pork?"

I nodded stupidly.

"Good. As soon as I mix this up, I'll put the bacon on."

"I can do it."

He shook his head. "Allow me this, Evie. You saved my life last night. Let me make you breakfast." His deep voice rumbled across my skin.

I stood there like an idiot. "Um. Okay."

A smile flashed across his face. "Good."

Padding over to the coffeepot, I poured us both a cup, passing one over to him. He gave me a grateful nod and kept working.

Bewildered, I took a seat at the table and watched the Shifter Lord, one of the most powerful people in the entire country, make a no-name Floromancer breakfast.

After a few minutes, I rose and went to Seymour, the flytrap worse for the wear this morning. His pot was chipped, and one of his extra traps was listing to the side. I'd almost forgotten about him. "Hey," I said, crouching down beside him. "Are you okay?"

Seymour quivered.

"I'm so sorry I didn't get to you last night. But I can help you now. Okay?"

The flytrap quivered again. I reached for Seymour, stroking a finger over the top of his main trap, and let my magic seep into every part of him. A minute later and the other trap had perked up, and Seymour was looking much better. "I can't do anything about the pot yet, but I'll get you something better, okay?"

Seymour thumped his broken pot a few times.

"Good. It's time to get you a larger one anyway." I gave him a final stroke and rose.

THIRTY MINUTES of almost silent cooking later, Caelan sat a large pile of French toast and bacon in front of me, then snagged my coffee mug and poured me another.

I waited for him to fix his plate before I took a bite. And when he settled beside me, and my stomach lurched, it took everything I had not to ask him a million questions in an incoherent ramble.

We ate a king's feast, and when the last of the bacon was polished off, I realized I probably could have eaten more.

"Evie," Caelan rumbled. "Who's Finn?"

My hand jerked, sloshing hot coffee all over my fingers. I hissed in pain, clutching my fingers to my chest. "Shit," I cursed.

Caelan leaned back in his chair and waited, his expression neutral.

If he was asking about Finn then…

"He's the one who attacked you last night." Horror rolled through my veins. While the severity of his wounds made sense now that I knew who was responsible, not all the pieces fit.

The Shifter Lord inclined his head. "He was. And he seemed quite enamored with you."

My eyes closed. He would know if I lied to him. Few people could lie to a shifter and get away with it. Lying to a Shifter Lord was tantamount to suicide.

"Why did he attack you?" Maybe I could distract him with questions.

One of his eyebrows rose. "I traced the rogue magic to the back of your property. Finn was waiting there. Watching for you, I assume. I told him stalking you isn't a good idea." A faint smile. "Finn did not agree."

"I'm so sorry," I whispered.

"I'm alive thanks to you. No harm, no foul, I suppose."

I licked my lips and tried to think of what to say.

"You met him in Scotland."

How much did he know? Shit. The walls pressed in against me, my secrets coming home to roost. I nodded. "Yes. I was on a trip with some girlfriends."

"After your divorce."

"As soon as the papers were signed."

"Did you date him?" There was something in his eyes I didn't like.

I opened my mouth to answer, then snapped it shut. "That's an inappropriate question."

Caelan's lips edged up into a smile. "Did you?"

I tipped the last of my coffee into my mouth and rose. "Thank you for breakfast. I appreciate it." After a quick rinse, I put my mug in the dishwasher. "I think your clothes are toast, so I can dispose of them if you put them in the trash. Do you need a ride home?"

"Evie."

"Also, don't worry about the cleanup here. You already got most of it up."

"Evie."

"I'll call someone to handle the floor and—"

"EVIE!"

His roar shocked me into silence. My jaw snapped shut, and I stared.

"Your dating life might not be my business, but Finn is a threat to my territory. He is now my priority. Why is he so interested in you?"

My magic hummed in my veins, the Chimera magic oddly silent. Every time I went into a healing sleep, my Floromancy power settled down, and I had a few days of reprieve from being forced to siphon off the excess. But now that I'd merged with the Chimera, I felt more settled than usual. Maybe Cernunnos was right. Maybe this was the path I needed to walk.

"He's someone who can't take no for an answer." It was the best way to describe Finn.

"You've rebuffed his advances?"

"Multiple times. He is persistent."

Power boomed through the room, the Shifter Lord's magic rising. His eyes glowed burnished gold, the light reflecting off the kitchen counter like the morning sun. "I will kill him," he snarled.

I touched Caelan's forearm, sending a small jolt of magic through his body to break him from his rage. "Caelan. It's not up to you to protect me."

"It is my job to protect this place; you are included in that duty."

"But it isn't the only reason," I said softly.

Caelan put his hand over mine, the heat from his palm burning against my skin. "Evie—"

Someone knocked on the door. I jerked my hand away and bolted to my feet. "I have to answer that."

Scurrying to the door, my heart beating a hundred miles a minute, I flung it open only to see Ben standing there. He wore jeans and a Henley shirt, his hair freshly washed. The scent of pine rose around us. A gentle aura floated around him, the Healer at home in a wild place like mine.

He held up his medical kit. "I didn't like the way we left things. As such, I made up a lame excuse to come check on you to see how you were doing after the attack."

Ben's nose twitched, his eyebrows drawing together. "Do you have company?" He brushed past me and entered the house, freezing when he spotted Caelan in the kitchen.

"Poison," I blurted. "He had poison."

Ben turned to me. "Someone poisoned Lord Caelan?"

I nodded.

The Healer frowned and set his medical bag down. "I'd like to examine you."

Caelan lifted his mug. "No need. Evie patched me right up." His slow, suggestive smile made me want to punch him.

Ben's jaw tightened. "Regardless, I am the Keep's Healer, and you, its Lord. An exam is protocol." His eyes swept over the living room, widening when he spotted the destruction.

Caelan raised his hands. "Fine. I submit."

Ben nodded once and flipped open his bag. I retreated to get another cup of coffee during the exam. Once Ben was finished, he rose. "Evie, your healing ability is unparalleled."

"I can't claim all the credit. The earth does most of the heavy lifting."

His gaze flicked to Caelan. "Poison doesn't usually look so cozy in the morning."

The Lord grinned. "Tell me, Ben. Do you always show up uninvited?"

I gave him a quelling look. "Ben is always welcome on my property."

"May I speak with you outside?" Ben asked.

"Keeping secrets from your Lord, Evie?" Caelan's taunting tone made me want to scream.

"I saved your life last night," I snarled. "Don't make me regret it."

Caelan's warm laugh followed Ben and me outside.

We hadn't made it off the porch before Ben spun to me. "What are you hiding? Is this why Caelan was attacked?" He exhaled. "What are you?"

I blinked. "Ben. You just threw a lot of questions my way."

He crossed his arms over his chest. "And you aren't going to answer any of them, are you?"

When I remained silent, Ben's face hardened. "I can't be the fool who continues waiting around for you to trust someone." He jerked his thumb over his shoulder. "If you harm the Lord, the entire Council will come down on you. Remember that when you decide you want to keep your secrets."

Ben hoisted his bag over his shoulder and jogged down the stairs, not looking back.

I threw up my hands and marched back inside. Caelan hadn't moved from his spot, the Lord looking like the cat who'd eaten the canary.

"A lover's spat?" he asked, sipping his coffee from my fox mug. I didn't even realize I'd given him that one. How fitting.

"It's time for you to go home. If Gianna finds out you stayed the night here, things will get complicated."

He rose, all lean grace as he sauntered over. "It's time for you to spill your secrets, Evie Quinn. Before they get someone killed."

Twenty-Four

T he shrill ring of Caelan's cell broke the tension. I stepped away, keeping a wary eye on him.

His lips pressed together as he snatched his cell from the coffee table. "This is Caelan," he barked.

His face went blank a second later. My hearing wasn't as sharp as a shifter, but it was better than a human's. The caller was female and agitated.

And from Caelan's expression, the caller was his soon-to-be wife.

I grinned and wiggled my fingers at him, hurrying to escape to the bedroom. "Show yourself out," I whispered.

It took a while, but Caelan finally vacated the house. I came back into the living room to find the rest of the debris picked up and Caelan's trash gone from the kitchen. The only evidence he was here was the destroyed couch and flooring.

And a note lying on the kitchen table.

With trepidation, I picked it up.

I had fun last night. Let's do it again, minus the blood, vomit, and property damage.

A smile tugged at my mouth. Folding the note, I tucked it into my pocket and went to get ready for the rest of the day. If Finn was stalking me, he must be waiting for me to let my guard down. Surviving him would mean being able to shift rapidly and on demand, while also using my Floromancy.

I fired off a quick text to Hazel to make sure she was okay. Knowing the witch, she stayed the night in the woods, but dangerous things prowled out there, and I needed to know where all the people I cared about were.

She responded right away and said she'd be home later.

Moira, Tess, and Ash were all at home, safe and sound.

I went to the back and put on a pair of workout leggings and a tank top. On the way out, I tied my hair into a ponytail and slipped on a pair of flip-flops. I didn't mind destroying some workout clothes with the practice I had in mind, but I didn't have many shoes. Mostly because I only wore them when I went to work or had to be in public. Other than that, it was bare feet all the time.

I moved away from the back porch and headed farther back into my property, far enough away from the house that if things went wrong, I wouldn't destroy anything. To avoid prying eyes, I sank onto the ground and dug my fingers into the soil, communing with the earth for a few minutes. When all the stress of the last twenty-four hours had sunk into the ground, I called the earth to form a barrier of plant life around me, ensuring I had enough room to practice and move around. The earth rumbled and cracked, and new trees and plants and vines rose from the ground, and I let it go until it was about ten feet high.

Take that, spies.

The only negative about the thick wall of protection was the lack of light. I folded the top barrier down, opening the area wider until I had enough daylight to see by.

Then I sank into my magic and practiced, determined to get it right this time. I let go of all my fear and all my worry and allowed the Chimera magic to function as it was supposed to.

I could barely muster an armful of feathers the first couple of hours, but by the time lunch rolled around and the sun was high in the sky, I managed a partial shift. A couple of hours after that, a half shift.

By evening time, I was sweaty and dragging ass but still trying to perfect the shift. From what little I knew of Chimeras, I should be able to shift into anything, animal or plant life. I stayed mostly in the bird family because my animal form was a wren, switching back and forth from wren to human to see if shifting to my fae form could help the shift to another one.

No dice. My fae magic was different from the Chimera and felt different. Shifting to a wren felt like second nature. The other magic felt like an unused, atrophied muscle I was trying to work out, stiff and unyielding.

I plopped onto the ground and lay like a starfish, arms and legs akimbo. My breath rattled in my chest, and every muscle in my body hurt. Why couldn't I do this? What was I missing?

Not having another Chimera to teach me the ropes was aggravating, but if they were all like Finn, I was better off learning on my own. With a groan, I rolled onto my side and got back up.

I'd give it a few more tries before I gave up for the day.

An hour later, just as I was about to throw in the towel, I decided to try something different. I wasn't just a shifter. I was a Chimera, and a Floromancer, and half-fae. Maybe the key was there?

Every time I tried to shift, I was standing up. My feet were locked onto the soil, but maybe I needed more contact. I frowned and thought what the hell. What could it hurt?

I dug a small channel with the back of my heels and planted my feet inside, digging my toes deeper into the earth. When I touched my Chimera magic, the change was immediate. My body exploded in a shower of light, and the shift rolled over me, power exploding in my veins.

Every cell in my body changed. Feathers rolled over my skin, and my head morphed into the sharply angled head of an eagle. I opened my mouth to scream my delight only for a loud screech to emit, startling me with its intensity.

Holy shit.

I flexed my wings, the size putting me off balance for a moment while I adjusted. A wren is a tiny bird. An eagle was a massive change from my normal form. But I could feel the strength in my wings and my claws.

A few test flaps later, and I launched myself into the air, screeching with delight. My heart beat a thousand miles per hour as I soared high into the air.

This was incredible!

Completely stunned at the transformation, I sailed through the sky, keeping to the boundaries of my property even as I yearned to explore everything. I could see everything. I rose high above my property, looking over Joy Springs at night. It was early enough for downtown to still be active, and the warm glow of lights cast the city in a magical haze.

I flew for a little while longer before landing, my body knowing what to do immediately.

Then I was Evie once more, my clothes thankfully still on, which was a cool trick.

"Awesome," I breathed. Maybe being a Chimera wouldn't be so bad after all. Not if I could do cool stuff like that all the time.

The protective barrier sank back into the ground after a quick command from me, and I hurried into the house. I was starving and had no idea if I had enough food in the fridge to scrounge up dinner.

I checked my phone to see a text from Caelan that simply said, *Continue with the red and white centerpieces and bouquets.*

I cringed but typed out an affirmative and asked how much leeway I had with the bonding ceremony bouquet. Not my wedding. Not my circus. Caelan was paying me handsomely to do what he asked, and that's what I would do.

Make it your own.

Are you sure? Not red and white?

I'm sure. Whatever you think I would like as long as it has your spin on it.

I grinned and put my phone back down, ideas already spinning in my head. The best part of owning a flower shop was people trusting me with a vision.

Dinner first, then I'd head into the shop tonight to put some things together.

Hazel and I texted back and forth before I left, and I mentioned the bonding ceremony in case Caelan hadn't. She said he reached out to her, and she was working on something for him, though she was a little confused about why he had contacted her and not someone local.

I didn't have an answer to that. Maybe it was Caelan being Caelan. Understanding his logic required a PhD.

I inhaled the last of my egg scramble, filled my to-go mug with coffee, and headed out the door, excited to put a few examples together for Caelan.

But when I got to the shop, my hackles rose. Nothing looked amiss, but there was an odd energy around the door. Silent as a ghost, I slipped out of the car, quietly clicking the door shut. Nothing to be done about the headlights when I had pulled in, but hopefully whoever might be in my shop hadn't seen me yet.

I sent a thread of magic inside, immediately reading distress coming off all the plants. Someone was inside. Another tug of magic on one of the pothos close to the door to wrap around and silence the bell above allowed me to slip inside.

I alerted the six deadly plants I had scattered in various places around the shop to get ready. Whether their poison could infect Finn was unknown, but I had no qualms about trying if he got close enough for them to react.

No one was in the front, but the noise of shattering pots made my shoulders stiffen. On silent feet, I ventured to the back, picking two of those plants up to take with me to the back.

I found him in the walk-in, systematically destroying my seasonal arrangements. The cursed bouquet lay quiet on the warded table, but I knew that damned thing was the reason Finn was able to get inside without triggering my ward alarms. I planned to destroy that thing as soon as I was done here.

If Finn didn't kill me first.

I came up behind Finn without him realizing it and watched as he gleefully shattered a three-hundred-dollar arrangement. Hate rose, a tidal wave in my blood. Silent as a wraith, I came closer, touched both of the plants I held in my arms and whispered a mental command.

Both vines lunged for Finn at the same time, poison leaking thorns appearing on the back of their leaves. As soon as they touched his skin, Finn froze, a hissing intake of breath the only sign of pain.

Without waiting, I spun on my heel and hauled ass from the fridge, putting both plants down on the stainless table, away from the cursed bouquet.

Finn walked out, casual and none the worse for the wear, though blood leaked down both biceps. Savage pleasure at the sight rang through me.

"It was far too easy to gain access to your sanctum, Evie."

"I'm sure it had nothing to do with that leaking pile of garbage on my table."

He smiled, and even though I knew he was cruel and without morals, I remembered a cold night in Scotland where I thought I was getting a fresh start. The memory was a visceral punch, reminding me of how hard I worked to get back on my feet and build a life for myself.

And I'd be damned if I let him take that away from me.

"You've always been so easy to deceive." He tucked his hands in his pockets, blood continuing to leak from his arms. A shifter should have been able to stop the bleeding by now, and I had an overwhelming urge to high-five my plants when this was over.

"But not so easy to beat. Otherwise, you wouldn't still be here trying to bend me to your will."

Anger glittered in his eyes, but his response was amused.

"What can I say? I've always had a weakness for strong-willed women." His fingers trailed over the ward on the bouquet. "Much like Caelan's fiancée. So strong-willed in personality, but so very weak when it comes to her desire for power."

I froze. "What did you do?"

"Nothing Gianna didn't allow. I'm not a monster."

"Yes, yes, you are a monster. That's why we're standing here right now."

He slammed a fist on the edge of the table. "You have no idea what a monster really is, Evie! I've been patient, allowing you to come to terms with what you are and what you mean to me. And you've betrayed me in a hundred different ways. I've even allowed your dalliance with the two shifters, knowing you would come to me eventually."

Finn swayed on his feet.

Two high-fives to those plants.

"Are you okay?" I asked sweetly.

Blood dripped from the edge of his lower lip. "This is the last time I ask. Come with me, Evie. Let me teach you what you need to know."

I snorted. "I learned all I needed from you that night in Scotland. You broke my already fraught trust in men and taught me I didn't need to be with a man to have a happy and fulfilling life. This is the last time I tell you, Finn. My answer is no."

Crimson magic rose in the air, Finn's entire body highlighted in an awful glow. He lunged, but I was ready. Vines whipped from the potted plants on the shelf behind him, wrapping around his neck and waist. Finn jerked off balance and crashed to the floor, a bark of pain cracking from his lips. He was up in seconds but stumbled, his face pale and sweaty.

"What did you do to me?" he rasped.

"Nothing you didn't deserve," I said sweetly.

His eyes flicked to the bouquet before settling on me once more. In a flash of crimson light, Finn shifted, a black puma stalking toward me.

Primal fear bleated through my bones. No matter how powerful I was, I'd never be unsurprised by a huge ass cat circling around me. Pumas were apex predators, and I was just a girl in a flower store hoping not to get murdered.

I reached for the poisonous vine again, holding it before me like a weapon

Finn chuffed, exposing brilliant white fangs.

The vine reached out and popped the top of Finn's head twice, reminding me of a pissed-off cat. He screeched and reared back, glistening poison slipping down his face, right into one of his eyes.

Claws sliding on the floor, the cat slammed into the rack of metal cabinets at the back of the kitchen. A thought niggled at the back of my mind, and on a whim, I destroyed the wards holding the bouquet and forced my hand into a tight fist, calling back every bit of life from that damned thing.

My magic was life, bright and green and earthy, but I could also use my power to take that life away. I used this magic only when a plant or animal's suffering became too much and I knew they wouldn't make it. But every time I used the power, it took something away from me, a little piece of Evie.

Today was the first time I had no regrets about taking a life. And I had no regrets about taking two.

The bouquet crumbled to ash, a fine layer of black glittering dust on the surface of the worktable. A flash of crimson light and an unending scream I'd hear in my nightmares ricocheted through the room. Finn's body bowed in a rictus of pain, his mouth wide open, and crimson veins pulsing against every piece of bare skin I could see.

A second later, he was gone.

I sank to my knees, a sob bubbling from my lips. Relief warred with worry because I didn't believe Finn was dead. Injured, probably severely. But not dead.

I'd never been that lucky.

Rising on shaky legs, I stood there for a long moment, marveling at the fact that I was here. I was alive.

The only thing that could have made it better was if Finn were dead.

Glittering dust lay in a pile on the table. Not liking the look of it, I used a scraper to carefully brush every single bit from the table into a glass jar. I'd give it to Hazel for disposal later. She'd know what to do with it.

Then I went straight to the regular fridge and got myself a bottle of wine.

A few hours later, I stumbled out of the shop, planning to shift into a wren and fly home when I spotted a shadowy figure leaning against my car.

Energy hummed in the air, the god a finely honed weapon. I wasn't drunk; the wine wasn't strong enough to affect me much, but I also wasn't in the mood to deal with the gods. "I'd be annoyed if I were driving home, but I don't need my car tonight."

"Too many spirits, little wren?" His teeth flashed white in the dark.

"We both know human wine does little more than give a temporary buzz."

"True. If you're nice, I can bring you some better spirits."

The offer was tempting because there were many nights I wanted to drink myself into oblivion. "I'm always nice," I said in a shitty tone.

Neit chuckled and snapped his fingers, an amber-colored bottle appearing in his hands.

"I shouldn't drive this evening, so I can't carry that home. Normally, I'd leave it in the shop, but..." My voice trailed off.

"Your security is compromised. I heard the commotion."

I stared at him for a beat. "You could have helped."

One dark eyebrow lifted, a mocking gesture I wasn't in the mood for. "My favors don't come for free."

Of course not. That'd be too much to ask. "And the booze?"

He shrugged. "Not a favor. A gift."

"How kind of you. I'm sure there are no strings attached. At all."

Neit's eyes danced with amusement. "Not all gods are cruel, Evie."

I inclined my head. "Maybe." Cernunnos wasn't cruel. Not yet anyway.

"This place," Neit said with a sweeping hand gesture, "is a house made of dry wood. And you, my dear, are a spark. Eventually, you will burn too hot and turn this town to ash."

Goosebumps rose over my flesh. "You know nothing about me."

"I know your mother, and I know you are nothing like her."

Thank the gods for that.

"Cliona is aware of her power, and she squirrels it away, living in fear. You are a bright light in a dark world, and you have no idea how brightly you can burn."

Neit held out his hand. "Come, little wren. Allow me to transport you and this lovely vintage Scotch home."

I eyed his hand but made no move to take it.

Neit smiled again. "Smart girl. I promise you, nor this bottle, will come to any harm on our way."

I still didn't move. "And when we get there?"

He laughed. "You are safe from me this night."

It was the best I could get from him, and we both knew it. "And the bottle, too?"

His laughter, rich and warm, rang through the night. "I will protect the bottle with my life."

I slid my hand into his, power snaking up my arm—ancient, staggering power. He wrapped an arm around my waist, pulled me tight against his body, and shot straight into the air.

My stomach leapt to my throat, and a scream ripped from me. Neit's deep laughter in my ear made my body stiffen. I slapped his arm. "Warn a girl next time."

"Why? It's so much more fun this way." He took me high into the clouds, up and up and up until I shivered in his arms.

Neit pressed me tighter against his body, a spark of magic on his palms rising and flowing over us, warmth flowing from my head to my feet. I sighed at the languid heat soaking into my bones.

"So," I said after a beat of silence. "You and my mom, eh?"

Neit snorted. "Not quite like that, little wren. Courtship with the fae is quite different from humans'. We were not lovers, not in the carnal sense."

"I don't understand. Mom says you're her ex-boyfriend."

The god's arm tightened around my waist. "A simple explanation from your mother, and not quite true. We were betrothed for a time."

"Holy shit! You were going to be my stepdaddy?"

"Impertinent child," Neit growled, though he sounded more amused than angry.

"Daddy, can I have a car?" I snickered to myself.

"Definitely not like your mother."

I opened the wards to allow Neit passage. We touched down in the middle of the yard, and the god released me immediately. His eyes swept over the property until they landed on me once again, a thoughtful look on his face. "You keep your land wild but well-maintained."

"I'm a Floromancer. That's kind of our job."

"You are not only a Floromancer, but you know that already, don't you?"

I stayed silent.

His teeth flashed in the darkness. "Very well, little wren." Neit handed me the bottle. "Be careful with it. A little goes a long way."

"Thanks for the ride." I still didn't understand why he was being so nice, so I tilted my head and blurted out the question bugging me from the moment I saw him. "Mom says you're here to kill me. Is buttering me up part of your modus operandi or something?"

Neith's smile fell away. "Your mother is a cruel woman, Evangeline, though I'm sure you know this already. Our children suffer needlessly due to our mistakes."

"Will I suffer?"

He took a step back. "That is up to your mother, little wren."

Without another word, Neit shot into the sky, a bolt of brilliant energy lighting up the sky.

One more thing to worry about. Awesome.

CHAPTER
Twenty~Five

CAELAN

T he Council gathered tonight, here for a strategy meeting first and the wedding second. We'd gathered around the war room's table, a map of the Keep laid out before us. Security was always a pain in the ass on a daily basis, but the wedding had made it much more difficult.

Gianna's guest list had gotten out of control, the numbers ballooning from a manageable two hundred people all the way up to five hundred. I was familiar with twenty percent of the people she invited and didn't see the need for that many guests roaming my property, but Gianna pushed, and I'd reluctantly relented.

She was more political than me, savvy when it came to manipulating people for good or ill, so I allowed her mostly free rein on wedding decisions. Except when it came to Evie's flowers, and even then, I'd eventually caved.

"It's easy to smell weapons, so no need for metal detectors," Donovan said, pale blue eyes sweeping the room.

"Technology advances every day. Plastic is used in many weapons, so we won't always be able to tell if someone has a weapon based on smell alone." Thorvin tapped the southeast area of the map. "This could be a weak point in your security with that many guests on the property."

"Simone is already aware," I said.

Rowan sipped whiskey from a crystal glass, his eyes hooded. He hadn't said much today, his mood shitty after a run-in with Gianna. Later that day, he'd found me in my office, shut the door, and sank onto one of my good chairs and sighed louder and deeper than I'd ever heard coming from him. "Caelan?"

Concerned, I put my pen down and watched him warily. "Everything okay?"

He scrubbed a hand over his jaw and let out a bark of laughter. "That woman is a stone-cold bitch, Caelan."

Silence fell. I could have said a million appropriate things, but this was Rowan. "Yeah. I'm well aware."

Rowan snorted. "Is there any way out of this?"

The deal with the god had never left my thoughts from the moment I made it. "I have one desperate last-ditch plan up my sleeve."

Rowan's eyebrows lifted. "You aren't going to share with an old friend?"

"Plausible deniability, my friend."

Rowan whistled. "That bad?"

"That bad," I agreed.

The other Lord held his glass up, turning it so the light flashed in a prism. "For what it's worth, I'm sorry."

I waved his apologies away. "This is why we have a Council. So we can all make shitty decisions together."

Rowan exhaled. "We can fix this. Somewhat."

"We can't. Not if I wed Gianna. She might be good politically, but she is a nightmare."

"I can marry Evie."

The words dropped like bombs, but Rowan continued navigating the minefield. "I like Evie. She likes me. You know she's safest with me, Caelan. We don't have to have a traditional marriage. Evie would be free to be herself."

Magic rose in the air, my power rising to the surface.

Rowan snorted. "Don't let your emotions override your good

sense. Would you rather see that poor woman with Donovan? Fuck's sake, man. She'd eat him alive, and we'd have even more of a nightmare on our hands."

A surprised laugh escaped me. "She would, wouldn't she?"

"Absolutely. Maybe she'd just feed him to one of her man-eating plants."

We both laughed, the tension broken.

Bringing us back to the here and now. Rowan's good cheer had faded when Gianna interrupted the meeting a few hours earlier demanding to be included in the security plans. Donovan had relented, but none of us wanted her in here and we had denied her request.

Gianna was not popular around the Keep, a precursor of things to come.

My cell beeped. A quick glance down revealed a message from Evie.

Finn broke into the shop.

My heart became encased in ice.

I managed to get a few good licks in. Poison first.

A smile tugged at my mouth. *Good girl,* I thought.

Destroying that bouquet damaged him. He won't be up and about for a while.

Do you need me?

No. Only keeping you informed.

I'll send scouts out to see if we can find him.

Be careful.

"Everything alright?" Ethan asked.

"Fine. Security update from Simone." I put my cell face down. "Where were we?"

The doors slammed open. Every Lord shot up from their seat.

Three shifters stumbled into the room, the first being Lucas Velt.

"Lord." Lucas went to his knees, the other two right behind him. "We are…awake."

I wasn't sure what I was seeing. "Lucas? What happened?"

The shifters were all filthy and bruised, but none of them looked feral. Lucas' eyes were confused but clear.

Lucas bowed his head, his fists clenched atop his thighs. "We've been in a fog for months, Lord. I—I can't explain it. But tonight, something freed us. I don't know what or how, but I woke up. Normal." A soft, broken sob. His shoulders shook with shock and relief. "I don't know what happened, but something freed us."

"And the other two?" They were lower-level shifters, too young to have any real power, but dangerous, nonetheless. Feral wolves were deadly, mindless with hunger and rage.

"Same, Lord." Lucas lifted his eyes. "I hate to ask this, but have you heard from my bride?"

No one had seen Rebecca for weeks. "I'm sorry, Lucas." I knelt beside him and placed one hand on his shoulder. Power seeped into the younger wolf, healing the rest of his wounds. I scraped through his mind and found nothing damaged or off. Lucas was telling the truth.

Something had broken the grip on his mind and body.

My gaze went to my cell phone and the message she'd sent me.

Finn. The damage he took. The bouquet. And now my wolves returning home, free of whatever bondage that had contained them.

"There was a voice, Lord," Lucas said, licking his lips. "Inside all of our heads. All of a sudden it was gone, and we came straight home."

"Be welcome, Lucas. Rise. Simone will be here in a moment to escort you to guest rooms. Clean up, get some rest, and she'll have the kitchens bring dinner up."

Lucas and the others rose. I pressed a button under the table connected to Simone's phone before escorting them outside. Once I spotted my Omega hurrying around the corner, I left them with the assurance I'd see them in the morning.

No matter how fortuitous and timely Lucas and the other

shifters' arrival was something wasn't sitting right with me about the situation. I didn't believe in coincidence, and that text from Evie had me wondering how she or Finn played into my rogue shifters returning home.

Tension had settled over the room when I walked back in. I grinned. "It looks like the issue of the rogue shifters is solved."

Donovan's cheeks flushed, his elaborate plans to seek dominion over my territory in its death throes. Rowan had perked up some, hiding a grin poorly behind his Scotch glass.

"We'll need time to investigate," Donovan said. "Your people might be home, but it doesn't mean the threat is over."

"And will the investigation take enough time for me to be married before it's done?" I said, my voice soft and deadly.

Donovan cleared his throat. "There's no way to tell how long it might take us."

Thorvin snorted. "He's not wrong, Caelan. We have to perform due diligence."

Rowan rolled his eyes. Ethan sighed, and Soren, who'd been suspiciously quiet, stared at Donovan like he wanted to murder the guy where he sat.

I stifled a laugh. "We will keep these developments to ourselves. Is that clear?"

Nods all around, Donovan's reluctant.

"We'll convene later to address the wedding security. You may stay the night in the Keep if you wish, but now that Council emergency authority is rescinded due to new developments—" I eyed Donovan, allowing a hum of power to shine in my eyes, "I expect you to vacate the Keep no later than ten tomorrow morning. Understood?"

"Crystal clear, Caelan," Soren said. "I have a date tonight. If it goes well, I won't be back." He wiggled his eyebrows and was the first to leave.

Ethan clapped me on the back. "I'll stay as long as your chef plans to put out more of that breakfast quiche." He kissed his fingers. "It's glorious."

"She does the quiche every weekend. It's Simone's favorite, too."

Ethan's eyes gleamed. "Is it now?"

Interesting. "That and the plum sangria on Saturday's."

"Thanks for the intel, Caelan. I'll see you in the morning."

"Best of luck, you poor bastard." Simone was notoriously difficult to get to know and even harder to get to agree to a date.

Ethan's hearty laugh made me smile. We didn't always get along, but when we did, I wondered whether, if it weren't for our positions, we might all be friends.

Donovan slunk out without saying goodbye. I sent Simone a quick text, telling her to put a man on the Lord for the night. He was way too invested in Gianna's success and my perceived failure for me to trust him.

Twenty-Six

CAELAN — A FEW WEEKS LATER

All attempts to find Finn turned out to be futile, and Donovan's "investigation" proceeded in exactly the way I thought it would—slow and full of barricades. My wedding fast approached and with it, a gray cloud of dread hanging over the Keep.

Bucking the established power of the Council to release myself from this farce of a wedding would cripple me and my people. Without their support, we'd be considered a rogue establishment, open to attack by every other territory in the country.

As much as I disliked my current situation, the Council and its Lords had me by the balls.

Rowan's suggestion of marriage niggled at the back of my mind, but every time I thought about it, I dismissed the option. Evie wouldn't marry anyone she didn't want to, and she was dangerous and volatile enough to destroy anyone who tried to force her. Never before had I let something or someone like her stay inside my territory boundaries. In the past, I would have thrown them out with little fanfare, but everyone knew I had a soft spot for the little violent Floromancer.

Time would tell if she became my downfall or my saving grace.

I hadn't heard from Evie since her update on Finn, and the more time I had to think about things, the more I had to assume the deadly Chimera and the man obsessed with the Floromancer were one and the same.

The question was, why did he want Evie so much? Was he as fascinated by her as I was or did he want her for other, more nefarious means? But more importantly, were there other Chimeras in my territory?

If there were, I'd have to handle them with extreme prejudice and exterminate them with no mercy.

The bonding ceremony was still on, Gianna self-assured of the god's blessings and her future place in my Keep. But she walked around with a new, odd stiffness in her posture, and she didn't throw as many barbs as before. Strange but I wasn't complaining.

I hadn't heard from the one I'd bargained with, but I felt confident the god would show up and throw the entire ceremony into disarray. What kind of disarray was still up in the air.

A message came through, and my heart stopped for a brief second when I saw it was Evie. But her message was short and to the point.

Bonding arrangement samples are on the way to the Keep via courier. Send me back the number you like, and I'll get to work on it. The others are almost finished. Warmest blessings on your upcoming nuptials.

My lips pulled back from my teeth at that last sentence.

Thank you for the update, flower girl. Any more signs of Finn?

None. With the bouquet gone, Finn should have no more access to the shop or my property.

We're still looking for him. Be careful.

Will do.

The office door burst open, revealing a travel weary, haggard Garrett. I hadn't seen the man in weeks once I'd sent him off to track down Halvard. Garrett might be a mean sonofabitch, but he was my friend and the best tracker in the entire country. His presence here today with no warning of his return did not bode well for Halvard's fate.

I gestured for him to sit and took a bottle of Scotch and two glasses from the tray by my desk. Without a word, I poured us both two stiff portions and pushed one over to him.

"He's dead, isn't he?"

Garrett drained the glass in a single swallow. I poured him another.

"Yes, Lord. Most assuredly so."

Something else had been tugging at my brain for a while now about Halvard and his link to Evie. "Any strange magic around the body?"

Garrett's fingers trembled. He drained the second portion. "Yes." His jaw tightened. "I've only seen this magic once before, many years ago when traveling through Europe."

Then Garrett said the words I'd been dreading for weeks now.

"I believe we have a Chimera in our midst."

CHAPTER
Twenty~Seven

"Those are hideous," Moira breathed.

Everyone stood gathered around the work table as I put the finishing touches on the last round of centerpieces and bouquets for the Shifter Lord's upcoming nuptials. Moira was right. They were hideous.

"They look like Christmas threw up all over an evergreen forest," Tess said.

"This is a candy cane hellscape," Ash added helpfully. "You're sure this is what his bride wants?"

"Confirmed multiple times," I said, an aggrieved note in my voice.

"What are her bridesmaid colors?" Moira asked.

It took me a beat to even say the words. "Navy."

Three equally horrified gasps rang through the room. "No," Moira breathed.

"I'm surprised you didn't fall into a dead faint when she told you," Ash said.

"Sometimes even pretty people have zero taste," Tess added.

"Not my wedding, not my monkeys." Those words were the mantra I was living by these days. "Caelan is paying us a small fortune to get this done."

"Even if the wedding doesn't happen?" Moira asked. "Because I would definitely second guess someone who thought this aesthetic gave off any other vibes than angry Santa Claus."

"Even if it doesn't happen," I said. "The bonding ceremony will determine whether the wedding continues, but even that should go off without a hitch. Rarely do the gods spurn a Lord's match."

Moira put her hand on my shoulder. "I'm sorry, Evie."

I put my hand over hers. "Not like I could have had a relationship with him anyway. If Caelan ever finds out what I am, he'll be forced to put me down."

"There are ways around everything," Ash said. "You haven't turned into an evil, slavering mess, so there's hope for you yet."

I snorted. "Thanks, I think."

"Ash is right," Moira interjected. "You've had some weird magical blips, but you seem the same old Evie to us."

I stopped twisting a bit of wire and glanced up. "Did you expect something different?"

No one said a word. "Guys?"

"Umm," Tess said. "Finn is a dick, and we wondered if that was because he was a Chimera...or if he was just a dick."

Ash let out a scandalized gasp. "Tess!"

Moira's eyes widened before a delighted giggle slipped from her lips. "I knew we'd finally bring her down to our level!"

"Probably just a dick," I said. "I'm hungrier than usual, especially after a shift, but other than that, I feel the same."

It was the truth and yet, not the entire truth. The Chimera magic had boosted my Floromancy gifts and now I had to use a delicate hand when I worked on anything in the shop or greenhouse. After an incident where a pothos vine punched right through one of the shop windows, I had to spend a lot of time practicing before I could work on any plant life without altering it on a fundamental level.

I'd gotten the hang of it, but things were dicey for a week or two.

Everything was unusually quiet. Around town, the shop, and in my life. No chaos. No Finn. No threats of rogue shifters, and no gods. Naturally, that made me nervous as a cat landing on tin foil. When would the other shoe drop? And once it did, would all the fallout be on my shoulders?

"What about the bonding ceremony arrangement?" Moira asked.

I held up a finger and reached under the work table. This one was my pride and joy. To avoid giving Gianna the middle finger on her wedding day, I stayed somewhat within the boundaries of the red and white theme, but I'd used peonies and Matsubara Red apricot blossoms, along with crimson dahlias, and a few artfully placed vanilla orchid blooms. For the final touch, I added delicate crystal beads and handmade glass berries throughout the arrangements to give it a sparkling and elegant appearance, along with a few thin bonsai branches selected by Ash.

The end result was a centerpiece that looked modern but also like a piece of art.

"Oooh," Tess breathed.

Moira sucked in a breath. "Evie. This is beautiful."

"Gorgeous," Ash murmured. "Gianna is a fool."

"The pièce de résistance," I said, triggering a button at the centerpiece's base.

A warm golden light encased the centerpiece as edible crimson and white glitter shot up from the middle, appearing and disappearing in an endless cycle.

"This is astonishing," Moira said. "How is the glitter doing that?"

I wiggled my fingers. "Magic."

"The Shifter Lord will love it," Tess said firmly.

I hadn't told the Lord everything about the piece. He'd seen the floral part, minus the crystals and glass berries, but I neglected to mention the lights and glitter.

"If the wedding isn't blessed, I won't trigger the glitter or lights." The device was activated by a tiny remote control I could hide in the palm of my hand.

"Good call," Moira said, "but I doubt Caelan will have that problem. The man was born blessed by the gods."

Maybe in other areas, but from the way he talked about the ceremony, I had my doubts about this one.

"Either way, I'm proud of this."

"We're going to be rich!" Ash exclaimed. "Especially when everyone books you once they see this piece."

Moira grimaced. "As long as they ignore everything else."

I laughed. "Even so, the cost of the wedding will sustain us for a long time, if need be."

"Caelan's checkbook must be on fire these days." Moira grinned.

Wasn't that the truth. I'd told her about Caelan's attack and the resulting damage to the house. True to his word, he'd sent over a more than generous check that covered the damage and then some, along with a recommendation for a dryad woodworker who worked as a contractor for people like me.

I'd called him over, told him what I wanted, then hired him on the spot because he knew exactly what I wanted and how to do the work.

"Good for us," was all I said. "He's good for it."

Despite my mixed feelings on the upcoming wedding, the Shifter Lord had been good for business, and once we'd announced our shop was the florist, our foot traffic had exploded, forcing us to implement new store hours and be much more diligent about our calendar.

Little Shop of Florals was booked months in advance.

Things were looking up.

"Don't forget we're closed tomorrow. I'll be out of pocket for most of the day, though I don't plan to stay for the reception." My contract required me to be on hand for the bonding ceremony and the exchange of vows to keep everything running smoothly. But once those were over, I planned to hightail it out of there ASAP.

Moira grimaced. "Gianna is a bitch for making you stay," she grumbled.

I shook my head. "I appreciate it, but we all know having the florist there is common. I plan to keep to the background as much as possible."

"Good luck with that," Ash murmured, an amused glimmer in his mossy green eyes.

"Away with you," I said, flicking my fingers at all of them.

Ash laughed and tugged on Tess's arm. Moira lingered behind. When everyone was gone, she leaned forward. "How are you doing? The truth this time."

Grief tugged at my heart. "Even if I wanted something, I can't have it with him. It's too dangerous. He's intelligent enough to put things together. The further away from him I am, the better for us all."

Her mouth turned down in a frown. "He might surprise you, you know."

Caelan surprised me all the time, and not always in a good way. "Nothing good will come from him realizing what I am."

"Maybe not at first. But don't count Caelan out."

I reached for her hand as she turned to leave. "Moira. You have to realize in twenty-four hours Caelan will be married. I've already acted like an asshat every time I've gone to the Keep. I can't keep seeing him. I'll screw up and I don't want to be the kind of woman who comes in between a husband and wife. I've already toed the line too much."

Moira's eyes filled with sadness. She squeezed my fingers. "I understand. But things have a way of working out. Maybe not on the timelines we want them to, but they do."

"I love you, vamp."

"I love you too, monster."

Moira trailed out of the back room, leaving me alone with my thoughts.

Tomorrow, I would watch the Shifter Lord marry, and I vowed not to do a thing about it.

I should have never gotten involved with him in the first place. Perhaps this was my karma to bear.

230

CHAPTER

Twenty~Eight

I t had cost me an arm and a leg even without the rush fee, but the gown I'd ordered from Caelan's tailor was at my doorstep when I arrived home later that evening. Gasping with delight, I snatched up the box and went inside, excited to see what she'd come up with.

I'd given her my measurements, told her why I wanted it, and given her free rein to come up with an appropriate ensemble. The dress lay encased in a mountain of navy tissue paper. With trembling fingers, I pushed the paper aside to reveal an emerald green dress, cut in a sharp A-line, embroidered with a belt of multi-colored flowers. The bodice was off shoulder, with short cap sleeves. Magic hummed from the satin fabric, but most of it came from the embroidery.

I ran my fingers over the belt, smiling as I felt multiple types of flowers sleeping inside the stitched pistils. The dress would show-case who I was and would also serve as appropriate attire for a formal wedding without upstaging the bride.

I slipped off my clothing and tried the dress on, marveling at the fit and how flattering it was on my body. Nude high heels completed the look.

Once I was dressed in normal clothing again, I carefully hung

231

the dress up, keeping it in the cedar lined part of my closet. Not that there were bugs inside the house. I scanned every few days for any rogue strays and gently ushered them out when I found them. But better safe than sorry.

After I fixed a quick dinner and poured myself a tiny bit of the Scotch Neit had given me, I brought my laptop over to the couch and went through the checklist for tomorrow one more time. The courier to help us transport everything was confirmed, and my van was all gassed up and ready to go. I'd put all the flowers and arrangements back into the walk-in, but I'd taken Caelan's boutonniere home with me because I had one more tweak to make.

As much as it pained me to force him to wear the candy cane colors of his wedding, I sucked it up and created him something with dark blue delphinium flowers and privet berries, along with the same blossoms I'd used in the bonding ceremony. Different, but still matching the bride and bridesmaids.

But when the ceremony and reception was over, I'd planned for the boutonniere to collapse into ash, the final link between us severed. The bonding ceremony arrangement would do the same. Those were the two pieces of Caelan's wedding that held the most of me. The other arrangements were just that…arrangements with no soul and no fire.

This wedding would definitively cut the bindings between us.

After tomorrow, we would no longer be Evie and Caelan.

He would be the Shifter Lord once more, and I would be the Floromancer who worked in town.

A knock on the door startled me.

With a curse, I slid everything off my lap and hurried to the door.

Simone, Caelan's Omega, stood there. I stared through the peephole for an astonished moment before remembering I'd added her to my wards. Once upon a time, I thought we might be friends.

Then Caelan announced his nuptials, and our relationship had turned downright chilly, and I'm still not sure how it happened.

I opened the door and stared at her.

Simone had the grace to look uncomfortable. "Evie."

"Simone."

If she expected me to fling open the doors and invite her in for a girl's night, she was sorely mistaken. When I said nothing else, Simone let out an annoyed breath.

"I had to," she snapped.

"Had to what?"

Simone's delicate nostrils flared. "Will you stop being an ass and invite me in? I can smell the wine on your breath."

"Why should I?"

Her eyes narrowed. "I don't grovel."

"I'm not expecting you to grovel."

"Fine. I'm sorry."

I grinned. "Sorry for what?"

"I swear. How Caelan tolerates you is one of the world's greatest mysteries."

"I am a mysterious person," I agreed.

Simone's nails tapped on the back of her iPad case. "I'm sorry for ghosting you. Things have been…difficult in the Keep since Gianna arrived."

I opened the door. "I might have some extra wine."

"Thank the gods," Simone breathed as she breezed past me.

It wasn't until after a few glasses of wine that Simone brought up the reason she came by. Part of the reason was the flowers, but part of it was something more.

"There's something off about her," Simone said, her eyes focused on the old coffee table I used to replace the broken one.

"Off how?"

Our eyes met. "She's always been cold, even when I knew her from a few years ago. But she's never been such a…"

"Bitch?" I supplied.

Simone snorted. "Yes, but she's also borderline cruel, too. I'm worried about what might happen if she becomes the Lady."

"Is there any way you can stop it?" I plucked an olive off the small snack board I'd made after she'd arrived.

"Not if I want to keep my job," she muttered gloomily.

"Then this is a venting session?"

She shifted and took a long sip of her wine. "There's someone else who could stop it, though."

"Like the Council?" They were the ones who put the order in place. Surely they were the ones who could halt the entire thing. But there were people flying in from all over, some who'd already arrived. If they had any plans to put a stop to this madness, they'd better do it soon.

"Not quite," Simone murmured, picking up another cracker to munch.

I stared at her for a long moment before starting to laugh. "You cannot mean me. Are you insane?"

"I'm going to tell you something that can go no further than this couch. Do you understand?"

I straightened, my stomach twisting in knots. "Yes."

"I'm serious. My job and my life will be on the line if you repeat this."

"Understood. I'm a vault."

"The Council has concerns about your power levels. They want you to sign a contract with them—"

"What?" I blurted. "I've never had any trouble until your Shifter Lord came into my life!"

Her look was quelling. "Or," she continued, "you marry a Lord of their choosing."

The air went out of me. I gaped at her. "Excuse me?" I wheezed. "They want me to marry one of *them*? That's ludicrous." The thought of marrying any of them set my teeth on edge. We lived in America, for crying out loud!

She lifted a delicate shoulder. "Not in terms of strategy. If you marry one of the Lords, you'll fall under Council rules. They'll be able to bring your power to heel."

"The hell they will," I grumbled. But I wondered why they wouldn't have forced Caelan on me if they wanted to bring me to heel.

Simone saw the question on my face. "Caelan is the most powerful Lord in the country, even if no one on the Council wants to admit it. They're afraid of what might happen if you and he get together."

"Got it. Not only do they not want me to ally with Caelan, they want me out of his territory, too." Damn. I thought it was bad getting picked last for group sports in school, but this was way worse.

Simone nodded. "And I suspect they don't know the half of your power, do they?"

That wasn't something I'd divulge to anyone but the three people in my shop. I gave her a tight smile that made her laugh.

"How long do I have before they try to strong arm me?"

Simone's mouth tightened with sympathy. "They're leaning more toward forcing a marriage than a contract."

I closed my eyes. "To whom?"

"Rowan has offered."

My eyes flew open. "Rowan…"

Something flickered in Simone's eyes. "A good choice, though Ethan has his moments, too."

"I'd consider Rowan a friend as much as I'd consider any Lord one," I admitted. "But I refuse to be forced into a marriage I don't want. We are not living in the Dark Ages."

"We are living in the time where the Council holds power over the entire country," Simone murmured. "What will you do if they revoke your stay here? You won't be allowed to move to any of the other states."

"What a bunch of bastards," I hissed. "Maybe Europe could use a good Floromancer and her team. It's been a while since we've had an overseas adventure."

"You'd run into the same problem soon enough. Maybe right away if word of your shenanigans has made its way over there."

"I'm going to stop refilling your wine glass if you don't stop being so negative."

Simone snatched the bottle. "Try and die."

My eyes narrowed. "Did you sneak out of the Keep?"

A guilty look stole over her face. "Gianna is everywhere these days. I've been trying to sneak out for weeks. But tomorrow's the wedding and she has tons of things left to do." Her smile held a slight touch of evil.

"Hypothetically, how do you think I could stop the wedding? Not that I want to." Lies. "But, if you think Gianna is so bad, maybe it's the right path?"

Simone shrugged. "Do what you do so well?"

I gave her a flat look. "And what's that?"

"Sow chaos and calamity?"

"Ha." I poured myself a glass of wine. "That will only temporarily delay the inevitable."

"A delay is a delay," Simone sang.

I broached a delicate subject. "What about the bonding ceremony?"

Her face paled. "Don't do anything to disrupt that." A delicate shudder rolled over her small frame. "None of us wish to anger the gods."

"I wouldn't do that," I said as I gave her the side-eye. "A little worrisome you think I'm that destructive, though. What I'm saying is what if the gods don't bless the wedding?"

Simone went still for a long moment before she carefully set her wineglass down. "And why would that be on the options list?"

I blinked at her. "Um. Because the gods are fickle and unpredictable?"

"Uh huh. And why does it sound like you have personal experience with them?"

"Err."

She closed her eyes and pinched the space between her eyebrows. "Right. Is there something you need to tell me?"

"What? No! I don't make deals with gods. That's crazy pants."

She let out a sigh of relief. "Thank the gods. There have only been a couple of times where the gods refused a union, but both times, the couple was terribly wrong for each other. Gianna, as much as I hate to say it, has the necessary pedigree and bloodline. She's politically savvy and ruthless. On paper, Caelan could do a lot worse."

"Then there's no reason for the gods to rebuff them."

"Right. Unless they know something we don't."

"It's possible." We ate and drank a little more before Simone rose, clutching her ever trusty device to her chest. "It was worth a shot, I guess. But if you decide to cause a shitshow at the wedding, maybe give a girl a little advanced warning?"

I sucked my teeth. "Sorry. Shenanigans are rarely planned, but I'll do my best."

Simone rolled her eyes. "See you tomorrow."

I waved. "If any of the Lords propose tomorrow, I'll be sure to let you know."

She laughed and headed out the door but stopped before she went out. "Evie?"

"Hmm?"

"I thought you should know that Caelan has never once planned a party or any event at the keep where flowers were involved until the day I dragged him into your shop." Her smile was sad. "Every other time was at his suggestion." She left before I could respond, plunging the house into silence.

I sat there for a long time pondering tomorrow and her words and wondering how Caelan's marriage might affect my life. But I'd be damned if I let the Council swoop in and try to dictate who I decided to marry, if I ever married.

On that note, I cleaned up the dirty dishes and headed to bed. I had a long day tomorrow.

CHAPTER
Twenty~Nine

We stood in a circle around a small, sparsely decorated table, the bonding floral arrangement in the center. A somber air had fallen in the Keep's chapel, the atmosphere tense and watchful. Caelan stood beside Gianna, his form powerful and sleek in a black tuxedo, the boutonniere I'd made him on his lapel. His jaw was tight and his eyes haunted. We'd locked eyes once on our way into the chapel, and I don't think I'd ever unsee the burning power in his gaze. We did not speak even though I had a million things I wanted to say, knowing I could let none of those words pass my lips. A sense of profound loss weighed on my shoulders as I stood there, watching Caelan marry another, but to say anything out of turn could ruin me, and as a way of collateral, everyone else I cared about, too.

Gianna wore a bright white gown with a startling thread of crimson on the bodice. She looked cold yet resplendent in her wedding finery, though there was a touch of exhaustion on her features I'd never seen before. Her lips were pinched tight together and her knuckles white around her bouquet.

Caelan had made the decision to only allow the Council and a few favored guests to view the bonding ceremony. Everyone else waited in the separate area of the chapel where most of the wedding ceremonies took place. This was a smaller room, one with stained glass windows and a pulpit for services—a warm and comforting place. Or it would be if we weren't standing around like we were lined up for a firing squad.

My skin itched. Weddings were supposed to be joyous times of celebration. Not this tense and terse affair.

"Are we ready to begin?" Hazel asked from right beside me.

The witch had left home for Scotland two weeks ago but had flown back for the wedding after Caelan had personally requested her presence. If I didn't know better, I'd say she had a soft spot for the Lord.

She was dressed in traditional robes denoting the type of witch she was, her wild strawberry hair tamed into a neat braid. Her face was devoid of makeup, and she wore no jewelry. Ceremonies like this required the witch to come in supplication to the gods the way they came into the world. Devoid of ornamentation and humble.

At Caelan's and Gianna's nods, the two clasped hands. I ignored the clench of my stomach and kept my expression neutral.

Hazel's words swept over the small chapel, a strange wind rustling our hair as she invoked the gods, inviting one to come forward and offer their blessing. A moment later, I smelled ice and wind, and a rush of cold air blew over my shoulder before it stopped abruptly, all the magic in the air sucked out like it had never been there. I glanced up to see Hazel's pinched mouth and a furrow between her brows. She cleared her throat. "Perhaps I should try again."

Gianna shifted uncomfortably, her face pale and wan.

What was going on? There was no blessing, and whatever presence had started to come in had abruptly left. From Hazel's expression, that was not the way it was supposed to happen.

The smell of ancient forests and glens roared through the

room, extinguishing all the candles. "No need, witch," a familiar voice said.

Oh no. I almost turned around before a tight grip on my hand reminded me to stay still. Hazel.

Cernunnos, king of the fae, came into my line of sight. Hazel and everyone else sucked in a shocked breath. I gave him a raised eyebrow look. Cernunnos winked and sauntered up to the altar. He reached out with a bronzed finger and touched the petal of the apricot blossom.

"Stunning," he murmured.

Had the fae king purposely shoved another god out of the way to be here?

Surely not.

That would be madness.

Right?

The king turned his attention to Caelan. "Your florist is immensely talented and powerful. You must give me her name."

I choked on a cough.

Caelan's forehead wrinkled. "Uh. Certainly. But she's standing right beside you."

Wicked humor glinted in his eyes as he turned back to me. He inclined his head, sharp antlers glowing with bioluminescent moss.

"Are you enjoying yourself?" I hissed in a whisper as I bowed to the king.

"Very much so," he responded.

When I rose, Cernunnos held his palm out, forcing me to place my hand in his. Power snapped against my skin. "It is rare when someone can manage to bring out nature's true, raw beauty. You have unparalleled talent. I would be honored to host you in my halls one day."

I blinked at him.

Go with it, his voice echoed in my mind.

"Um." I licked my lips, shoving down the hysterical laugh threatening to bubble over. "It would be my honor, sire."

Do not interfere in what happens next, Evangeline.

I stiffened, the words making my worst fears come true, even as a sliver of hope slid through my heart. Why?

It is between me and your Lord.

He is not my Lord. Who knew a mental voice could sound so salty?

"I will be in touch," Cernunnos said before he turned his attention back to Gianna and Caelan.

Cernunnos. Don't do this.

They are not meant to be.

It doesn't mean they shouldn't marry.

Cernunnos stilled and glanced behind him. *Do you want this Lord to marry this creature?*

I almost laughed at his description of Gianna. *I want him to be happy. That's all.*

And you believe he'd be happy with her?

I didn't say that.

His ancient stare burned into my heart before he turned once more.

You will thank me for this one day.

He overestimated my ability to be grateful for taking my choices out of my hands.

"You are the seekers of my blessing?" Cernunnos asked.

Gianna's face had lit up at Cernunnos' presence. The physical manifestation of a god had never been documented at such an occasion, so this was already one for the books.

Caelan bowed. "We are. Your presence in my domain gives me the highest honor."

Cernunnos didn't acknowledge Caelan's words. His attention went to Gianna. "How long have you been pretending?"

Gianna froze. "Sire?"

The smile he gave her held barely leashed violence. "You cannot fool a god."

Gianna's pleasure upon seeing the god slid off her face like melting wax. Her eyes went cold, but Cernunnos appeared to be done with her.

Confusion flashed over Caelan's face as he watched the byplay between them. He opened his mouth to speak, but Cernunnos interrupted.

"Ancient traditions dictate the gods' blessing on certain occasions. A celebration like today is cause for joy and wonder, but I see none of that before me. The Lords sit in their pews like they are above our law, waiting for this woman to bring about your downfall."

I closed my eyes for a brief moment, knowing somehow even though Cernunnos was going totally rogue and I had no control of what a god decides to do, that somehow, I'd be blamed for this going awry.

The Lords in question shifted uncomfortably. All except for Rowan who was watching this with unfettered delight on his face.

I bit back my smile.

"All except for one who honors you with his loyalty and friendship."

Rowan blinked in surprise, awe overtaking the amusement.

Cernunnos continued. "Love might be considered a tradeable commodity in your world, but I believe in a union blessed by a joining of two compatible hearts. Your bride has misrepresented herself to you and your Council, and you, Lord Caelan, have hidden the deepest truths of your heart in order to perform your duty as someone else has dictated it be done."

Caelan paled.

Cernunnos turned to the Lords, his ancient gaze sweeping over them. All sat in awe of the god, except for Donovan whose forehead was beaded with sweat. "As of today, any practice of forcible marriage is banned in this country. Any law of your Council attempting to enforce such is hereby deemed illegal."

Hazel's grip tightened as my knees threatened to collapse from under me.

What was happening right now?

Rowan's eyes were suspiciously wet. If only he and I weren't such good friends, I might have pursued him. He was a good man with a good heart and how he'd landed on the Council…

But Cernunnos wasn't done. He returned his attention to the couple.

"You will not receive my blessing today, young Lord. Whether you decide to move forward with your wedding is up to you, though I would urge you to think long and hard about the secrets you hold in your heart before taking such action. Some things aren't meant to happen right away and will require a long, difficult fight." Cernunnos' gaze flicked to me for a brief moment. "But sometimes those fights are worth it."

Gianna's lips curled with fury.

"Return to whence you came from, Gianna. I daresay you won't be welcome in this Keep very soon."

If I could sink into the floor, I would. My hands were gripped in tight fists, slick with fear. I was waiting for Gianna to lunge across the table and try to claw my eyes out, but she stayed frozen, her eyes blazing with rage.

Cernunnos turned to me. "Nice dress."

And with another wink, he was gone, golden oak leaves falling from the sky in the wake of his presence.

No one said a word for a long moment.

"Is it too soon to ask if there's a refund policy?" Rowan asked, breaking the thick tension.

Caelan snorted.

Gianna turned on her heels and stormed from the chapel.

Hazel finally dropped my hand and leaned in. "Is there anything you want to tell me?" she whispered.

I shook my head frantically.

"Liar." She sighed. "I have a flight out in a few hours. Be very careful over the next few weeks," Hazel murmured. "You've got a target on your back."

Nothing new there.

I hugged the witch, and she hurried from the room, tossing her robes off to reveal a sleek magenta pantsuit.

Sassy.

A warm grip around my upper arm turned me, and I found myself facing Rowan. "I'm here to escort you out," he whispered. "A lot of the Lords are furious."

"Take me to the restrooms so I can get out of this dress."

Rowan's eyes glittered. "Is that an invitation? We might be friends, but I'm not blind."

I slapped his arm. "No. My clothes don't go with me when I use my other form. The fastest way I can get home is to fly."

He shook his head and led me out the door. I didn't dare turn to look at Caelan. "Not a chance. If Caelan catches me holding your dress and lacy underthings, I won't make it out of this Keep alive."

"Ass," I groused.

"An ass who likes to live. I'll drive you home. No one will accost a Lord."

"Evie." Caelan's voice came from behind.

Rowan stilled.

"Keep walking," I demanded.

He hesitated.

"I'm going to drop my panties right on your fancy shoes and fly away if you don't keep moving."

Rowan kept walking.

"Evie!"

"Walk faster."

A minute later, we were in Rowan's car flying down the road.

CHAPTER

Thirty

CAELAN

My territory was officially Gianna free, though I still didn't know what the price would be.

I sat in my office stroking the back of Seymour's main trap, the plant brushing against me like a cat.

The ashes of my boutonniere lay on the desk before me, a last fuck you from Evie.

Cernunnos' presence at my wedding had stunned me to speechlessness, but it was his familiarity with Evie that bothered me more than the spectacular failure of the bonding ceremony.

And what had he meant by Gianna pretending?

I pressed my hands against my eyes and groaned. Gianna hadn't waited for me to kick her out. She hadn't even bothered to gather her clothing. The woman had called a car and hightailed it from the Keep within a half hour after Cernunnos' rejection of our union. Every other guest had slowly left after heatedly gossiping in the main chapel for hours afterward.

Even the Lords had retreated, Cernunnos' warning no doubt still ringing in their ears.

My territory was safe once again, but my victory felt false.

A single oak leaf floated from the ceiling to land before me.

I stilled, searching for the scent of rising magic, but there was nothing except for the glittering leaf.

A few words were burned across the middle.

Payment is deferred. For now.

Dread pooled in my stomach, the unknown future looming ahead of me once again fraught with peril.

But the worst part of everything?

I still didn't have Evie.

The knock on my door wasn't unexpected, but I hid the leaf in my top desk drawer anyway to avoid questions.

"Enter."

Ben walked in, eyes wary. Our relationship hadn't been the same for a while, but I hoped to repair it over time.

"Please have a seat."

The Healer sat down and said nothing.

I never had to tiptoe around subjects with Ben, so I laid out my plans.

"Halvar is dead. I'd like you to take his position."

The only reaction was a slight rise of his eyebrows. "Leaving you free to pursue Evie."

"Pursuing Evie and actually getting Evie are two wildly different things. As I'm sure you know."

Ben sighed and crossed his arms. "I accept the position."

I opened my mouth to argue with him until his words sank in. Having expected him to argue with me, I'd come up with a large list of counterarguments. My mouth closed, and I studied him warily.

"Evie is dangerous, Caelan."

"One of the many reasons she appeals to me."

He scoffed. "You would take that like some kind of positive challenge, wouldn't you?" Ben scrubbed a hand through his hair. "No. I mean she's keeping secrets that are going to get us all killed. She's fae, man. And you know how fickle those creatures can be."

I'd seen zero evidence of Evie ever being fickle. Reticent, deliciously violent, even unhinged at times. Never fickle. She'd protect those she loved even if it cost her life.

"I'd argue the woman I almost had to marry was worse."

Ben cracked a laugh, the first thawing I'd see from him in weeks. "Where is the ice queen, anyway?"

"Fuck if I know. Not here. That's enough for me."

"When do I leave?"

"As soon as you want to. Halvard's territory will hold for now."

"I'll be gone in three days." Ben rose. "I'm serious, Caelan. Be careful with Evie."

I would do nothing of the sort. "Thanks for the warning."

Ben walked out without another word.

Beside me, Seymour let out a sad little whine.

"I know, buddy," I said quietly.

Seymour thumped his pot closer and clamped onto my sleeve.

Epilogue

Rowan had left after a cup of hot chocolate and a tour of my greenhouse.

With Hazel gone and everyone else off for the day, I basked in the silence and feeling of freedom.

But when oak leaves began falling from the sky, I knew my peace wouldn't last. I poured two cups of hot cocoa, topped them both with whipped cream, and turned to see Cernunnos in my living room, his bare feet propped on the old coffee table. He was staring down at the damaged floor.

"I can fix that for you."

A surprised laugh bubbled from me. "Sure, but I'm already under contract with a dryad. They take those very seriously."

Cernunnos waved a hand. "I've already cleared it with him."

I set the mug down on the table beside him. "Of course you have."

"Sit with me awhile," he said. "I'm tired."

I took the chair opposite him. Cernunnos picked up his mug and took a hesitant sip.

"What is this?" he demanded.

"Hot cocoa. You've never had it?"

"No. It's delicious."

A smile tugged at my mouth. "It's popular during the colder months."

"I see why."

We fell into a comfortable silence. Cernunnos didn't speak again until he finished his cocoa. He rose and gestured with his massive antlers. "There is something you must see."

"Do I need a jacket?"

"Not with me."

Curious but unafraid, I followed Cernunnos outside. He led me through my property until we stood close to the boundary at the very back. A mound of freshly disturbed dirt in an oblong shape lay before us.

A sickening feeling crept up my throat. "Is that what I think it is?"

"Trouble comes your way once more, Evangeline. Be prepared."

"From the Chimera?"

"From everywhere," Cernunnos said.

"That is surprisingly unhelpful," I muttered. "Why do you continue to help me?" A terrifying thought had come to mind after the wedding, but I'd squashed it down, refusing to believe it might be true.

"I'm afraid my capacity for assistance is limited in many ways due to my...role in the fae kingdom. But certain things, like your Lord's wedding, do not fall under fae purview."

"Even though not giving your blessing can cause a wedding and long-standing political clout to crumble into dust?"

Cernunnos chuckled. "The fae love their loopholes, my dear."

He lifted a hand, glowing power at the edge of his palm.

"Wait," I blurted.

Cernunnos stilled, his eyes burning. "Ask your question, Evangeline."

I licked my lips, my heart pounding against my ribs. "Are—are you my father?" If he was, it would change everything. About me. My power. My life. Everything.

Cernunnos' power rumbled the earth, disturbing the fresh mound. Pale skin was revealed, along with a tangle of cool blonde hair.

"She's been dead for at least two weeks."

I sucked in a shocked breath as Gianna's corpse came into view, her skin stretched against the bone due to decomposition.

"Impossible. The wedding was—" My words cut off. "Finn," I snarled.

But Cernunnos shook his head. "Not Finn. Not this time. The Chimeras rise once again, Evangeline, and your world is under threat."

"You didn't answer my question."

Cernunnos' eyes glowed with power. The sky opened, revealing a wide swath of pale, ghostly riders, glowing with warm fae light. "The ride awaits. I will return."

"Cernunnos!"

Lightning cracked through the sky. "It is not time to answer that question. The truth will be revealed soon." His eyes glowed with unholy power as he rose into the sky. "Until we meet again, Evangeline. Beware the man with too many teeth."

"Um. Okay?"

Cernunnos winked and disappeared, the sky closing, revealing a clear night sky, no evidence of the god's presence anywhere.

My shoulders slumped.

Can't a hybrid, shapeshifting florist ever catch a break?

Also by S.E. Babin

Shifter Lords

Shift of Heart

Shift of Morals

Power Shift

Shifting Winds

Shifting Resolve

Shift of Rule

Shift of the Wild

OTHER SERIES

A Shelf Indulgence Cozy Mystery Series

Book of the Virago

Trailer Park Transylvania

Psychic Cleaner

The Magical Soapmaker Mysteries

The Goddess Chronicles

Cocktails in Hell

About the Author

Sheryl likes cake too much and can be found hoarding it while hiding from her children in the pantry closet.

Follow her on Amazon at: https://www.amazon.com/S-E-Babin/e/B00J1J236A

f

www.ingramcontent.com/pod-product-compliance
Lightning Source LLC
Chambersburg PA
CBHW020419110726
47899CB00006B/2051